Dear Reader:

Amazing is the only word that can truly describe this novel *Silent Cry* by Dywane D. Birch. In *Beneath the Bruises*, Birch gave us an eagle's eye view of what happens when a woman, Syreeta, endures years and years of domestic violence. Now, in its sequel, K'wan, the son of Syreeta and her abusive husband, Randall, struggles with dealing with the effects that the abuse has on him and his four younger brothers.

Too many women honestly believe that remaining in an abusive marriage for the sake of the children, suffering so that they can have a father in the household, is going to benefit the kids in the long run. Not at all. K'wan ends up in the system with a lot of other young men whose tempers also get the best of them when they attempt to save females not willing to save themselves. This is one of the most powerful novels that I have ever read because the message is so deep. *Silent Cry* needs to be used in juvenile institutions, domestic violence counseling centers and in women's prisons across the globe. Domestic violence has become an epidemic and a horrific cycle of chaos, heartache, and toxic results.

As always, I appreciate the support of myself and the authors that I publish under Strebor Books. We try our best to bring you cutting-edge literature from powerful and diverse voices. Please visit www.Zanestore.com for a complete list of our titles. I can be found on Facebook at www.Facebook.com/AuthorZane and on Twitter @planetzane. Thanks for the love.

Blessings,

Zane

Publisher
Strebor Books International
www.simonandschuster.com/streborbooks

Silent Cry

ALSO BY DYWANE D. BIRCH
Beneath the Bruises
Shattered Souls
When Loving You is Wrong
From My Soul to Yours

ZANE PRESENTS

Silent Cry

DYWANE D. BIRCH

SBI

STREBOR BOOKS

NEW YORK LONDON TORONTO SYDNEY

Strebor Books
P.O. Box 6505
Largo, MD 20792
http://www.streborbooks.com

ISBN 978-1-59309-389-1
ISBN 978-1-4516-5108-9 (ebook)
LCCN 2012933941

First Strebor Books trade paperback edition October 2012

Cover design: www.mariondesigns.com
Cover photograph: © Keith Saunders/Marion Designs

10 9 8 7 6 5 4 3 2 1

Manufactured in the United States of America

For information regarding special discounts for bulk purchases, please contact Simon & Schuster Special Sales at 1-866-506-1949 or business@simonandschuster.com

The Simon & Schuster Speakers Bureau can bring authors to your live event. For more information or to book an event, contact the Simon & Schuster Speakers Bureau at 1-866-248-3049 or visit our website at www.simonspeakers.com.

This book is dedicated to Kyle Warren for being an inspiration!
Even when the storms were raging in your life,
you kept the faith, you persevered, and you continued to soar,
never giving up on your dreams.
May the world continue to be a better place with you in it!

Acknowledgments

It's been four years since the release of *Beneath the Bruises*. And although this sequel was a very difficult book for me to write, it was one that I felt had to be, needed to be, written. And for that, I am truly thankful for being given the voice to do so. My blessings continue to come down because the praises always go up to the One who continues to guide my feet, my hands, and my heart. It is through His grace and mercy that I am who I am because He allows me to be!

To my family & close friends: Thank you for always loving me. I am truly blessed!

A special shout-out to Angela Coleman for being more than a loyal reader, but a friend as well. Auntie Orange, I have nothing but love for you. I appreciate your never-ending support of my literary work, and for always sharing a laugh with me. You are one of a kind!

Much love, much respect, to Zane and Charmaine for their undying support of my literary endeavors. You are both rare gems in a haystack of craziness! And I appreciate the both of you immensely! To the rest of the Strebor/Simon & Schuster staff: thank you for all that you do! And last, but not least—a special thanks to Yona Deshommes for always having my back!

To Sara Camilli, my agent, for always being supportive and encouraging. I appreciate you more than you'll ever know.

To Keith Saunders/Marion Designs: Thanks for the banging cover! You are a creative beast! I appreciate all that you do!

And to all the readers (and book clubs) who have continued to support me over the years, thank you, thank you, thank you! I am forever grateful to you!

Soulfully,

Dywane
Email: bshatteredsouls@cs.com

2010

"Your Honor, given all of the extenuating circumstances in this case, we ask that the charges of possession of a deadly weapon and attempted murder against my client, K'wan Taylor, be dismissed. Given the testimony from expert witnesses, and by his mother's own account, my client lived in a home of violence. He feared that one day his father would kill his mother and the night of the incident he believed that fear would come true. Over the years, my client has overheard threats made against his mother by the victim and he has seen bruises on his mother as a result of that violence in the home. And there is one documented incident that resulted in aggravated assault charges and a restraining order being executed against the victim.

"K'wan has no history of severe mental illness nor does he have any history of delinquent behavior. What happened is a tragedy, your Honor. This whole experience has been extremely traumatic for both my client and his family. What he did was done in an act of desperation to protect his mother during a domestic violence situation in which she was being strangled by the victim. In this case, his father."

One

Sometimes I wish I were dead. There, I said it! And, no, I'm not suicidal. I'm too much of a punk to actually kill myself. And I could never do that to my mom or my brothers, anyway. They are the only people I truly love. Still, the thought of one day not waking up lingers in the back of my mind. Death to me would be the ultimate freedom. I toy with its possibilities. Fantasize about its finality. Yet, no matter how much I wish for it, no matter how many times I dream of it, death doesn't come. Instead, I awaken still breathing, still chained, still hoping to be free. Free from this anger that burns deep inside of me. Free from my mom's screams that still haunt me in my sleep. Free from my father's blood that has been stained on my hands by the knife that I plunged into his back and side. But I don't share any of this with anyone. I keep it to myself—locked away from nosey counselors and busybody social workers and strange-looking psychiatrists trying to be all up in my business—attempting to get all up in my head, probing and prodding to get me to open up.

That's what they expect you to do here. Talk. Talk about your past, about the things that have hurt you. Talk about your present, about the things that bother you in the here and now. Talk about your future, about the things you hope to be different.

Talk.

Talk.

Talk.

For what? To explore my anger? To face my fears? To fill their space with words about how I feel and about what I want? So they can talk about me behind my back? So they can have secret meetings to discuss me? Maybe I don't know what I want, maybe I do. It's not their business. So why should I allow any of them inside my head? Why should I talk about my fears? I've already faced them. Why should I talk to any of them about my anger? I know why I'm angry. I don't need them or anyone else to help me figure out what I already know. I wanna be left alone.

So, no, I am not talking. I refuse to give them what they want. Before everything in my life fell apart, no one was concerned about what *I* wanted. No one was interested in hearing what *I* had to say. So why should anyone care now? All any of these people here need to know about me is what others have already told them, or what's written on paper. My name is K'wan Taylor; I am fourteen and the oldest of five brothers; my address and zip code are synonymous to gated communities and pretenses. Before the police, and court hearings, and detention center, I attended a prestigious private school; I played on the Lacrosse team and was a straight-A student in an advanced honors program with mostly juniors and seniors. I still am—a straight-A student, that is.

But it doesn't take brains to know that this is not where *I* need to be. And it shouldn't take much for these *so-called* educated and trained professionals to realize that I am not interested in hearing anything they have to say. They, the treatment team staff here— a buncha clueless people who sit around making decisions about what they *think* is best for me when they don't know crap about *me*—know that my parents are divorced (finally!); that behind the closed doors of our big, fancy house, *he* used to beat my Mom— never in front of me and my brothers, though—well, not really; and not all the time. Not that any of that makes a difference.

Because my brothers and I still heard and we still lived our lives in fear.

"What were you most fearful of?" a social worker at YDC—the youth detention I was in, once asked me. I tilted my head and stared at her. *That he would kill her.* I opened my mouth to speak, but the words would not follow. What I wanted to say, what I heard in my head, somehow got lost in the mix of my own anxiety of having to relive the idea, the frightening promise, that one day I would wake up, or come home from school, and my mom would be dead; that *his* big hands would have squeezed the life out of her. And my brothers and I would be motherless. The words became stuck in the back of my throat. So I closed my mouth, folded my arms across my chest and sat in defiant silence. Still, they know that my charges of possession of a weapon and attempted murder were downgraded to aggravated assault for stabbing *him*. And that I am here.

But what they don't know is that many times (when my parents were arguing or times I felt something bad was going to happen) I would sneak out of my bed and tiptoe down to their bedroom and press my ear up against their door—listening and waiting, holding my breath. That I would stand there, sometimes, for what felt like hours.

They don't know that I would quietly turn the doorknob to peek in, but it would always be locked. They don't know that I would often hear my mom's muffled cries and pleas for *him* to stop; that I would hear her begging *him* to keep his voice down, then the next day she would act like everything was okay. She would go through her cooking and cleaning and running his errands and tending to me and my brothers, never complaining; most times smiling. But none of them know that I know—that I've always known, she was pretending. She was hiding bruises. And not always the ones on her arms, or face, or shoulders, or back. I'm talking about the ones that chipped away at her character. The ones that made her think it was okay to make excuses for them.

My mom always said, even when I was, like seven, that I was much older and wiser than my age. That I didn't act or think like most kids my age. I still don't. I see beyond the surface of everything. And I saw the bruises, even when there were none. The invisible scars—the ones that had been sliced into her spirit were the ones most frightening to me, even more than the ones I could see. Image has been important to her. How people perceived her, us, has always mattered. Maybe not so much now, but in the past it was. We had to always look good in the eyes of others. God help us if anyone ever saw how screwed up our picture-perfect world really was.

Still, I don't share crap with these people about my hurts or my pains or my fears. I don't tell them how angry I am at her for letting that man move back in when everything was going fine with him not being there. I don't tell them how much I hate him. How bad I wanted to kill him. How I wanted him dead. And I still do. No, these things I keep to myself.

I sit and stare and blink at them, waiting for them all to disappear. I pretend to be invisible to them. And I am. Yes, they see me in the physical sense. My body is here; the shell of my existence. But, that's it.

I do not speak. I do not share. I do not allow them a glimpse into my soul. Nor allow them the opportunity to peel me apart and dissect me, slicing me into tiny little pieces so that they can put me under a microscope, inspect me, then try to put me back together again. No, there is no need for that.

I am not crazy.

I am broken.

TWO

"Is Daddy coming back home?"

"Why? Do you want him to?"

"No."

Why not?

"Because I don't like him."

"That's not a nice thing to say about your father."

"He hits you and makes you cry."

"Your father doesn't mean to hurt me. …He doesn't know how to handle his anger when he gets upset…your father and I have to work on some things before he can come home."

"I heard him yell at you and say nasty, mean things to you. I'm scared he might hurt you really bad. And then we won't have a mommy. I don't want him to hurt you anymore. Can he just stop hitting you and being mean to you?"

"I won't let him."

"You promise, Mommy?"

"I promise."

Promises, promises! I hate when people make promises they can't keep. Promises they have no intentions of keeping. And I hate myself for being no different from any of them! Then, again, promises are made to be broken, right? *I promise.* I repeat the words in my head and feel my chest tighten. *I promise.* I close my eyes and try to steady my breathing.

Inhale.

Exhale.

Press my eyes shut tighter.

I am ten again.

My eight-year-old brother, Kyle, and I are peeking out of our bedroom window. Red and blue lights are swirling and flashing. We count three police cars. The neighbors are looking out of their doors, and peering out of windows, waiting. Kyle and I hold hands, also waiting. Still, afraid to see. And then he appears. Hands cuffed in front of him. He is being taken out of the house by two police officers, barefoot with only his pajama pants on. An ambulance is in the driveway. And then...

I open my eyes, blink. Try to bring the images into view. Yet, the rest of that night is one big blur. I take in a deep breath. Close my eyes again. Force myself to remember. It's the morning after.

Kyle is standing at the foot of Mom's bed, staring at her face and neck. She puts a hand up to her throat, trying to cover the bruises around her neck. Her lip is swollen. Her right eye is puffy and swollen. I can see his fist, the print—angry and menacing, punched around her eye.

I sit beside her on the edge of the bed and hold my head down. I am angry...very angry!

"We saw the police take Daddy last night," my brother Kyle says. *"Did he hurt you?"* He sees what I see—the bruises, yet he still asks.

We both watch her, and wait. *"It's not as bad as it looks."*

"I hate him," I blurt out.

"Who?"

"Daddy." My nose is flaring. I am opening and closing my fists.

"Don't talk like that. He is still your father."

"I don't care. I still hate him. And I hope he never comes back."

"Look at me. That is not a nice thing to say. No matter what your father and I are going through, he loves you."

No matter how many times she said it—"he loves you," tried to convince me of it, nothing he did felt like love to me. How could he love my brothers, my mom, or me when he spent so much time hurting her, and scaring me?

I blink, blink again. I don't want to remember. But I don't want to forget, either. I have to relive this. I can't escape it.

I feel trapped in this memory.

I blink again.

Shut my eyes, tighter.

Allow my mind to go back.

"Does Daddy love you?" Kyle asks, narrowing his eyes.

"Your father loves me very much."

"Then why does he hit you?" I ask, feeling my anger boil over.

We watch as her eyes dart around the room. She tries not to look at us. But Kyle and I have cornered her. *"Because..."* We stare at her, waiting for her to say more. But she can't. So she doesn't.

We see tears in her eyes. But she doesn't want us to see her cry. She gets out of bed. And we watch as she straightens her shoulders, lifts her head, and walks into her bathroom, closing the door behind her and shutting us out.

"Is Mommy going to be okay?" Kyle whispers to me.

"Yes," I tell him. *"She'll be okay. I'm going to keep her safe."*

"Me too."

I made a promise to keep her safe. And I couldn't. I wanted to. But at ten, I simply didn't know how.

I blame myself.

I hate myself.

He could have killed her. And I can never forgive myself.

I close my eyes, again. I am standing at their door, my ear pressed up against the door. I am thirteen.

"Randy, I think you should leave before things get out of control."

"I'm not leaving. You leave…"

"And go where at this time of the night?"

"You figure it out. But if you think you can put me out of my own house, you have another thing coming. I'm not going anywhere, not this time."

"I'm calling the police."

There's scuffling, then a slap.

"Ohmygod, I can't believe you hit me…"

"Well, believe it. It's what you wanted. You must like being smacked up."

There is sniffling. *"I want you out of the house. You begged me to give us another chance. Promised your sons, and swore to me, that you'd never put your hands on me again. And you've hit me! You… you promised…"*

"Yeah, I did. But guess what, after everything you put me through, promises are made to be broken."

I snap my eyes open, glancing over at the clock. It's 3:15 A.M. I place a hand over my eyes. Press my thumb and fingers into my temples. I am fighting back a headache, and fighting back tears that are sure to follow.

Three

open my eyes. Rub the sleep out of them, then yawn. I have overslept, again. But I am relieved that the nightmares did not disrupt what little sleep I was able to get last night; well, early this morning. I stretch, glancing over at the clock; 8:47 A.M. I have missed breakfast from 7:15 to 8:30. If you miss breakfast, then you have to wait for lunch, which is served from 12:15 to 1:15. I don't really care about missing breakfast. My stomach is in knots, anyway. I have IPC—Individualized Personal Counseling— that's what they call it here, at nine o'clock with Mrs. Morgan. She's not a doctor, but she has a bunch of degrees behind her name. A Licensed Clinical Social Worker, I think.

I have IPC on Tuesday and Thursday mornings. Then right afterward, I am in group for an hour and a half. And on Monday, Wednesday and Fridays, I have school from nine in the morning to three in the afternoon. Then study hall for two hours. Dinner is from 5:15 to 6:30. Seems like that's all we do here. Shuffle from one appointment to the next. We become robots to their schedule; become puppets dangling by a string of rules and expectations.

This place—Healing Souls, the residential program I'm in— programs you to death. Everyone wants you to participate, to work the program, blah, blah, blah. I wish they'd all leave me alone. I have my good days and bad days here. Some days aren't as bad as others. Today, it's horrible. Although on some days, it beats being locked up in the detention center. Being confined in a cell most of the day and having to deal with crazy-acting CO's who act worse than some of the residents—what we're called in detention, is enough to drive anyone crazy. But, then there are other days when I'd rather be confined to a cell, away from everyone here. When I really think about it, what's really the difference between being locked up there or being locked up here? There is none. Either way, I am not given free will to walk out the door and go home. I am still held against my will.

I glance over at the empty bed on the other side of the room, then over at the pile of clothes that fill the corner by the foot of the bed. My roomie, Ja'Meer, is already gone. I'm glad. All he ever does is talk my head off, seemingly unfazed by the fact that— save from an occasional head nod or shrug of the shoulder—I don't respond back to him. He just wants, maybe needs, someone to listen to him. The way I did. Still, he seems cool enough. He calls me Green Eyes when my eyes are gray. At first I thought he was maybe color blind or something. Then he told me he knows that my eyes are gray, but sometimes they look green so that's what he's gonna call me. I almost laughed. Hearing him call me that is kinda funny.

My brow furrows as I climb out of bed. If I were talking, I'd have to confront him about his nasty ways. His side of the room is junky. His bed is unmade and, when they do room inspection today, he'll be written up for his mess. *Not my problem*, I think, walking into the bathroom. I am mindful to keep the light off. I take a leak, flush the urinal, then shuffle over to the sink and wash my hands. I avoid looking in the mirror. Avoid its constant reminders of who I was, who I am, and who I may become. My past and my present all wrapped around memories, good and bad; painful and happy. Somewhere buried beneath layers of hurt, there's happiness. I know there is. But why can't I dig those rec-ollections up and remember the good times? Why am I only able to summon up the bad?

I blink.

I am home again. Kyle and I are downstairs in the game room, playing PlayStation 2. They are upstairs in the kitchen, above our heads. *He* is yelling.

"For Christ's sake, Syreeta! Can't you do anything right? I asked you to handle one simple task for me. Pick up my suits from the cleaners. And what do you do? Forget! You're home all day and you can't even get that right. I don't know why I even bother with you."

"Randy, please. The boys. They'll hear you."

"Well, maybe they need to hear me. Then they'll know how useless you are…all you want to do is lie around on your fat ass all day, spending up my money. I'm sick of you…"

"I'm not fat."

"You're fat if I say you are. And right now you're a fat, lazy ass!"

"Randy, please don't call me names."

"I'll call you what I want. And if you don't like it, you can pack your shit and get out!"

Kyle and I look up at the ceiling, frightened. Something breaks, smashes to the floor. We hold our breath. Wait. Then slowly exhale when there is silence.

Kyle has tears in his eyes.

I put my arm around him. *"Don't cry."*

"I can't help it. I'm scared, K'wan."

"Don't be. I'm going to take care of everything."

"How?"

I shrug, uncertainty unraveling around me. I did not have a plan, but I had to stop him…one day. *"I don't know, yet. But you have to trust me, okay?"*

Kyle looks up at me. His eyes wet with tears, he slowly nods. I hug him. And he hugs me back. I tell him that we have to be strong for Mommy, for each other. But, how were a ten- and eight-year-old supposed to be strong? How were we supposed to not cry when we had heard more than once *him* threatening to kill her?

"You think Mommy's okay?"

"I hope so. You stay here. I'll go check."

I hurriedly get up from my seat, dropping my controls to the floor. I take the steps two at a time until I reach the top of the stairs. Quietly, I peer around the corner into the kitchen. There she is, pressed up against a counter. There he is. His large hand around her neck, squeezing.

"I will snap your neck. Do you under—"

"Daddy, please! Don't hurt Mommy!"

He shoots me a look. *"Boy, get back downstairs. Now!"*

"But, you're hurting her," I beg. I am on the verge of tears.

"I said, get back downstairs!"

Mom gives me a pleading look. There are tears in her eyes as well. My lips quiver. I am so scared for her. *"Go on, sweetheart. Listen to your father. Mommy's okay."*

It is a lie. It is always a lie. I know it is. But I do as I am told. Afraid if I stay I will make things worse. And it will be my fault. But she wasn't okay. And I left her, anyway.

It's always my fault.

I blink back to the present. Glance up at my reflection, then quickly shift my eyes away. I do not like what I see. Even in the dimness of the bathroom, I am haunted by the image. I have my mother's skin tone and her eyes. But I do not see her. My forehead and nose and lips…they do not belong to me.

I feel so disconnected.

I do not feel as if I am my own person.

My thoughts, my feelings…they do not seem to belong to me, either. And that frightens me.

I remember reading a pamphlet about domestic violence my mom had lying on the counter at home and there was one thing written that sticks in my head and frightens me: "Children who are victims of domestic violence are much more likely to become abusers themselves."

I repeat this over and over and over in my head. My chest tightens. I am afraid. I don't want to be an abuser. Do not want to be violent. But I am afraid it is in me.

I run the water, make it as hot as my hands can possibly stand, then lower my face into the sink and splash my face with it. Maybe if I submerge my face, my thoughts, my fears, in water, I will drown out the reflection. Maybe I can wash away the image that keeps staring back at me. The person I do not ever want to be…my father.

Four

I am almost anxious to hear what Mrs. Morgan's going to talk about today, even though I never respond. Every session, she sits and patiently waits; every so often saying something she believes is encouraging.

"Things can get better." *For who?* I hear myself thinking every time she says that.

"You're not in this alone. You have to trust us to help you."

Sorry, lady, I'm all out of trust. The last person I thought I could trust beat my mother.

"Your family needs for you to get better."

I'm not sick! I scream in my head.

Each session, I sit and stare at her, emotionless. Even when she smiles at me, I don't smile back. Still, I kinda like coming to see her, although I don't tell her this. And I don't act it. She's kinda cool, actually. And she's nice to stare at, even with all of her makeup painted on. Although she's a little heavy on the lipstick and eyeliner, I can tell she was kinda hot when she was younger. Some of the kids here say she looks like a circus clown. They say a lot of mean things about most of the staff here, but I ignore it. I usually sit and stare at her, wondering what she'd look like now underneath her mask if she removed it; seems like everyone wears some kind of disguise. I wonder what she's hiding from.

"Good morning, K'wan," she says when I approach her office

door. As always, she wears a wide smile on her face. My eyes zoom in on the wide gap in her teeth. Her lips are painted with an orange-colored lipstick today. It's kind of hard for me to figure out how old she is since she looks young. But her neck, with its loose skin, makes me think she's mad old, like in her forties or fifties. I can hear my great-auntie Edie saying, "Good black don't crack."

I guess.

She motions for me to come in. I already know to shut the door behind me and take my seat in front of her. She's grabbing an ink pen from out her penholder as I walk toward her desk, scribbling something on her notepad. The date and time, I'm sure. We both know that today's session will be like any other session. She will ask me a few questions. We'll sit and stare at each other for a while, then she'll break the silence between us with some words of encouragement before telling me my session is over. Then I will get up and leave her office, with her crisp white pages still blank.

"How are you today?"

How the heck do you think I am? I'm stuck here!

I don't respond. Truth is I'm tired. I was up all night, thinking. And even that was difficult with my roomie snoring most of the night. Still, I stared up at the ceiling and thought about how much I miss my life back home—being in my own bed, in my own room, watching my own TV and eating my own food. I miss the triplets barging in my room, bugging me about whatever. I never thought I'd miss them three bad-asses. But I do! I miss my brother Kyle, too. I miss going to my private school with all of the other uniformed preppy kids who get good grades and speak proper English. This shit here is for the birds, being around all of these disrespectful kids who curse out adults and pick fights. Bullying and stealing from each other.

"This is not my life!" I hear myself screaming at her. "I didn't ask for a father who beat my mother! I didn't ask to have to witness it, or hear it! I didn't ask for any of this crap!"

I stare at the two framed posters hanging, centered, on the wall in back of her. The poster in the middle is of a black woman resting her cheek up on her hands. Her head is tilted. The caption reads: DOMESTIC VIOLENCE IS THE LEADING CAUSE OF INJURY TO WOMEN

The second poster is a white woman holding her face in her hands. The caption reads: EVERY 7 SECONDS A WOMAN IS BEATEN

I swallow.

"Why couldn't he keep his hands to himself?" I want to ask her.

"K'wan," she starts off, clasping her hands in front of her. "I want to talk to you about forgiveness, especially toward your father."

I blink.

"You're probably out whoring while I'm at work…Are my sons even my kids?"

"What? OhmyGod, Randy, I can't believe you'd ask me something like that. Of course, our sons are yours. The only man I've ever been with is you."

"Yeah, right."

"It's the truth. And I don't appreciate what you're implying."

"Well, I don't appreciate you being a whore."

"I'm not a whore."

"I want a blood test."

I cringe.

No one knows I overheard him saying all that to her. But I did. I kept it to myself as I did other things because I didn't wanna get in trouble, or worse…him to take it out on my mom. So I held onto it. And let it boil inside of me. No one knows that it bothered me to hear him accuse my mom of cheating on him and calling her a *whore*. It really hurt my feelings that he would think my brothers and I weren't his kids. That really had me looking at him differently. Who does that? I mean, what kind of person suggests his wife is *whoring* and that his own kids aren't his?

Him hitting her was bad enough. But to accuse her of sleeping around on him made it that much easier for me to not want anything else to do with him. How could I? Why would I? He didn't believe I was his son. So why would I want him as my father?

Why should I have to forgive him? I feel like my whole life is screwed up because of him. I never, ever curse, but I feel like he effed everything up. That he didn't give a damn about my mom. And he definitely didn't care about my brothers or me. There's nothing he can say to make me think, feel, or believe otherwise. His actions spoke for him. After all, it was him who always said all a man has is his word. If he isn't a man of his word, then he isn't someone easily trusted. Those were his words, so how can he ever be trusted after all the promises he made, then turned around and broke them?

"Promises are made to be broken..."

I narrow my eyes at her as if she can hear my thoughts.

Maybe she can.

Mrs. Morgan folds her hands on top of the desk. "Sometimes the people we're supposed to be able to trust are the same people who hurt us the most. There is no simple answer to explain why they do what they do. Intentional or not, they all have their reasons. And their choices are what hurt the ones they love."

Then how can they really love you?

How could he love my mother if he called her names and beat her?

How could he love my brothers and me if he kept us living in fear?

He had to know we were afraid.

I stare at her.

She continues, "Right or wrong, people who say they love us, *choose* to hurt us. But we still have the power to forgive them. We can choose to let go of what they've done to us. Or choose to hold onto it. Holding on to resentment keeps you imprisoned…"

And if I let go, will I not still be locked up? Unless you people are unlocking those iron gates out front and letting me leave, I am still imprisoned. So what's the difference?

"The mere sound of any references being made to your father makes you uncomfortable," she says, eyeing me cautiously. "I see it in your eyes, K'wan. The hurt and rage you have toward him. It isn't healthy for you, or to you. What you experienced, the abuse you witnessed your father inflict on your mother, isn't something that should ever be condoned or overlooked. It happened. That can't be changed. But the way in which you deal with what has happened in your life can. We can control our actions. We are responsible for the choices we make. And we can choose not to allow bitterness and anger to consume us. And it can start by forgiving…"

I fold my arms, defiantly.

I will never forgive him!

I am not trying to hear anything she is saying. Not about forgiveness. What he did to my mom, what he put me and my brothers through, is unforgiveable.

I shift my eyes away from her stare.

"Can you look at me, please?" I take a deep breath, reluctantly bringing my attention back to her. "We all know how hurt and angry you are. But that bottled up rage is dangerous. It eats away at you. Holding onto it will only destroy you. K'wan, forgiveness is an act of courage. And I believe, we all believe, you are a courageous young man…"

I blink. You don't know what I am. There's nothing courageous about someone who's failed to protect their mom.

"That wasn't your job, protecting your mom…"

Then whose job was it? Surely not his!

"K'wan, forgiveness is not about overlooking or excusing what has happened. And it's never about accepting the unacceptable. Forgiveness is about you. Not the person who has wronged or hurt you. Or anyone else." She pauses as if she's trying to give me a chance to hear, understand, what it is she's saying. I hear her, but I am not listening. And no, I am not understanding; not because I can't but because I choose not to. She continues, "Forgiveness is about releasing you from all of those negative feelings you keep bottled up inside of you that are toxic and destructive. It's about releasing yourself from a very hurtful past."

I wonder if she has kids.

Who do you need to forgive that you haven't?

I blink.

"Forgiveness helps us to move on. Like with your father," she pauses, gauging my reaction. There is none. "Sometimes we have to know when to surrender, so that we can work on letting go. I'd like to help you work on forgiving yourself. Then work on forgiving him. But we can't help you, K'wan, if you won't open up and let us in. Let us help you."

Why now? Where were you and all of your help when I needed it?

She waits for me to give her a sign, any indication that I am receptive to her help, and the idea of forgiveness.

I am going to kill you, Syreeta!

I stand up, open the door and walk out, leaving behind my answer.

I can't forgive him.

I can't forgive myself.

I can't speak.

I can't surrender.

No. I will suffer in silence.

Five

"Okay, gentlemen," Miss Daisy says, glancing around the circle. She's a short, brown-skinned woman who wears her hair in long, black micro-braids that she usually rolls up in a big twist. She has really big feet, too. But she's probably one of the nicest counselors here. She's also the one that most of the guys like being in group with. I could not care less either way. "Let's get started. Who wants to go first?"

There are twelve of us in group today.

I hate group. But, this is where I sit—with other delinquents, okay residents, first-and-second-and-third time offenders who have been charged with a violent crime—miserable, forced to sit in a whack circle, expected to share all things personal.

Here, you are either a) a troubled kid from a good home, b) a good kid from a troubled home, or c) a troubled kid from a troubled home. Most of the guys in group seem to be from the latter. My guess is they're kids who didn't have much of a chance from the start. I suppose I should feel lucky, perhaps blessed. But I don't. I can't see the blessing in living in a home where your mom is being beaten. I don't see anything good in living in fear. So exactly where is the blessing in that?

I shift in my seat.

Miss Daisy's deep brown eyes sweep around the circle looking for a willing participant. No one ever wants to go first. She lands her stare on Jarrod, this tall, lanky kid who's really good at playing basketball. Someone said he's here for vehicular manslaughter. But the kids here lie, so it's hard to know what's fact or fiction around here. And since I haven't heard him say it, I take it to be not true. Not that I care.

"Jarrod?"

He shifts in his seat, folding his arms. He narrows his eyes. "Nah, don't look at me. I'm not beat."

She looks over at this kid, Anthony. A thick, muscled, seventeen-year-old Italian guy from Bayonne who's here for beating up his sister's nineteen-year-old boyfriend, then running him over with his car when she told him that he was the one who had blackened her eye and broke her nose. His sister's sixteen.

I'm glad I don't have sisters.

"Anthony, how about you? Would you like to start off?" Her question sounds more like a plea, almost desperate.

He shrugs. Balls up a letter he has finished reading. He seems agitated.

She smiles at him. "Great. What's on your mind?"

"Nothing." He squeezes the ball of paper as if it's one of those stress balls.

"Well, it seems like there's a lot of something going on. You look upset. Does it have anything to do with what was in that letter you crumpled up?"

The muscles in his jaw tighten. "My sister's back with that fucking asshole!"

I look away.

"Your father's moving home…"

Miss Daisy nods. "How does that make you feel?"

Angry!

He gives her a stupid look. "How do you think it makes me

feel? I'm pissed. I mean, like, what the fuck, man. I'm sitting up in this bullshit-ass place for beating him up. And her dumb ass goes back to him. What kind of bullshit is that?"

"Beating her boyfriend up was a choice you made," Miss Daisy says. "Did your sister ask you to beat him up for her?"

He huffs, eyeing her. "No."

"Then why'd you do it?"

"Because she's my sister. And I was pissed that he put his hands on her."

"So since *you* made the choice to assault him, *you* have to be the one to suffer the consequences. It's as simple as that. And since your sister has made the decision to reconcile with him, you will have to work on respecting her decision and being there emotionally for her when she needs you."

He grunts, shaking his head. "Yeah, I made my choices and now she's made hers, so we'll both have to live with them. He can snap her neck for all I care. I no longer have a sister."

She steadies her gaze on him. "You don't really mean that, do you?"

He matches her stare. "Yeah, I mean it.

"Sounds like you're speaking out of anger. But let's talk about that."

"No, let's not," he says. "She did what she did. And that's that. I'm done with her."

"Anthony, many times we say things we don't really mean out of anger."

I hate him! And I mean it!

I cut my eyes over at Anthony, wait to hear his response. He shrugs. "It is what it is."

"You're upset, hurt, maybe even disappointed. And you have a right to feel all of those things. But we both know you still love your sister. It's only natural to want to protect people we love. In hindsight, do you think you could have handled that whole situation differently?"

He shrugs.

I keep myself from shrugging, too. I repeat the question in my head.

"Promises are made to be broken…"

"Syreeta, I will kill you, the kids and me if you ever try to leave me…."

There's only one answer for me. *No.*

"I guess," he says. "But, I didn't like him anyway so I still would have knocked his block in."

"So you were looking for a reason to fight him?"

"Basically. Still, he had no business putting his hands on my sister. And she had no business going back to him."

I blink. I am twelve.

"K'wan and Kyle, your father and I have been doing a lot of talking lately and we both want all of us to be a family again. He's been out of the house for almost a year now and he's ready to come home. Ever since he finished his counseling, he seems to have changed. He wants to be back in our lives. He'll be spending a lot more time here with us. How do you boys feel about that?" she asks this, sounding like her mind is already made up, regardless of what we say, think, or feel.

"I like our family the way it already is," I tell her.

"Me too," Kyle agrees.

"Why can't he stay at his own house? I don't want him here with us."

"Well, sweetheart, I guess he could keep living where he is. But that's not what we really want. Your father misses being here with us. Don't you boys miss him being here with us?"

I frown. *"No. I don't like him."*

"I know this whole experience has been hard on the two of you. It's been hard on me, too. Your father loves us. And he deserves another chance. He's changed."

"But what if he hits you again?" Kyle wants to know.

I stare at her.

She shifts her eyes. *"He promised he won't ever hit me again."*

"But what if he does?"

She reaches over and touches the side of Kyle's face. *"Oh, sweetheart. You don't have anything to worry about. I'm not going to let that happen again. I promise. We'll talk about this more when your father gets here tonight, okay?"*

Kyle nods. She hugs him, then reaches for me.

I walk off, angry.

"…I'm her brother," Anthony says, slicing into my thoughts. "And I feel like she chose that asshole over me. And I'm the one who was trying to protect her."

I hear myself saying, "I feel the same way!"

I shift in my seat.

A few guys groan. Comments, like a slow building fire, start to spread around the group.

"Man, I'd be pissed, too," this kid, Jackson, says. "I beat dude up and get all hemmed up tryna help you, then you go back to his ass. Nah, I'd be ready to take it to her head, too."

"Yo, that's fucked up, man," says this kid, Westley.

"Yo, if my sister did some shit like that, I'd beat her up my damn self, for real." This kid, Jake, says this.

"Man, some chicks like getting their asses beat," this kid, Corey, says. Most of the group seems to agree with what he's said. He seems pretty cool, but the kids here say his feet smell like corn chips. I'm glad I don't eat those things.

"Why can't you just do what I ask, huh? Why do you make me have to act ugly to get you to fucking listen, huh? You must like your ass beat…"

I blink. I don't want to think my mom liked getting beat on. But now I have to wonder. Maybe she did.

Miss Daisy looks over at him. "Corey, what makes you say that?"

"Because they keep going back...."

"That's the problem with you, Syreeta. You don't fucking listen!"

"If they didn't like bein' beat on, why would they keep taking the nig..." Miss Daisy raises her brow. "Oh, my bad. I mean, dude, back?"

Miss Daisy clasps her hands in front of her. "Well, that might appear to be the case to those who don't understand domestic violence, or the damaging effects it has on the human spirit. But, let me be clear. That *is* not the case. No woman wants to be beat on." She eyes all of us. *Then what is the case?* I lean forward in my seat, waiting to hear her explanation. Hoping she'll say something that makes sense to me. I want to be able to wrap my mind around it. Maybe if I can understand it, I won't be so mad at my mom for taking him back.

"Then why these broads keep letting a muhfucka..." Corey pauses, putting his hands up. "My bad, Miss Daisy, but you know what I'm sayin'. He either beatin' that thing-thing down real good and he got her hooked on it, or she gotta be straight-up dumb."

"Yo, real talk," this kid, Aesop, says, punching a fist into the palm of his hand. Sometimes I wonder what his mom was really thinking when she named him that. A few weeks back I overheard him tell these kids at a table he was sitting at that his name meant "Great One." Dude was clueless about Greek history. Probably doesn't even know what a fable is. I kinda stared at him in disbelief, shaking my head. He shakes his head. "Yo, I know some chicks who will jump up in a dude's face and come at him like she's ready to get it in, darin' him to hit her, then when he tries to step off, she calls him all kinds of punks and pussies...my bad Miss Daisy, but you know what I mean...for not hitting her. She be beggin' for dude to knock her fronts out. Then the minute he runs his fist up in her mouth, she's good."

A few guys laugh.

"Or she runs and calls the police," Aesop adds, "after *she* was the one who was asking to have her snot locker punched in, in the first place."

More laughter.

I see nothing funny about any of this. It actually sounds sad and pathetic.

"Yeah, they like that shit," Jake agrees.

"No emotionally healthy woman wants to be hit on," Miss Daisy counters. "No woman wakes up and decides today is the day I want to be beat on. That's not to say that there aren't some women who have been programmed—almost brainwashed, if you will—to believe that being hit is a sign of someone really loving them. It's almost like saying, 'I beat you because I love you.' That kind of warped thinking is dangerous. Abuse is not love."

"Your father loves me…"

"Then why does he hit you?"

"Then she should bounce," this kid, Marco, says.

"That's sometimes easier said than done," she explains. "Some women may never leave. And the ones who do, oftentimes will find themselves right back in the same type of situation, if not with the same abuser, then with someone else."

"See what I'm sayin'," Corey huffs. "Straight-up dumb."

Miss Daisy nods and listens. She never makes anyone feel like they're being judged. Even if what they say makes them look really crazy. "Going back to an abusive partner," she says, "is more common than not. But a woman's reasons for going back are very personal choices. They go back for many different reasons. And those reasons aren't always easy ones to make."

Anthony sucks his teeth. "Yeah, 'cause they're a buncha stupid bi...I mean, broads, like my sister."

"They're not stupid," Miss Daisy says, calmly. "They're women who are emotionally attached to men who have dark sides. Many of them go back because they are afraid of letting go—it's easier said than done for many. Or they're simply afraid of being alone, especially if they've been brainwashed to believe over and over that no one else is going to ever want them. These women who you see as stupid are, in most cases, filled with anxiety, shame, and guilt. They blame themselves for the abuse."

"I'm so sorry for what you and K'wan have heard your father say..."

"It's not your fault, Mommy," Kyle says to her.

I stare at her.

"Still sounds crazy to me," Corey says.

"Well, answer this," Miss Daisy says, eyeing the group. "How many of you have been in relationships?"

I am the only one who doesn't raise his hand. I feel embarrassed.

"Yo, son, let me find out you've never been with a girl," Jarrod teases. "You do like girls, right?"

I don't respond. I turn my head toward the window. There's a neatly constructed cobweb in the lower corner between the screen and window, a lonely fly dangling from a string of silk—trapped, the irony of my life.

"Nah, that little nigga scared of pussy," this kid, Lenny, says. He's sixteen and one of the Healing Souls' bullies. He's here for pulling a gun out on his mom's boyfriend. "He probably sucks dick."

"Lenny, watch your mouth," Miss Daisy warns. "I will not have that kind of talk in here."

"Yeah, yours," Jarrod says, laughing. A few other guys in the group laugh with him.

I ignore them. I've had girls that I've liked, or who have liked me. And I have even kissed a few. But the truth is I am a virgin. *I just turned fourteen! I shouldn't feel like there's something wrong with me because I haven't had sex, yet!*

"Jarrod, that's enough," Miss Daisy says, cutting her eyes at him.

"Yo, don't play me, son," Lenny says defensively. "I don't roll like that."

"Yeah, whatever," Jarrod says back.

Lenny gets up from his seat. "Yo, son, what'd you say? I'll knock your skull back for real, yo…"

"Lenny, get back in your seat," Miss Daisy warns him.

Jarrod remains sitting, smirking at him. "Do you, bruh. It's whatever."

Jarrod has been looking for a reason to fight Lenny. Someone needs to shut him up. I don't like him. But I wouldn't start a fight with him or anyone else. Nor would I let anyone reel me into one. Not unless they hit me first.

"Lenny, get back in your seat, *now*," Miss Daisy warns again. "Aggression is not allowed in this group. And it will not be tolerated. Nor will those kinds of remarks about someone's sexuality, or lack of sexual experiences. Now take a seat or be escorted out of here in restraints."

He eyes Jarrod, then cuts his eye at Miss Daisy. She waits for him to make his decision, her finger hovering over the panic button. He takes his seat. She brings her attention to Jarrod. "And you, Mister. That was uncalled for."

"You right, Miss Dee; my bad."

She eyes everyone around the circle. "If none of you have anything constructive to say, then I'd suggest you do one of two things. Either sit there and keep quiet, or get out. Do I make myself clear?"

Everyone says yes, except Lenny. He narrows his eyes. "Yeah, aiiight."

"No. It's not 'yeah, aiiight.' It's yes. Now do you understand?"

He grits his teeth. "Yes."

"Good." She looks around the circle of faces; Black, White, Hispanic, and Asian. We are all from different backgrounds and experiences. All here because of something we did. "Now back to my question. Out of twelve group members, eleven of you raised your hands indicating you've been in relationships before. Now out of those who've raised their hands, how many of you have been in relationships where you've been hit, or had your personal belongings destroyed?"

Seven hands go up.

"Okay," Miss Daisy continues. "And how many of you ended your relationships because of it?"

No one raised their hands.

"Interesting. And how many of you were hit or had your belongings destroyed more than once in your relationships?"

Five hands go up.

"And out of the five of you, how many of you ended your relationships right after that?"

No one raises their hands.

I imagine myself sitting here staring at them all, shaking my head. Instead, I sit with a blank look on my face.

"So does that mean you stayed because you liked being slapped on or having your property damaged?"

"Nah," most of them say.

"Yo, I can't speak for anyone else," Corey says. "But when my girl hit me, I wasn't beat to bounce on her 'cause she's a girl. It's not like her slaps really hurt me; like I could hurt her, if I'd smack her up."

Miss Daisy tilts her head. "So, then what you're really saying is that because she's a girl, it's okay for her to do what she does; is that it?"

"Nah. I'm not sayin' that it's cool for her to be puttin' her hands on me. But, she's a girl."

"So," she pushes, "it's more acceptable. Is that what you're saying?"

He shrugs. "I guess."

"That still doesn't make it right," Westley says.

"Yo, eff what ya heard," Jackson says. "A broad puts her hands on me, I'm knocking her light switch out; period, point-blank. No questions asked."

Corey laughs. "I heard that, man. But, nah. I can't put my hands on no chick, yo. My moms would spazz out if I did some shi...I mean, mess, like that."

Miss Daisy keeps her eyes on him. "And you stay with this girl-friend who hits you, why?"

"A lot of reasons," he says.

"Like?" Miss Daisy probes.

"She gives good head."

Everyone laughs, except me.

Miss Daisy doesn't seem fazed by the sexual comment. "And?"

"The sex is good."

More laughter.

"And?"

"I dig her."

"So by staying with her you must *dig* getting smacked, right?"

He frowns. "Nah. It pisses me off. But I know she's crazy, so it's whatever."

"What makes her crazy?"

He shrugs, shaking his head. "She just is. She stays goin' through my stuff and wantin' to argue 'bout dumb stuff. And she's mad jealous 'bout e'erything. She's just like her moms. She does that dumb shit—my bad, Miss Dee—to her pops. It's crazy."

Miss Daisy nods, taking in what he's said. "If in fact your girl-friend is doing all of those things you say, then it's safe to say she's learned them from her mother, or from witnessing someone else in her home displaying those types of behaviors."

"Nah," Corey says, shaking his head. "It's safe to say she's effen crazy, like her moms."

The guys laugh.

Miss Daisy crosses her legs. "And have you broken up with her because of it?"

"Yeah," he says. I blink. He must have forgotten he was one of the guys who didn't raise his hand when she asked if anyone had ever broken up over being hit. I wonder if anyone else has picked up on it. If they have, no one calls him on it. Not even Miss Daisy. "Well, I mean. Not really. I just spin-off on her and don't answer my phone for a few days."

"And then what?"

"She starts trackin' me down, callin' my peeps and shit—my bad."

"Then what happens?"

"I call her. We talk. Or she comes over. We talk, then put on the slow jams and have make-up sex."

Several of the guys laugh.

"Now that's what I'm talkin' about," Jackson says, giving him a pound. "Make-up sex is the best kinda sex."

Is that what kept Mom with him; the make-up sex?

Miss Daisy seems intent on getting to the bottom of why Corey stays with his girlfriend, who he labels as *crazy*. I wait for her to prove a point. My guess is that he's a hypocrite. That he's the crazy one. That he's no less stupid than those girls he believes are for staying with someone who hits on them.

"Okay, so you have 'spun-off' on her, as you say. But the two of you have also broken up at some point, no?"

"Yeah, I guess."

"How many times?"

He shifts in his seat. He is starting to look like a deer caught in headlights. "I don't know. Maybe seven or eight times."

"And, even after she's physically assaulted you on more than one occasion, you still went back to her?"

"Yo, Money, don't do it, man," Jake says, leaning forward. "She's fishin' you, son."

Miss Daisy shoots him a look. He shifts back in his seat.

"Nah, it's all good," Corey says. "Yeah, we made up."

"Mmmm. So then I guess going back to her makes you just as crazy as the women who you feel are stupid for going back to a man who beats on them, right?"

There's laughter.

"Yo, son, she just played you," Jarrod instigates.

Miss Daisy eyes him, then shifts her attention back over to Corey. "I haven't played anyone. I'm simply asking a question. And I'm trying to understand his thinking. Through your own admission you've stated that you feel that some women like being beat because they go back to the abuser. Am I correct?"

"Yeah."

"Then why'd *you* take her back? She sounds abusive."

His eyes get wide.

Miss Daisy has him cornered.

Everyone stares at him, waiting.

"Because I'm stupid," I hear him say in my head. But that isn't what he says.

He shrugs. "I guess…" He pauses, fidgeting in his seat.

"Well," Miss Daisy pushes. "Why do you keep going back to her?"

Corey sighs, realizing he has put his smelly feet deep into his own mouth. "Because I love her."

Love? *Yeah, right. Try stupidity*, I think, giving him a pitiful glance. For some reason, Auntie Edie's voice finds me again. This time she whispers one of her favorite passages in my ear. Corinthians 13:4: "Love is patient. Love is kind. Love is not jealous..."

I wanna tell her that someone's lied to her. I wanna scream if love was so patient and kind, why did it beat up on my mom? If love wasn't jealous, why did it always question my mom's whereabouts? Why did it always accuse her of cheating?

Love is what love does...

If love is lived out by words and actions, then how can someone honestly say they love someone when they show them nothing but hate? It makes no sense. Maybe I'm too young to understand it. But it doesn't seem right. Subconsciously, I frown. *Love is what love does...Yeah, right!*

I know from my English class and the dictionary that love is both a noun and a verb. It's not just in telling, it's in showing, too. I get that. Still, there seems to be a lot of room for misinterpretation and confusion.

"Your father loves me..."

How? From what I've seen about love—his love, it yells and screams. It beats the mother of its children, and insults its wife. And it subjects its children to yelling and screaming and seeing black and blue bruises. Love threatens to kill you. That's what love does!

Isn't love supposed to inspire your actions? *Sometimes we hurt the ones we love.* I do not understand this. To *intentionally—maliciously*—hurt someone is not my definition of love. I can't accept it as such. And, yet, I'm so very confused.

Yeah, love is real kind, all right.

Six

I t was deliberate…stabbing him.

I knew what I was doing. There was no lapse of memory, or judgment. I had played it over and over and over in my head a thousand times. Every night, I'd check and recheck to make sure it was there. I could not sleep, not knowing. I would not sleep until I saw it. The butcher knife. Sharp and shiny and neatly tucked in the middle of my bed—sandwiched between my mattress and box spring, waiting to be used.

I had rehearsed the moment in my mind until I had committed it to memory. Had lain awake night after night, waiting to hear the muffled sounds of fists hitting flesh, of whimpers for the beatings to stop. I didn't want there to be—the hushed threats, the mounting tension that would swell into a blister, then pop. But I knew, and feared, one day it would come—the storm, pounding of fists and name-calling and curse words and crying and screaming. I'd lie in the stillness of the night surrounded by fear, sometimes holding my breath, listening, fighting back sleep. Afraid that if I fell asleep I'd wake up and she would be gone, her life taken away from us.

I had to be ready.

I blink back tears.

The adults—the people who have been making decisions about my life—say I shouldn't have taken matters into my own hands.

That I should have let the police handle it. But they weren't there. They didn't have to live it. They weren't the ones who felt helpless and were fucking scared to go to sleep at night. They weren't the ones having nightmares of finding their mother's body. I was.

Flashes of what it would be like to plunge that knife into him played nonstop in my head for hours, for weeks, until the moment finally came. I will not make any apologies for what I have done. I did what I had to do.

I had to protect my mom.

And I have no regrets.

"K'wan, I am going to ask you a few questions."

"Have you had thoughts of actually hurting yourself?"

"Have you ever attempted to harm or kill yourself?"

"There's a big difference between having a thought and acting on a thought. Do you think you might actually make an attempt to hurt yourself in the near future?"

"Have you ever heard or seen things that other people could not hear or see?"

The questions that have been asked of me since the night of my arrest rattle around in my head. My responses to them all, always the same: a blank stare.

"Yo, Green Eyes, you have a visit," Ja'Meer calls out, disrupting my thoughts. His deep, manly voice ricochets around the room. He's standing in the doorway. I am sitting at the desk, doing my calculus homework. Well, staring at the formulas; my mind has been wandering in every direction other than on solving equations.

I look over at him. He's holding a ping-pong paddle in his hand. "Yo, you need to stop punkin' out on me, son-son, and let me whoop you in another game real quick. Don't worry. This time, since you're my roomie,"—he swings the paddle as if he's hitting an imaginary ball—"I won't be too hard on you."

I will myself not to crack a smile, or to laugh at him, shaking my head. Truth is, I let him win. At home, Kyle and I would spend hours down in our game room playing table tennis. And I was the reigning champ. I give pause to my thoughts. Maybe Kyle was letting me win as well. Maybe it was all in my head. After all that has happened, I am no longer certain of anything anymore.

I close my math book, get up from the desk, pulling off the Harvard T-shirt I have on. I slip a Yale sweatshirt over my head and into my arms, then head toward the visiting room.

I overhear two residents that I vaguely know half-talking, half-whispering as I walk by. "Damn, yo. You see his moms, son? Word is bond, she bad. I'd definitely tag that."

"Yeah, man. I'd tip drill that. She's da truth. Look like she gotta fatty, too."

I eye them. They eye me back.

I know without them saying it, who they're talking about—my mom. And it takes everything in me to keep walking. I have to keep reminding myself that it's only talk. That they're a buncha ignorant fools. Still, it's annoying to hear these disrespectful kids talk about my mom like that every time she visits, even if she is kinda fly; that's still my mom.

They have no respect for women, I think, walking into the visiting room. The triplets, Karon, Kason, and Kavon, jump up from their seats and race over to me. They hug me tight, asking a buncha questions without giving me time to respond to any of them.

I miss them so much.

"When are you coming home?" Karon wants to know.

"Do you like it here?" Kason inquires.

"Don't you wanna come home with us?" Kavon asks.

"Mommy says you're gonna come home soon. Are you coming home soon?"

"Why do you have to stay here?"

"How come you won't talk?"

"You boys come on and let your brother sit down," Mom says, standing up as we walk over to her. She smiles. I don't reciprocate. I am still too angry with her. My body stiffens, then relaxes as she gives me a hug. "Hi, baby," she says. Her voice is low and soothing. "You look tired. Are you sleeping okay?"

I stare at her. *What do you think?*

She hugs me again. "It's so good to see you, sweetheart. I'll be glad when this is all over and you can finally come home. I miss you so much."

"Then why'd you let him move back in?" I hear myself asking her. I imagine myself struggling to get the words out; the back of my throat burning as I open my mouth and attempt to speak.

I swallow.

My eyes scan the room as I take a seat across from her. Lenny, the bully, is sitting on the left of me with a dark-skinned man. He looks too old to be his dad. But I can tell they're related. He shoots me a look, scowling. His eyes look wet, like he's trying not to cry about something. I shift my eyes around the other side of the room, then land my stare back on Mom, questioningly.

"Kyle couldn't come tonight," she answers as if she's read my thoughts. "He had practice this afternoon, then a dentist appointment." Kyle plays basketball. Although he's only in the seventh grade, he's good enough to play on the high school varsity team.

"'Cause he's getting his braces off," Karon says to me. "Right, Mommy?"

She smiles. "That's right, sweetheart. He really wanted to come tonight. He told me to tell you he'll see you this weekend."

I slowly nod, looking away. These visits are becoming more awkward every time she comes up here. If I look at her long enough,

I can see faded bruises around her neck where he had choked her. If I stare hard enough, I can see the fear she's skillfully hidden for many years behind designer sunglasses and painted smiles. I want to ask her if she's still afraid of him; of being without him. Want to know if she has nightmares. Want to know what she felt that night. His body hovered over hers, his hands gripping her neck.

I am scarred by the memory.

I can still hear his ferocious roar.

"You want me to kill you, don't you?!"

"You're going to die tonight, bitch!"

I blink.

Swallow back the anger that rises up in me.

Somehow, I am ten again. And that part of the night I couldn't remember—before she swung open their bedroom door, crawled down the stairs and called the police—creeps up in my mind. I am not sure why my life at ten keeps resurfacing. But it does. The night we get back from Nana's surprise birthday party. He hadn't wanted her to go; hadn't wanted her taking us, either. *"They can't go…"* That's what I heard him yelling to her. But she defied him and went anyway, with us in tow. Then he showed up, unannounced, unwanted. I saw it in her eyes. The shock and disappointment of him being there threading its way around the room as he made his way to her, kissing her on the lips. Everyone seemed happy to see him, except for Mom; except for me.

I blink, again. The plane ride back comes into clear focus. Mom seemed really nervous. He was silent the whole flight, sitting in the aisle seat next to her; the muscles in his jaw twitching. I kept watching him. Kept watching her, knowing a storm was coming. I think my brothers felt it, too—maybe not the triplets. But definitely Kyle and I could sense it. The tension, building like an angry sea.

During the car ride from the airport, my brothers fall asleep. And I pretend to fall asleep as well, barely breathing. Through tiny slits of darkness, I watch him as he drives. Watch him as he cuts his eyes over at her—a quiet rage swelling inside of him. The silence—save the light snores of my brothers—during the car ride home was deafening and eerily frightening. The storm was coming.

I blink.

Mom is staring at me. The triplets are staring at me, too. For some strange reason, I feel disoriented, trapped in a wordless maze. Mom leans up in her seat, reaches over and touches the side of my face. "Are you okay, sweetheart? You don't look well. Do you want me to call someone over?"

I shake my head; my only form of communication with her the whole visit.

She gives me a faint smile. She looks pained that I do not talk. I stare at her, wondering what bothers her most. That I am not talking, or simply that I am not talking to her. "Oh, before I forget. Your aunt Janie sends her love. She asks about you every day. She said she's written to you. Did you get anything from her?"

I look away.

"Sweetheart, you have to start talking. They're saying you're not being responsive to treatment. You can't keep what's bothering you…"

I blink, wondering how long it will be before she drops the restraining order against him this time. *"Your father deserves a chance…"*

A chance to do what, kill you?

I close my eyes, then open them, bringing into focus snapshots of my life.

There is yelling and screaming. Kyle is standing at the bedroom door, blocked in by a gate, clutching a teddy bear and crying. He is three. I am standing at the top of the stairs, looking down, crying. Mom is lying on the floor. I can see it. I know what happened. I saw him push her. But that is not the story I remember hearing her telling. Still, I know what I saw.

She is tryna get away from him.

I know what I heard.

"Don't you walk away from me when I'm talking to you..."

I see him yank her by the arm. I know I did. I see her snatch it away from him. I am there. I am five, scared and crying. But I know what I see. Then again, maybe...

I blink.

Now I see something I didn't see before. I see his hand up. I hear it slap across her face. And she stumbles. He slaps her again. And she tumbles backward.

She's right.

He's right.

He doesn't push her down the stairs.

He *slaps* her down them.

But the lie...that she tripped, and fell, is her truth.

And it is his.

Not mine. I know what I saw. I know what I heard. Yet, sometimes I still don't know what to believe.

"Shut your trap before I put my fist in it! You're nothing but a fucking liar..."

Mom touches the side of my face and the memory disappears.

She is looking at me, her eyes wet with worry. "...Sweetheart, it hurts my heart to see you like this. I wish you'd talk. Please. Let the professionals here help you. Your brothers and I miss you so much, K'wan. Don't you want to get better so you can come home?"

I don't respond.

Don't you want to get better? She asks this as if I have some debilitating illness. As if I am afflicted. I want to yell at her, "I am not sick!"

"How come you won't talk to Mommy? Are you mad at us?" Kavon wants to know, tapping me on the arm. I bring my attention to him. I want to tell him that I could never be mad at them. That I love them. That I miss them. And want to be home to protect them. But the words won't come out.

Kason and Karon watch and wait. I take them in, their eyes curious and wide. They are still innocent. Untainted—I hope—by the ugliness of what we had to live through. Maybe what I did has shielded them, maybe saved them, from the kind of pain I have experienced. Even if I didn't succeed at killing him, maybe I stopped him from doing any more harm. Maybe I have protected my brothers from the demons that haunt me. I hope. I truly pray. Only time will tell.

I swallow the lump in my throat.

"Are you gonna come home with us?" Kason asks.

I shake my head.

"Why?" Karon asks.

I pull all three into me and hug them, holding back tears.

I can't.

Seven

My grandma Ellen always says everything happens for a reason. Then when things go wrong, she'll say things like: "This too shall pass" and "God doesn't give us any more than what we can handle, or I'm going to keep it lifted up in prayer." I don't know if I believe her. I mean. What is the reason for someone having to live in fear? Why would God wanna give anyone that? I am trying to figure out what it is (or was) that I am supposed to get out of all of this. I can't see the point, or the purpose behind it. Yet, I am supposed to believe that there is a lesson in all of this. I am supposed to believe that there is a light at the end of the tunnel. Well, I don't know what the lesson is. And I definitely don't know what I am supposed to find when I finally get through this proverbial tunnel and to the light. What am I supposed to see? I guess the answers, as Grandma Ellen says, will come. But for now, what I do know is the only thing I do see is a buncha long days and nights ahead of me. And a long, dark winding *tunnel* that is leading me nowhere. As a matter of fact, I don't see any way out. I feel trapped. I feel stuck. I feel lost. I want out of here, but the illusion of freedom comes in clipped images.

Death, escape, release.

All three ways out; still remain fleeting thoughts of possibility. I am doubtful that any of the three will happen—today. Still, I try to remain hopeful, too. Yet, the one with the most immediate probability is…death. Yes, I am still toying with it. It's concept. Death, dying, dying…dead!

If it's your time to go, that's the one thing that no one can stop from happening, whether you're ready for it or not. At least that's what I've been told. And, it's what I also believe. I suppose I should be thankful it isn't my time to die. That I am still alive, even though I am…numb. I am still breathing, but I do not feel as if I am doing it on my own. It feels as if someone has me on a ventilator, mechanical breathing being done for me.

I do not feel like me…K'wan. I don't even know who I am anymore. Or why I am still here. Not here at this place, but here, alive. It is obvious, that it is a force greater than, more powerful than, me that keeps me still breathing, still moving, still existing; still asking the same question: Why am I here? Why can't I close my eyes and never wake up again? Why, why, why?

Death would be so much better than this.

Maybe I am already dead. I mean, my spirit. At least that's how I feel. How can anyone live without their spirit? If you are robbed of your spirit, at least it is something that you can eventually gain back, right? I think it is. But what if someone kills it, your spirit? A spirit can be killed right? When it's dead, can it be resurrected? Is it something you can ever really get back?

Without a spirit, you are a shell. I am a shell. A walking ball of hollowness.

"*I will fucking kill you…*"

Those words, his voice, remain with me. No matter how many times I try to forget them; no matter how hard I try to run from them, they always find their way back to me.

"*I will fucking kill you…*"

The threat wasn't directed at me. Its warning wasn't meant for me. It never is. I mean, it never was. Still, I am affected by the looming intent. Even now, despite there being a restraining order, what will stop *him* from hurting my mom? What will stop *him* from breaking it?

Nothing!

And there's nothing I can do about it.

"How are you feeling today, K'wan?" Mrs. Morgan asks. Her voice sounds laced with concern. But I can't be for certain. She is nice, but that doesn't mean she cares.

I run through the list of feelings in my head. *Trapped! Frightened! Worried! Confused!*

Choose one!

"How was your visit with your family?"

How do you think? They get to go home. I don't!

I shrug.

Her usual smile is etched on her neatly painted face. Her plump lips are shiny and painted pink, and look bigger than usual. I take a seat in the chair closest to the door, wondering if she's been stung by a bee or if she's used some kind of lip plumping product or something. She considers me for a while, then goes right into counselor mode. She clasps her hands in front of her. I glance at her fingernails. They're painted in bright, multi-colors with gem-stones on each nail. I stop myself from frowning. In my head, I hear my mom telling me it's not nice to stare. I shift my eyes.

"I'm hoping you were able to give some more thought to what I spoke about in our last session. Were you?"

What was it she wanted me to think about? Oh right. Forgiveness. I turn my head, pulling in my bottom lip. Where was forgiveness when Mom was trying to fight that man off of her? Where was it when he was pounding her face in? Where was it when she was screaming out for help? It was nowhere to be found. So, no, I do not wanna hear crap about forgiveness. Forgiveness wasn't there to protect her. And it can do nothing for me.

I inhale deeply, shutting my eyes.

"I see," she says, resting her arms up on her desk and clasping her hands together. "My heart goes out to you, K'wan. I can only imagine what it must have been like for you and your brothers, especially for you, growing up in a house where there was violence."

I open my eyes and stare at her.

Unless you've lived it, you will never understand. I want to ask her what exactly it is she thinks she can imagine. The feelings of helplessness? The confusion? The fear? The not knowing when the next big blowup would be?

I envision telling her about the silence being the worst part of it all; him coming home, not talking to Mom, and her running around looking lost, trying to figure out what she had done wrong, or what she didn't do. How he made her invisible and barely acknowledged us—his own sons—simply because he wanted to punish her for whatever wrongdoings he believed she had done. If he felt slighted, he slighted us, too.

What kind of person does that?

Oh, wait. He didn't think we were his anyway. So it really didn't matter. We didn't matter. How could we? So, of course, he'd ignore us. It's easier to ignore what you don't feel connected to, isn't it?

"Everything we do in life is a choice..." That's what my guidance counselor, Mr. Crenshaw, has always said. "You can choose to treat people the way you want to be treated, or not to be treated. It's up to you..."

I imagine telling her about him expecting dinner to be ready and served at the same time each night and him making us sit at the dinner table, waiting for him to grace us with his presence, if and when he decided to eat with us.

I blink.

"K'wan, please go upstairs and tell your father that dinner is ready."

I climb the stairs to their bedroom. He's in the sitting room that's on the other side of their huge bedroom. He's watching CNN. His feet propped up on the leather ottoman. *"Daddy, Mommy said dinner's ready."*

"Tell her I'm not coming down. Y'all go on and eat without me. I've ordered food."

He doesn't look up when he says this.

I feel myself getting pissed. She slaved over the stove cooking two separate meals because he only ate certain things, then he doesn't eat what she's cooked. It was another way for him to punish her (not my thoughts, but what I once overheard her telling Aunt Janie). But that's what she allowed him to do to her. She'd turn her back to us so we wouldn't see the disappointment pasted on her face. No matter how many times she tried to hide the hurt in her eyes from us, Kyle and I saw it. We always saw it. It was burned into my memory. That man was thoughtless and selfish. And he treated Mom like shit. And she took him back; even after everything he put her through. She wanted to still love him. Still wanted to give him chance after chance. Still wanted to make excuses after excuses as to why he hit her, or called her stupid, or fat, or worthless.

But why?

"I love your father very much. And he loves me. No matter what we are going through, he would never do anything to hurt me..."

How could he love her and hurt her at the same time? That is the million-dollar question that no one will ever answer and it make sense to me.

My fists clench.

"K'wan, I want to help you," Mrs. Morgan says, soothingly. Her voice brings me back to the present. I blink. "But I can't if you won't let me. Whatever it is you're feeling, you don't have to go through it alone. You have all these wonderful people in your family who are there to love and support you through all of this if you'd let them…"

I turn my head. Stare at the colorful wall mural on the right side of the room, a collage of multi-ethnic facial expressions: angry, sad, smiling, frowning, perplexed faces.

I am angry that I am here. Angry that my mother let *him* back into our lives. And I am angrier that she allowed *him* to disrupt it.

"Your father wants to move back home…"

"We all make choices we have to learn to live with…" the social worker from the youth detention said to me in one of our many one-sided sessions, like this one. *"And some of those choices have adverse consequences for those whom we care most about."*

How did moving him back in the house benefit me, or my brothers? It didn't. It's obvious to me that it was for her benefit rather than for ours.

"The next time you call the police on me it'll be for something worthwhile…"

"Aaaaah…HELP!"

"You stupid bitch! You want me to kill you, don't you?!"

Mom's yelling; her voice pleading for her life randomly slips into my thoughts. They live within me, in my head.

Stuck and unwanted!

I feel like my whole life is a recording on repeat. His threats hover over my head, like a dangling noose—a constant reminder that my mother's life meant nothing to him; that it could be snatched at any time.

I wonder if something is wrong with me. If I am supposed to feel sorry for what I did, I don't. If I am supposed to be remorseful, I am not. I don't regret stabbing him. My only regret is not killing him.

"...Are you okay?" I hear Mrs. Morgan asking. She has gotten up from her seat and is now sitting in the matching chair next to me with a box of tissue in her hand. She places her warm hand over mine. I look at her. "Where did you go?"

I blink, unaware that I have tears rolling down my face. I pull several sheets of tissue from the box, wipe my face with them, then roll the wet mess into a ball. In my head, I thank her. Tell her I found my way back to hell.

"K'wan, I only know what's on paper about what happened that night; what your parents have reported. And the thing is, everyone has their own perception of what life must have been like for you experiencing violence in your home. I can't begin to imagine what that was really like for you. But I'd like for you to help me better understand it so that I can help you. I want to hear your side. So that I can help you sort through it—that painful place you just visited—so that you can heal from it, grow from it, and be able to fully move on from it."

I look at her.

She smiles. "I want you to know, you're not responsible for your parents' choices. You are not to blame for their stuff, their choices, or their issues."

I steady my breathing.

Unclench my fist.

You wanna know the worst part? I hear myself asking her.

That not knowing when or how the bomb would explode. Not knowing what trigger would detonate it and set him off. *I need for you and your brother to keep the triplets quiet when your father comes home... Don't do anything to upset your father tonight... Your father's under a lot of stress, try not to make him angry..."*

Why did his moods have to become our responsibility? Why did we have to be the ones to walk around on edge, hoping we didn't do anything to cause him to take his frustrations with us out on our mother?

For Christ's sake, Syreeta, why are they crying? Will you do something to shut them up!

"Whatever guilt you might be feeling at this moment, K'wan, I want to help you work through it."

I blink.

I'm not the one who needs help! Why am I here? And he gets to be out on the streets on four years probation?

"Guilt and worry are two very useless emotions," she continues, keeping her eyes locked on mine. This time I hold her stare. *You can't break me. I'm already broken.* "They make it very difficult for people to let go of past hurts and disappointments so that they can move on with their lives. People consumed by guilt spend so much time being immobilized by past behavior, that they miss out on the present. It is in the present that we can change. That real change begins. What has already happened, our pasts, can't be undone."

I shift my eyes.

"Guilt speaks to us about not being good enough, about being a failure—in our own eyes, because it becomes a way that we can beat up on ourselves. It is a very toxic emotion that can be used to manipulate, to accuse and blame. It pushes us to make poor decisions; decisions that are not thought through. Guilt is a self-inflicting punishment, K'wan. Holding onto it doesn't hurt anyone except you." She squeezes my hand.

I stare at her, unblinking.

"Why are you punishing yourself, K'wan?"

Why are you touching me?

I pull my hand from her.

"K'wan, what happened in your home is not your fault. You do not have to own it."

I am starting to feel like I am listening to a sermon, the Gospel According to Mrs. Morgan. I wait for the tambourines and drums to start up. She means well; she is only doing her job. But, damn! Enough already!

I feel a headache coming on.

"It's about that time," she finally says, getting up and walking back around to her desk. I let out a sigh of relief. I'm exhausted.

"But before we end our session, K'wan, I want to say this: You can begin to change your attitude and thoughts about any self-imposed guilt you may have, if you really want to heal. Holding onto it does not help. Don't let the past control you."

But the past still haunts me!
The past still affects me!
The past is my present!
I can't run from it!
I'm too tired to run from it!
There is no escaping it!
I get up and walk out.

Eight

"**W**ho wants to tell me why they think some people have problems taking responsibility for what they do?" Miss Daisy asks, looking around the circle. Today there are ten of us in group, well, now eleven, since The Bully has walked in. Miss Daisy gestures toward the empty seat next to me and the hairs on the back of my neck stand up. He isn't happy about sitting next to me either.

At least we have that in common.

"Yo, Jake, man, let me get your seat and you sit here"—he cuts his eye at me—"next to this lil'—"

Miss Daisy cuts him off. "No one is switching seats. Next time get here on time if you're so worried about the seating arrangements in here."

He huffs, mumbling under his breath as he snatches the chair. It hits my foot, and I am certain he's done it deliberately. "Punk-ass."

I take a deep breath. Then smile to myself as Grandma Ellen's voice plays in my head. "That little fresh-mouthed heathen is gonna have me smack the peapods out of his knotty head in a minute if he keeps messing with my grandbaby. Don't you worry yourself about that little disrespectful S-O-B. He's nothing but the devil himself. But, if he keeps picking with Grandma's baby, I'll beat the fire out of him."

I bite the inside of my lip to keep from chuckling to myself. Grandma Ellen doesn't play.

"Now, as I was saying before Mister Late came through the door disrupting group, who wants to tell me why some people minimize their violent behaviors, deny them, or make excuses for their behaviors instead of owning their actions and accepting responsibility for them?"

Because no one makes them, I answer in my head.

Westley says, "Because people keep letting them do ish to 'em and makin' excuses for them."

"Because they keep getting away with it," Jackson adds.

"There's definitely truth to that," she agrees. "When there's no real accountability, there's no motivation to make real changes in behavior, or at least get honest enough to look at it for what it is. So, yes, because they keep getting away with it. Anyone else?" She pauses, glancing around the circle, waiting for someone else to speak. "What about you, Marco?"

He shrugs. "If they don't think they did anything wrong, then why would they?"

"That's true. Okay, anyone else?" She waits a beat, then continues, "When people minimize their behaviors or go around pretending that what they did wasn't so bad, or that the situation itself wasn't as bad as others are making it out to be, then they're not taking responsibility for their actions. For instance, when people have committed acts of violence toward others, not taking responsibility might allow them to not feel bad about what they've done. If you're not the one responsible for your violence, then it means you don't have to do anything about it. Like Marco said, if you don't think you've done anything wrong, then there's nothing to address. If you're not the one responsible for the violence, then there's no point in trying to change your behavior."

I see myself raising my hand and saying, "I know what I did was wrong, but I don't feel bad about doing it." I hear, "Anything after but is bullshit." I'm not sure where that's coming from, but it's what I imagine Miss Daisy saying.

Like everyone else in this place, I feel he got exactly what he deserved for treating my mom like that for all those years. If I were talking, I'd tell her that there's only so much a person can take before they go off. Then I imagine her saying something like, "Going off is still a choice one makes."

"So, let's talk about blame. How many of you blame someone else for you being here?" Seven hands go up. Marco is the only one, along with me, who doesn't raise his hand. "Marco, why not?"

Because I wanted to do it, I answer in my head. *Because stabbing him was all I thought about doing.*

I shift in my seat, glance over at Marco when he almost says what I was thinking. "Because I wanted to do it, knowing that there was going to be consequences. But, at that moment, I didn't care."

"Do you regret what happened?" Miss Daisy wants to know.

"Nah. I don't regret takin' it to him. I regret gettin' caught. As far as I was concerned, he had to get got so it is what it is. I wish my moms woulda never got involved wit' his crab-ass from the rip."

"So you think you should have gotten away with what you did?"

He looks at Miss Daisy as if she's asked something crazy. "Heck yeah."

A few guys laugh.

"He's gotten away with doin' what he's done to my moms for mad long, so yeah, I shoulda been able to get away with it."

Several guys in the group agree with him.

"On some real, I should have waited until I caught him somewhere by himself slipping, then masked up and shut his lights out."

Several guys laugh.

Miss Daisy doesn't find any humor in it. "And what would that have really accomplished?"

"Well, for one, I wouldn't be here."

"But what would it have changed? Granted you might have gotten away with assaulting him, but would it have stopped your mother from being with him? Would it have forced him to change his behavior?"

Marco shrugs. "Maybe not."

Miss Daisy nods, knowingly. She glances over at me and I nervously shift in my seat.

She leans over in her seat. "K'wan, how about you? Do you take responsibility for what you did?"

I hope you die!

I hate you!

Yeah. I swallow, keeping my eyes locked on hers. Then nod. That's the most I can offer her. She smiles, understandingly.

Lenny sucks his teeth. "This is some BS, for real. This mofo sits up in every group and says nothing and you let him. But let one of us not open our mouths and you wanna threaten us with sanctions and whatnot."

"Leonard, you know what?"

He shoots Miss Daisy a look. "I told you, stop calling me that. That's not my name."

I will myself to not smile. Miss Daisy only calls him by his whole name when he's being an obnoxious prick.

She doesn't back down. "That *is* your name, young man, whether you want to own it or not. It's what's on your birth certificate, so get over it. Now, I've had about enough of you and your disruptiveness. I have not once sanctioned anyone for not wanting to share in group, nor have I ever threatened anyone in doing so. What I have done is sanction young men like *you* who remain troublesome in my groups. I keep telling you, if you spent more time on your own stuff and less time on everyone else's, you just might get out of here and stay out."

He folds his arms across his chest and mumbles under his breath.

"Well, he does kinda have a point, Miss Dee. No disrespect," Jake says. "We don't even know why he's here."

"He's here because of the choices he's made, like everyone else. When he's ready to share more with the group, he will. And believe me, one day, Mister Taylor will. For now, he will sit and he will listen. And if the rest of you wish to sit and not speak, you can do so. And we'll simply sit here for an hour and a half, staring at each other. Would you prefer that?"

They all groan.

"Nah, I'm good," Aesop says. "I don't know about anyone else, but I like talking in group."

Good for you. I turn my attention to the window.

"Man, you like hearing yourself talk; that's all that is," Jake says.

"Nah, for real, yo," Aesop explains. "I'm not gonna front. At first I wasn't beat to be here. But, listening to some of the other guys' stories and listening to some of the stuff Miss Dee says to us kinda got me thinkin' about different things."

"Like what?" Miss Daisy wants to know.

"Like maybe I need to change. I mean, I don't wanna keep gettin' locked up, or put in programs. I've been in and outta programs since I was twelve. And this is like my third one. I'm tired of it. But if I don't learn how to be different, I will if I keep doin' the same things. You said people only make real change when they're beat to change."

Jake corrects him. "Nah, she said when peeps get sick and tired of being sick and tired, then they'll change."

"Same thing," Aesop counters.

I think about my mom and wonder what she was like before she married him, before she had my brothers and me. Did she change over time, or was she always who she is. I wonder if she and Aunt Janie ever saw Grandma and Grandpop fight when they were growing up. Then I wonder about *him*. Did he see Grandma Ellen and Grandpop Bill fight growing up? Miss Daisy says violence is learned. So, then, where did he learn his? I wonder if he ever really thought about changing. I quickly dismiss the idea. It's already obvious had he really wanted to change, he would have. He would have done things differently after the first time Mom called the police on him. But he didn't. He came back home and did the same things.

Maybe 'cause he didn't think he had to change.

Right now, my brain is all jumbled up. In my head, everyone is pointing fingers at everyone else. I am pointing fingers at my parents. They are pointing fingers at each other. Still, I think, no, I believe, I wouldn't have stabbed him had he not given me a reason to. Maybe I would have liked him. Maybe I still wouldn't have. Still, none of us would be in this mess had he changed, or just stayed the heck outta our lives. Or better yet, had he never put his hands on Mom in the first place.

"I've actually said both," Miss Daisy says, bringing me back to the group. I glance around the circle, taking the group in. I hear her saying, "Your choices are what brought you here. And your choices are what will keep you out. It is all up to you."

"Aesop, why don't you tell us what's going on with you."

"I talked to my moms last night," he shares. "She says things are better at home."

Miss Daisy raises her brow. "Oh? How so?"

"She says that ni…I mean, dude…is really trying to change. That he's not yelling like he was. And not drinking as much."

Miss Daisy nods. "Mmm, I see. And hopefully that's the case. Change takes time, and it takes work."

"Do you think people like that can ever really change?" Aesop asks. I'm surprised at how talkative he is today. Even though he says he likes talking in group, he isn't always this chatty. He must really have a lot on his mind, like me. "I mean, my moms always says he's gonna change because that's what he keeps telling her. And obviously that's what she wants to believe. But I don't see it. I mean, damn! How stupid can she be? I mean, don't get me wrong. I love my moms"—he sighs—"but she be on some dumb shit sometimes, especially when it comes to him. It's real frustratin'. She keeps saying she doesn't wanna give up on him. But I'm like, get real. He's dead weight. But she don't be tryna hear nothin' I gotta say. I don't think he's ever gonna change. He doesn't even think what he does is wrong." He shakes his head. "My moms is delusional."

Miss Daisy crosses her legs. "It's not that your mom is delusional, as you say. She believes what she believes because that's what her heart allows her to see. Hopefully he does change. Thing is, in order for change to happen, people have to put in the work toward being different. They have to genuinely want to be different. Stopping behavior doesn't necessarily mean someone has changed. Putting down a drink for one or two days, or for several months, doesn't mean anything's different about your drinking. Same thing goes for abuse. Just because someone hasn't hit you or screamed at you doesn't mean they won't do it again. We all know how to stop doing something. But once the spotlight is off, we'll go right back to doing what we've always done. True change happens when we internalize our actions, invest in our choices, and commit to becoming better human beings."

She glances at her watch. "Well, gentlemen. It's about that time.

Does anyone have any last minute thoughts or concerns they'd like to share?"

As always, no one does. She dismisses us. Everyone starts scurrying outta the room. Lenny bumps into me, and I know it's done purposefully.

"Yo, watch where the fuck you goin', fag-ass bitch."

I stop in my tracks. Stare at him.

Take a deep breath.

He steps up to me. "Whatchu wanna do, yo?"

"Yo, c'mon, L," Aesop says, pulling on his arm. "It ain't worth it. Let's get outta here, man. Leave that dude alone."

He scowls. "Yeah, you right. Fuck this pussy-ass nigga."

I take another deep breath, pulling in my bottom lip.

I am really trying to make the right choices. But I don't know how much more of his bullying I can take before I snap on him.

I don't wanna fight that boy, but I will if I have to. And I promise I will beat his face in.

Miss Daisy calls for me. She wants to know if everything is okay. She stares at me, hard, as she asks this. Concern appears etched on her face. I tell her everything's great. Yeah, it's a lie. But so has most of my life—one big ole lie. So what's one more? Besides, what could she possibly do if I told her, *no*, everything wasn't okay? Nothing, so there's no point.

"I see how Leonard and a few of the other residents try to antagonize you. Try not to let them bother you too much, okay?"

I nod, shifting my eyes, then walking off.

Nine

Later that night, there's a knock on my door. I start to ignore it, but whoever it is knocks again. *It's probably someone looking for Ja'Meer.* I sigh, getting up from the desk where I am doing my homework. I peek through the glass strip and see that it's Aesop. I open the door and hope my face doesn't show my feelings of shock at him standing here.

"Yo, man," he says. "About earlier, don't pay L no mind, yo. He's a good dude; just kinda fucked up in the head sometimes, that's all."

Are you his personal messenger? I look at him, wondering why he feels the need to tell me this. I am not interested in his story. All I want is for The Bully to leave me the heck alone. Stay outta my face. I'm not interested in being his friend. I'm not even interested in getting along with him. So I don't know what the heck his problem is with me. And truth be told, I'm not interested in getting along with Aesop, either. He seems kinda two-faced and he has, as my grandma Ellen would say, devilish eyes so I'd rather keep my distance from him, too. My gut tells me he can't be trusted.

"Yo, you feel like playing a game of chess?"

He's been wanting to play me in chess ever since he heard I was good. But, like I always do, I shake my head no. He tells me if I change my mind he'll be in the rec room, then walks off. That whole encounter feels strange, but I do not give it much thought. I go back to studying Calculus formulas.

Ten minutes later, there's another knock at the door. I push back from the desk and let out an annoyed sigh. All I wanna do is study in peace. I open the door. This time it's one of the counselor aides, Mr. Lenton. He's really old, like in his fifties or sixties. And he has a bunch of gray hairs coming outta his ears and nose, out from the back of his neck. The kids call him Wolfman behind his back. One time I googled something on men with hair growing outta their noses and ears and learned that it was called hyper-trichosis, or something like that. Whatever. Mr. Lenton's always been nice to me so I don't care if he has a patch of hair hanging outta his ears, or annoying hairs that curl outta his nose.

He tells me I have a visit, then walks off.

I quickly use the bathroom, wash my hands, then change into a Seton Hall basketball jersey and a pair of jeans, anxiously look-ing forward to seeing my mom and brothers. I step out of my room and head down the hall.

As I am walking, I find myself wondering when I'm gonna be allowed to be a kid again. Or if those times are gonna pass me by and before I know it, I'll blink my eyes and be a grown man. Sometimes I don't feel fourteen. I feel like, I don't know…old. Older than I should be. I try to remember when I ever really feel like a kid. Thinking about school makes me sad. It is the only time, or place, that I ever really feel like a kid, where I can laugh and be silly and play sports and not think about anything other than being my age. It's when I would walk through the door of my house that I would start to feel the pressure. The strain to stand watch weighed heavily on me. To look after my brothers, to watch after my mom, to make sure they were safe. As much as I don't wanna admit it, being here gives me a break. I mean, I don't wanna be here. I'm still stressed, but not in the same way. It sounds crazy, feels crazy. All I wanna do is be a kid, but I don't know what being a kid means anymore. So much has happened. So much has changed. I feel like something was taken away from me. I feel so different.

I am different.

And for now, I do not know if that is a good thing or a bad one. All I know is nothing will ever be the same for me.

I step into the visiting room and freeze. *He* is not who I expect to see. Seeing him causes many different emotions to creep up in me. Anger; sadness; hurt. Why he keeps coming here when he knows I do not want to see him or be bothered with him makes no sense to me. *He* stands up to greet me. I do not acknowledge him. I turn around and walk out.

Twenty minutes later, Mr. Lenton is back at my door. This time to deliver a note. Mr. Lenton runs a hand over his mouth, then pulls at his goatee. "You know, son," he says as he hands me the folded piece of paper. He pauses as if he's trying to choose his words wisely. He narrows his eyes. "I'm sure you have your reasons for not wanting to see your father. And it isn't any of my business why. So I'ma say this, then leave it alone: A father can only love his son the way his son allows him to love him. And that's not always easy for either of them. Parents sometimes have to be reminded that they are as much a student as they are a teacher in their relationship with their children. I know you are angry with your father. But try not to shut him out. Give him the opportunity to make amends. I get the sense that he is realizing how important you are to him. And hopefully, one day, you'll realize it, too."

I shrug.

Mr. Lenton pulls in his lips. "Whatever it is your father did or didn't do, I'm sure he is fighting guilt that whatever he failed to do has stolen a piece of your innocence. And he has no one to blame but himself."

Mr. Lenton walks off, leaving me standing in the middle of the doorway, gripping the folded paper in my sweaty hand.

⊕

I am in bed, restless. I have my headphones on, listening to Rick Ross. But all he has done is given me a headache. Sometimes I think these rappers brag about stuff that isn't really true; that they rap about stuff that makes them appear greater than what they really are. I don't know. It's my opinion.

I remove the Soul by Ludacris headphones from around my head, placing them up on the nightstand that sits between the two beds. I glance over at Ja'Meer. He is snoring; not as loudly as most nights, but he still loud enough to make trying to get sleep unbearable. As annoying as Ja'Meer can be sometimes, tonight is one of those nights I wish he were up, talking my head off. Sometimes he keeps me distracted long enough to not get caught up in my thoughts. But tonight, I do not have any distractions. Not even music relaxes me.

He invades my head.

"I want to apologize to you and your brothers," he had said to Kyle and me one night when we were at his house. I hadn't wanted to go, but Mom made me. She told me it was the right thing to do, even if it didn't feel right to me. "I never meant to hurt your mom."

"But you were mean to her, Daddy," Kyle had said. "And you made Mommy cry."

"I know, son," he offered. "It was wrong of me. Your mother didn't deserve that."

"Then why'd you do it?" I had asked, narrowing my eyes at him. I'm not sure how long he had been outta the house, but I was happy he no longer lived with us. I was happy that the police had put handcuffs on him, and that he was gonna be outta our lives. At least, that's what I thought. Kyle and the triplets were always happy to see him. They were always excited to spend time with him; to stay the weekends with him. Not me. I wanted to be home. Closer to Mom. And away from him.

"I'm not going to lie to either of you. How I treated your mother is inexcusable. No man should ever put his hands on a woman, or mistreat her. What I did to your mother was wrong. She didn't deserve to be treated the way I treated her."

"Then why'd you do it?" I asked again. I remember Mom telling me to behave while I was with him, to not give him attitude. But I couldn't help it. I didn't like him. And I didn't wanna be there with him. But I was. I don't remember anything he said. Can't remember if he ever explained why he beat up Mom. Why he called her names and yelled at her. He was talking but nothing made sense to me. I remember staring at him, frowning.

"I've been stressed with work. That still doesn't justify what I did, or make it right. I know I was wrong. I feel really bad about it."

"Are you going to come back home?" Kyle asked.

"One day, I hope. If your mom will have me back, I want nothing more than to be back home with you and your brothers. I miss my—"

"I don't want you to come home," I snapped. "I like it better with you gone."

I remember the stunned look on his face. He was surprised that I would tell him that.

"Noooo," Kyle whined, hitting me. "Don't say that, K'wan."

"Don't hit your brother," he said. "It's okay if that's how your brother feels. If I were him, I wouldn't want me home either. Not the way I was, anyway. He's entitled to his feelings." He looked over at me. "I promise you, son. I'm getting help. I'm going to do whatever I need to so that I never do anything to hurt your mother, or you and your brothers again."

I folded my arms tightly across my chest. I didn't believe him. Everyone else wanted to, but I couldn't. I wouldn't. And I still won't. I don't trust, for one minute, that he ever wanted to change. If he had wanted to, he would have. It wouldn't have had to be an afterthought; not simply words, but actions as well. He would have been a man of his word. But he wasn't. So how can I ever trust what comes out of his mouth? Promises are made to be broken. Those were his words, not mine.

I stare up at the ceiling, counting backward in my head, hoping sleep finds its way to me. I am tired. My head is pounding. Thinking, remembering, hurts my brain.

Why can't he leave me alone?

Why does he feel the need to bother me?

He has to know I want nothing to do with him. He has to.

"I am never giving up on you. No matter how many times you refuse to see me, I will not stop visiting you. I am not going to stop being here for you."

"Leave me the heck alone," I mumble to myself rolling over on my side, facing the wall. I want to sleep, but I am afraid that tonight the nightmares will come. Thanks to him. Still, I am fighting to keep my eyes open; fighting to keep the imps at bay. But I am too tired to continue fighting. I am being pulled under. Reluctantly, I give in, shutting my eyes and allowing sleep and its demons to take me away.

Ten

I am sweating. My heart is racing. I awaken to the same nightmare I've had since I was eight years old. It's dark out. Kyle and I are standing over a grave. Our eyes are swollen and red from crying. We are all alone. There is a black headstone. Its inscription etched into my memory:

LOVING MOTHER & DEVOTED WIFE
SYREETA COLLETTE TAYLOR
JUNE 3, 1975–

My mom's grave is prepared, the ground opened and ready and waiting for her coffin to be lowered into the earth. Her tombstone is erected, a symbol of her untimely death at the hands of her abuser. Her gravesite, the place my brothers and I will mourn our loss, and remember our mother.

There is a beginning and an end to life. Mom's beginning, her date of birth, is already engraved in the marble at her resting place, her final destination. Her ending comes at the hands of *him*. But *when* remains a mystery. Still it taunts us as we are standing there, at her grave—despite its emptiness, waiting, snotty-nosed and tear-stained faces, preparing for the moment we've both feared, when the nightmare would become a reality.

"Why is Mommy's name on this stone?" Kyle asks, touching the marble, his small finger tracing each letter.

My voice falls to a whisper, "This is Mommy's grave."

"Why does she have a grave?"

"Because she's gonna die."

"How is she gonna die?" Kyle wants to know. He doesn't look at me. His eyes stay locked on her tombstone as he sniffles.

I am choking up, fighting to hold it all in, but I fail. Everything comes rushing out in a wave of tears. "She's gonna get *killed*." I can't stop them from rapidly falling from my eyes.

"I don't want Mommy to be killed," Kyle cries out, then hugs me tightly. "Is Daddy gonna kill her?"

I stare grimly down into the dark, empty hole. "Yes," I push out in between sobs.

I will kill you!

We jump at the sound of screaming. A woman's cry out for help echoes around us. And I am frozen still. Afraid.

I jolt up in bed, my heart racing and hands shaking. My lungs are tightening. I clutch my chest, gasping. I do not have asthma, but I feel as if I am having an attack; maybe it's asthma. No, it's panic. I am frantic and alone. This nightmare always ends with me either waking to the sounds of Mom's screaming, or a black-gloved hand covering her mouth and nose until her body falls limp. A few times I have awakened to her body being slowly lowered down into the ground.

I blink. For a moment, I am disoriented, almost forgetting where I am.

"Yo, K'wan, man," Ja'Meer says in a raspy tone, "you aiight over there?"

I don't say anything; just shake my head, pulling in deep breaths, holding the air in my lungs, then breathing it out slowly, trying to calm my shaky nerves. I have to get out of here. I have to get home. He hasn't killed her, yet. But what if he does? What if he decides that he's had enough of being without her and finally makes good on his threats? What if she drops the restraining order again and lets him move back in?

"I will fucking kill you…"

How can I not take those words seriously? I was raised to always think before I spoke. To never say anything I did not mean. "A man should always say what he means, and mean what he says." That's what *he* always told me. So I have to believe he's meant what he's said. He's said it too many times for me not to.

I wipe my eyes with the back of my sleeve, then close them and cover my face as Ja'Meer clicks on the lamp that sits on the nightstand between our beds. I slowly open them, trying to adjust to the unwelcomed light.

He studies me. "Yo, my dude; you look shook. You aiiight?"

I nod my head.

He sits up in bed, keeps his eyes locked on me. "That musta been one helluva dream—I mean, nightmare. You were tossing and turning and talking in your sleep. Sounded like you were crying."

I give him a shocked look, then lower my eyes in embarrassment. I am curious to know what he overheard me saying in my sleep.

"Look, K'wan, man, real shit. I know you can talk but for whatever reasons you ain't beat to, so it's all good. No pressures. You still aiiight wit' me, feel me? Somethin' really fucked up happened to you that you don't wanna talk about but, man, listen for real, for real, if you ever wanna talk about it, I got you. I'll just listen. And you have my word it'll stay between us, aiiight?"

Now it's my turn to study him. I take him in for a moment, then slowly nod. Although I'm not sure what to do with it, I feel like he's tossed me a lifeline. And for the first time since I've known him, I actually smile—not a complete smile, but it's a start—and nod, appreciative of the gesture.

I wanna ask him what he heard. I open my mouth to attempt to speak, but nothing comes out. I strain to form words.

He's looking at me. "Yo, you aiiight?" I nod, forcing out a yawn and stretching. "Aiight, cool. Remember what I said. Whenever you wanna talk, I got you." I nod again. "Cool. Now take ya ass back to sleep. We gotta be up in four hours. If I oversleep, I'm blamin' it on you, pickle head." He tosses one of his pillows at me. I toss it back and he laughs, catching it. "Yo, man, on some real shit. If you ever wanna get outta this hellhole you're gonna have to talk. There's no way around it. When I first got here I wasn't beat to fuck with anyone here. I didn't trust none of these muhfuckas, for real. I mean, I wasn't on some mute-type shit like you, feel me? I just had no convo for 'em. But, I gotta say, if it wasn't for Missus Ellerson, I'd prolly still be on level one, like you. She made me feel comfortable, and I finally started to trust her enough to talk. And talking has really helped me a lot. You should try it." He pauses, then snaps his fingers. "Yo, maybe you should request Missus Ellerson. She's cool as hell."

I shrug. I don't really wanna change counselors. Even if I don't talk to her, Missus Morgan is nice enough. She doesn't pressure me. But I know what he's saying is right. If I want to leave here, which I do, I'm gonna have to find my voice so I can tell them whatever they wanna hear so I can go home. I take a deep breath.

"Aiiight, I'm goin' back to sleep. No more nightmares." He reaches over and flicks off the light, then rolls over on his other side, pulling the sheet and blanket up over his head, leaving me feeling alone.

For some reason, his brother comes to mind and I am curious to know more about him. What happened to him? Was he hurt? Killed? I don't know if I could handle it if something were to ever happen to one of my brothers; especially Kyle.

I lean back against the wall, and welcome the quiet. In the darkness, I close my eyes and try to recall the first time I heard *him* threaten my mom. I swallow. The back of my throat burns.

I will kill you!

I inhale deeply, allowing his words to ricochet in my head. I think back, try to shuffle through the deck of memories that have been tossed around in my mind. Memories I've tried to put into neat piles, discarding those that are too painful. But they are the ones that seem to be the hardest to get rid of. They are the ones that haunt me.

I close my eyes, and the moment comes into focus. I am six. No, five. Even at that age, I understand—I know—the implication behind the threat.

I awaken in the middle of the night, frightened from a bad dream. I can't recall what the dream is about. But I remember climbing outta bed and walking out into the hallway, then down to their room. The bedroom door is open, but the room is empty. I remember walking back to my room, then standing and listening. The house is quiet, almost spooky like. And then I hear faint voices; a few minutes later, it's quiet again. Another beat passes, then I hear his voice. He's mad. The sounds are coming from downstairs. I follow the sound to his study. They are arguing, but there is no yelling, if that makes sense; just hushed angry words. The door is cracked. I strain to listen to what is being said.

"I want a divorce," I hear Mom say. *At five, I don't really know what a divorce really is, but it sounds bad in my head.*

"A divorce?" he snorts out. *"You can't be serious."*

"Oh, I'm very serious, Randy. I can't keep living like this. You're constantly on edge and I've taken your verbal abuse long enough. You can see the children anytime you want, but I think it's best we separate."

He kinda laughs at her. *"Syreeta, don't be absurd. And where will you go? Without me, you have nothing."*

"And even when I'm with you, I have nothing. Janie said the kids and I can stay with her and Rodney until I can get on my feet."

He huffs. *"It figures your meddling sister would be behind this nonsense, putting a bunch of ideas in your head."*

"Janie has nothing to do with this. My decision to leave you, Randy, is of my own volition. I'm tired of the fighting. I can't take the disrespect any longer. The stress is not good for me."

"You're not taking my kids out of here. And you're definitely not taking them anywhere out of state. If you want to leave, you can leave. Go live your life stress-free. But my boys stay with me."

"Randy, you can't be serious. I'm not leaving my sons behind with you."

"Then you had better come up with another plan because before I let you leave me and take my sons away from me, I will kill you." He says this as his eyes meet mine. I have pushed the door open and I am now standing in the doorway, my hand over my mouth, chest heaving in and out—frightened at what I've heard.

Mom rushes to me, wraps me in her arms and kisses me on the forehead. "Sweetheart, go on back to bed. Mommy and Daddy are having grownup talk, okay?"

I shake my head, struggling to breathe. "But I don't wanna go to bed. I heard Daddy say he's gonna kill you. Mommy, I'm scared."

"Oh, sweetheart, no. There's nothing to be scared of. Daddy didn't mean that. He's upset." She looks over at him. And he says nothing. "Randy, tell him."

"Listen to your mother. Go on back to bed." That's all he says. No I didn't mean it. No I'm sorry. Nothing. I am shaking in my mom's arms.

I am coughing and crying. "Why is he going to kill you?"

She is rubbing my back; does her best to console me. "He didn't mean that, Sweetheart. You have to believe me, okay? Sometimes grownups say things they don't really mean when they're upset, okay, sweetheart."

I don't believe her. I want to. But it is how he said it that scares me most, like he really meant it—every single gruesome word of it. I look over at him with pleading eyes, hoping he says something—anything that will sooth my worry; ease my fears. He does nothing.

I take a deep sigh, lightly banging my head back against the wall. Ja'Meer's snoring resonates through the room, disrupting my thoughts. I want to get up and shake him, to tell him to cut down on all that racket. But I leave him be.

How many times did he threaten to kill her?

I count: One...two...three...four times that I know of, that I heard with my own ears. I can only imagine how many other times he might have said it, how many times it went unheard. I may be only a kid, but if you ask me, once is too many.

"Is Daddy gonna kill you in your sleep?"

I'll never forget the look on her face when I ask this. Her brows crease with worry. She bites her bottom lip, reaching for my hands. She looks me in the eyes, intently. It looks as if she's about to cry. *"You have nothing to worry about, sweetheart, okay? Your father would never do anything to hurt me, okay?"*

I nod.

"Anything you've heard your father say to me, you have to promise me you won't repeat it to anyone. Your father and I are going through some things right now, but we're going to work it out. I promise you, okay?"

Nod again. She hugs me. And I start crying.

"Don't cry. Everything's going to be okay." She wipes my tears with her thumbs. *"You're Mommy's big boy. And I love you so much."*

I am crying and hiccupping. *"But you gonna get a divorce. And Daddy said heeee's gonna kill you. I don't want Daddy to kill you…"*

She pulls me into her bosom and rocks me like she used to when I was three. I remember that being the place I felt most safe, in her arms; close to her. "Sssssssssh. You have nothing to worry about, sweetheart. Look at me." I lift my head from her chest and stare into her wet eyes. "You have nothing to be afraid of. I'm not going to divorce your father. And he's not going to do anything to hurt me. Everything's going to be just fine, okay?"

I nod again, and she pulls me back into her. She keeps reassuring me that everything is okay; that I have nothing to worry about. In her arms, where she rocks and hums and pats my back, I feel loved. And at that moment, I want, need, to believe her—that I have nothing to worry about; that everything is going to be okay—even if she doesn't really believe it herself.

Now that I'm sitting up thinking about it, after all that's happened, I have to wonder if it's my fault Mom stayed. Maybe if I hadn't been scared—maybe if I hadn't heard him threaten to kill her that night she would have taken me and my brothers and left him. Maybe none of this would have happened. I hear Mrs. Morgan saying, "You're not responsible for your parents' choices...."

Yeah, right. Then why am I blaming myself? Why am I feeling so down?

Because it is my fault!

Eleven

Today's session with Mrs. Morgan is no different from any other session. She greets me with a smile, then waits for me to take a seat in one of the chairs in front of her. Wait. There is something different today. Her eyes. She's wearing hazel contacts and an orange-colored eye shadow that makes her eyes look like they're glowing. I wonder why she'd do that. I mean, wear that kinda stuff here. I thought there were different kinds of makeup for different things. I'm thinking orange eye makeup with those colored contacts isn't for this kind of place. It's a distraction. But, okay, it's none of my business what she wears.

I shift in my seat and watch as she writes something in my chart. The date and time, I'm sure. "How are you?" she asks, looking up at me.

I blink, then shrug. That's the best I can offer her. The nightmares are really starting to get to me, again. They've gotten worse since I was arrested, since my stay in the detention center, and now here. I wasn't having them as much before all this. But now it's almost every other night. I am tired.

She sets her pen down and folds her hands in front of her. She studies me. Or at least that's what it feels like she's trying to do. "K'wan, I'm going to be very honest with you..."

Uh-oh. I shift in my seat.

"You are probably one of the most challenging cases I've had in my entire career."

She says this and it sounds as if I am some case study that has gone wrong. I play with the definition in my head. I do that sometimes. Read the dictionary and memorize words and their meanings. Case study is one of those terms I committed to my memory, because that is how this whole situation—the stabbing, the arrest, the court hearings, everything—has made me feel.

I know what its purpose is for: to find patterns and causes of behavior. All she has to do is read my chart. Read the police reports. All she has to do is question my mom, let her tell her how many times I cried to her. How many times I asked her if he was going to hurt her again. And how many times she told me she wouldn't let him. How many times she promised me. There goes your pattern right there. And there goes your answer to the cause. Still, Mrs. Morgan is sitting here, sounding disappointed that she has not been able to analyze me—my life. That she has not been able to successfully crack open my shell.

I wanna tell her, don't bother. There's nothing inside.

"...I want to help you. Really, I do. But, honestly, I don't know how. You coming into my office twice a week with me doing all the work—the talking for both of us—isn't helping you. I've discussed your case in treatment team. Everyone who has contact with you all say the same thing—that they find you likeable; that you're not disruptive, but that you are not an active participant in any of the treatment process. This is your treatment; not anyone else's. You've been here for almost two months and none of us know you. It's hard to monitor progress or measure change when you've given us nothing to work with. We can't help you get better unless you let us."

I'm not looking for help. And I never asked to be here.

"We all want to help you. To help you begin the process of trusting and healing. But we can't do it alone."

How many times do I have to say it, I don't need help. I don't want it.

I glance over at the wooden sign hanging over the door: BREAK THE SILENCE

I don't remember ever seeing it—the sign—hanging there before, until now. I take the words in, repeat them in my head, then wonder how anyone breaks their silence when they can no longer speak for themselves, when their words have become lost, siphoned outta them, somewhere stuck in between fear and mistrust, uncertainty and anger.

"We want to help you find your voice, K'wan...."

Why? My voice didn't matter before. So why would, should, it matter now?

"And K'wan..."

I shift my gaze back to her.

"We're not giving up on you. Deep down inside, we believe you want help, too."

I lean over in my seat, clutching my sides as if I am going to be sick.

"Do you want us to help you, K'wan?"

I shift my eyes from her and shrug. I'm starting to think I don't know what I want anymore. My head feels all screwed up right now.

"Well, the Executive Director of Healing Souls has taken a special interest in your case. In conjunction with continuing your sessions with me, I think you would do well working with Dr. Curtis as well."

For what? Why?

I shoot her a look of confusion. My mind scrambling with whys. Why does he have an interest in me? Why do I have to see him? Why can't I just sit here with her and not be bothered?

I wonder if Mom has called up here requesting that I see him. There is nothing he can do for me. He couldn't even help her keep my father

outta our house. She let him back in. She let him beat her and almost kill her. She...

I swallow. I don't wanna blame my mom. I don't. But I do. I am frickin' angry at her. At *him*—my father. At Dr. Curtis. At everybody.

"Doctor Curtis is a great psychologist who has been working with women and children, and even men, for many years." She tells me this as if she senses my apprehension. "You'll have nothing to worry about. I'm not going anywhere. I will still be your primary counselor. You'll have one IPC session with me on Tuesdays and your second IPC with Doctor Curtis on Thursdays."

I shouldn't be surprised that he wants to see me, but I am. Doctor Curtis was—maybe he still is—my mom's therapist. And he's the founder of this place. He's also the reason I'm here. He's the one who spoke on my behalf at court. I'm sure as a favor to my mom. Still, I don't wanna see him. I don't wanna talk to him, or anyone else. What will he say or do that will be any different from what Mrs. Morgan has already tried? Besides, he is, or was, my mom's counselor. Isn't that like a conflict of interest?

"You'll be in good hands," she assures me. "Doctor Curtis is one of the best. He rarely takes on a case, but like I said, he's taken a special interest in you."

I stare at her, wondering if she knows he's my mom's therapist, or if knowing that information even makes a difference. The point is I'm not interested in hearing anything he has to say. Then again, maybe he'll help me understand why my mom did what she did. Maybe he can tell me what she was thinking by letting that man back into our home 'cause, up until now, nothing she's said has made any sense to me.

I looked Mom in the eyes and told her I was scared for her. Told her I didn't want him to move back home, but she let him anyway. Shouldn't grownups at least listen to what their kids have to say? I don't know. Maybe my mom did listen. But, maybe, she didn't really care about what I said, or felt. That's how I feel, like she didn't care.

"Your father and I have decided to give our marriage another try; he wants to be with his family...he loves us..."

Why? That's all I want to understand. Then maybe I won't be so angry with her. I don't wanna be pissed at her, but I am. I mean, I love her. But what she did—taking him back, disrupting what was working for us—well, for me—is something I don't know if I can get over. I was always nervous with him home; scared for her. Doesn't she realize that many times—well, in the beginning when I was seven and eight—I'd fake being sick just so I could be home, close to her. But then I really would become sick. My stomach and head would really hurt. I'd worry myself sick. Shouldn't that have mattered? I know I'm only a kid and I don't really have any say over what adults do, but shouldn't what your own kid wants matter?

I guess not.

"How about this, before I actually set your sessions up with Doctor Curtis, you and I will meet once, twice more, then we'll go from there. I want you to give this some serious thought. Really think about the endless possibilities there is to being in treatment, opening yourself up to the process and allowing room for self-discovery. As you grow in your awareness you will better understand why you feel what you feel? And it also allows you to understand why you behave the way you do."

Self-discovery. I sift through my mental files, pull its meaning out. Then mull over it. The process of achieving understanding or knowledge of oneself. There is nothing more for me to process or understand about myself. These people just don't get it. I have discovered, uncovered, all there is to know about me.

I am already exposed and naked.

I am already empty.

What more can she possibly expect me to see, learn, understand, about myself?

I hear Grandma Ellen's voice in my ear. "I am going keep you lifted in prayer, baby."

I wanna tell her the next time she's on her knees having her special conversation with God to please ask Him why He's putting me through all this hell. Why me? Sometimes I wonder if God even exists or if He's simply a figment of every believer's imagination.

"I will fucking kill you..."

"K'wan?"

I blink, looking up at her.

"Are you okay?"

I nod.

But I am not okay. I am never okay. Those words—I. Will. Fucking. Kill. You—are harsh and scary. What kinda person threatens to kill someone they say they love? I can't, I won't, accept that as love.

"There are some things I'd like you to think about for our next session. I am going to give you a homework assignment."

I frown.

She smiles at me. "It's painless, I promise." She pulls out a black and white composition book and opens it. She starts writing. "There are three very important questions I want you to consider. Then I'd like for you to write your answers in here, fair enough?"

Yeah, I guess.

I nod, again.

"Good." She slides the composition book over to me. "Life, your life, K'wan, isn't a destination. It is a passage of exploration. And, this is where your journey begins."

When my session is up, I stand up, grabbing the book. I walk out feeling no better than I did when I walked in. But, surprisingly, I am eager to open the book she has given me to see what three questions she has asked of me. But I won't. I will wait for when I am ready to respond. If ever.

Twelve

The cafeteria—or dining hall, which is what they call it here—is always filled with a buncha useless chatter to me. The noise around me sounds like a buncha nothingness cluttering up the air. *I can't even eat my food in peace. God, I hate this play.* I hate that I am here surrounded by this madness. Hate that I am here because of my own madness. Everything seemed to happen so fast. That night. No, it started out fast, then rolled in slow motion, then sped up again. I blink, and the video—the permanent recording of that night—plays over and over and over in my head. I wish there was a way I could get out of my own mind, but I am lost. Lost in the memory. Lost in the screams. Lost in the blood. Lost in wanting to save my mom.

There's so much blood, lots and lots of it. The knife is still in my hand. I remember grabbing it. Remember stabbing him. Remember the handcuffs being placed on me. Remember my heart beating hard. But I do not remember what I was feeling.

I am lost in all of these broken pieces of my life. Shards of anger scattered all around me colored by swollen eyes, black and blue bruises, and busted lips. Those are the things that stick into my brain like needles. I have become a pincushion. And I am hurting.

Right now I wish I could close my eyes and lose myself, quietly slipping away where no one will ever find me, or even miss me. I'm desperate to disappear.

"Yo, Green Eyes, you aiiight?" Ja'Meer's voice breaks me outta my haze. "You look like you're about to cry or something. What's good?"

I swallow and try to pretend there is something in my eye.

"Ain't no one in here fuckin' with you, is it?"

I shake my head. Outta the corner of my eye, I see The Bully as he walks over toward the table with his tray. He sits at the far end of the table with two other residents. I hear him say, "Yo, look at that pussy ass nigga. Fuckin' punk ass." I am not sure who he is speaking of, but he says it loud enough as if he wants me, along with everyone else in earshot, to hear it. I try never to say anything bad about people, but he is such an asshole.

Ja'Meer sneers at him. "I'm tellin' you, if I ever see that cat out on the bricks, I'ma slide his wig back; for real, yo. That bitch-ass nigga's lucky I'm tryna get the fuck home, or I'd been did him dirty by now. I hate niggas like him."

His brown eyes seem to darken as he says this. His nose looks like it's swelling. I wonder what his issue is with The Bully. It's not like he ever says anything to him. "Yo, niggas like that need to be put outta their misery; for real." I watch as he shovels food in his mouth. He looks up from his plate and eyes me. "If that nigga ever steps to you tryna put some work in, you come holla at me, aiight?" I don't nod or shake my head. I just stare at him. "I'ma stomp his lights out. Yo, you gonna eat the rest of that?"

I glance down at it. The only thing left on it is the grilled chicken. I've only eaten the broccoli. I am still full from breakfast. Thursday mornings, they usually serve pancakes. This morning, we had a choice of blueberry or plain. I chose blueberry. And they almost taste as good as the ones at IHOP.

I slide him my plate, standing up. I only have twenty minutes before I have to be in group. My head hurts. "Oh, you out?" he asks; his mouth stuffed with food.

I nod.

"Aiight, yo. Remember what I said; if that nigga fucks with you, let me know."

I shake my head, dismissively. Then squeeze between chairs, holding my tray up high so that I don't bump into anyone. The last thing I need is to give someone else cause to pick a fight with me. I already have one enemy here. I don't need two.

I dump my tray, wondering how someone can hate someone who has never said or done anything to them. *He hates me because he hates himself.* Whatever! *That dude has problems.*

Thirteen

Today there are only nine of us in group: Marco, Aesop, Jackson, The Bully, Jarrod, Corey, Westley, Nelson—this Spanish kid from Jersey City, and me.

"Okay, who wants to get started?" Miss Daisy asks, looking around the circle.

Everyone shifts in their seats. I keep stone-still.

Miss Daisy's eyes land on me. She smiles. "K'wan, how about you? Are you ready to share?" Her tone sounds hopeful. Sadly, I dash any optimism she might have as I have for the last twelve group sessions.

I match her stare, seemingly longer than I should. Under different circumstances, I would tell her she has nice eyes. I shift my gaze, shaking my head.

"Yo, that's fucked up," Lenny says, cutting his eye over at me. "Why this little nigga get to sit here and not speak?"

Since being here I've been called all kinds of *niggas* and *bitches* and *muhfuckas* and *pussies* at least once or twice a day, mostly by him. I ignore it. And I ignore him. He's irrelevant in my life. And I bet he feels he is too—insignificant. Most bullies do. Still, my patience is wearing thin, and I'm slowly becoming tired of him.

"Yo, I heard his moms cut out his tongue," Jackson jokes. I'm sure in an effort to impress The Bully. Seems like everyone—well, almost everyone—wants to try to make an impression on him in some way.

My grandma Ellen always says that the ones with the loudest barks are the ones who are usually the most troubled. I am starting to believe her. Lenny's bark is definitely the loudest of the pack. I cut my eyes over at him. He is sitting with his arms folded tightly across his chest. His face is an ugly scowl. Yeah, he's not only trouble. He's very troubled, too.

"Lenny, your language," Miss Daisy warns. "Jackson, that's enough."

Jackson apologizes. "My bad, Miss Dee. I was only kiddin'. Dude knows I didn't mean no harm."

Yeah, right!

I keep from rolling my eyes up in my head. They say cruel things, then try to pass it off as harmless jokes. I am glad that I have thick skin.

She regards Jackson with a nod, then shoots her attention back to The Bully. "And, Lenny, you know we don't use the N-word in here. I don't know how many times I have to have this conversation with you—to mind your business and worry about your own treatment. As I've said many times before, everyone has a story to tell. And when K'wan is ready, he'll share his." She leans over in her seat to get my attention. "Isn't that right, K'wan?" She smiles again. It's one of the nicest smiles I've seen today.

I turn my head and look out of the window.

"Soft-ass pussy," Lenny mumbles. I shoot him a look. "What, nigga?"

I bite down on my lip. Turn back to the window.

I remind myself of how insecure he is. Remind myself that I am not here to make friends or be liked by him. That I will never have to see him again once I leave this place.

"Yeah, just what I thought."

"Lenny," Miss Daisy states, sounding annoyed. "I've already

warned you to not use that language in here. You've just earned yourself two days of lost rec privileges. Another outburst and I'll make it for a whole week. Do I make myself clear?"

He grits his teeth. "Yeah."

She glances at her watch. There are no clocks in any of the counseling rooms. They don't want anyone, like me, staring at the clock, counting the time, or getting lost in it. "Good. Since no one wants to share, then we'll sit here quietly for the next hour and stare at each other. How's that for fun?"

Everyone groans.

"Then someone needs to start talking."

"What you wanna talk about?" Nelson asks. He's fifteen. He came here a week after I did for aggravated assault. He hit some guy in the head with a brick and knocked him unconscious because he felt disrespected when the guy bumped into him and didn't say, "Excuse me." Nelson always tries to act like he doesn't wanna talk, but once he gets started, he yaps nonstop the whole time. No one minds, though. Well, at least I don't.

"Let's talk about you. How was your visit the other night with your family?"

He shrugs. "It was aiiight, I guess. Pops is still locked up. The board denied his parole. Moms just lost her job and might not be able to keep making the mortgage payments. She's worried we might lose our house."

"And how does that make you feel?" Miss Daisy asks.

"Mad as hell. I should be out there to help her. Not sitting up in here." She wants to know how he thinks he could help. He looks at her as if she's asked one of the dumbest questions in American history. "Get a job. What else?"

"Okay, but at fifteen, what type of job do you think you'd get that would help your mother's current situation?"

He shrugs. "I'd get two jobs. And if that wasn't enough, then I'd do whatever I had to do to make that paper."

"And what about school?" she wants to know. "What would you do about that?"

He shrugs. "What about it?"

"Without a high school education, or at least a GED, your options will be limited. And it prevents you from getting into college, makes it difficult to land employment, and becomes a barrier to competing successfully in the workplace."

"Yo, Miss Dee, no disrespect. But, look at me. I'm in the tenth grade and can barely read or write. School hasn't done shit for me. So no matter if I finish or not, I'm still gonna be overlooked. I'm still gonna have it hard. And keepin' it real, an education can't do shit for me if my moms 'n 'em are somewhere out on the streets. Do you think a diploma is gonna feed my little brothers and sister? Hell, nah. My pops is in and outta jail so I gotta man up and step up to the plate and do what I gotta do to take care of my fam."

"Yo, that's real talk, fam," Westley cosigns. "Make that bread however you can."

"And I hear what you're saying," Miss Daisy continues. "But without an education, it puts you, all of you, at a greater disadvantage."

Westley snorts. "I can't speak for anyone else, but I'm black. The color of my skin *is* a barrier. It's a permanent badge that goes wherever I go. So I'm already at a disadvantage." He cuts his eyes over at me. "Some of us weren't born with silver spoons in our mouths."

"Real talk," Nelson agrees.

Lenny smirks. "That mufucka wouldn't last a day in the hood." He says this so that I can hear him, but low enough to hope that Miss Daisy doesn't.

"Lenny, what was that?" Miss Daisy inquires, raising her brow.

"Nuthin'," he lies.

She narrows her eyes. "Oh, I thought I heard you say someone wouldn't last a day in the hood."

He shifts in his seat. She lets him know she can hear through walls so he had better watch himself. A few guys snicker. Lenny shoots me a nasty look. Miss Daisy sees that as well and tells him she also has eyes on the side of her head. "Lenny, how about you tell the group what your problem is with K'wan since you seem to have a lot of animosity toward him. And he hasn't said a single word to anyone since he's been here."

Oh God, why did she do that?

She tilts her head.

I shrink in my seat.

"I don't like him."

Good, I don't like you either. You're rude, obnoxious, and disrespectful.

I turn and look out the window. Miss Daisy wants to know what I've done to him for him to not like me. He says I think I'm better than everyone else.

WTF? That's far from the truth. And now I'm convinced that this dude is really pathetic. But whatever! His opinion, his feelings, and he's entitled to them.

I am surprised that no one else has chimed in. I know they consider me the privileged one. The one with the life filled with promise and opportunity. They seem to hate me for not having the same experiences as them. Envy me for being different from them. Sometimes I wanna snap on them for thinking my life has been one big, happy fucking rollercoaster ride. Yeah, if you're standing on the outside looking in, you'd think it is. They have no idea.

"So let me get this straight. You don't like someone, not because they've done or said anything to you, or tried to personally hurt you or your family, but based on an assumption that you have about them?"

I turn to the group for a quick moment to see how many foreheads are stamped with STUPID on them; so far, only one. And he can't even come up with a response that doesn't make him sound dumber than he already looks. He's judging me based on what he thinks I have, or what he thinks I come from. Dude's a hater. And Miss Daisy has proven that, along with his ignorance.

Yeah, okay. I may not have had to live with the kinda worries that they've had to live with. And they're right. In many ways, I am different from them. While they're obsessed with girls and sex and drinking and partying and being stuck on stupid, I'm stuck trying to piece together what's left of my life. While they were busying cutting school and disrupting classes, I was concentrating on physics and chemistry and calculus, trying to take all the right classes that would gain me entry into one of the country's prestigious universities—all things that mattered, to me; to my parents. So, yeah, in that respect, I am different than them—well, the majority of them. And I'm not going to apologize for it, or be made to feel guilty about it. I didn't choose my life. And I didn't choose the way my parents raised me or provided for me. But I am also like many of them. I know what it's like to hear yelling and screaming and see your mom get beat on. I know what it's like to be afraid. And, if that isn't enough, then let's try this: I'm here. I'm pissed. I'm pained. And so are they.

A Langston Hughes poem I read last year in my AP English Lit class comes to mind as I sit here. "Mother to Son." I hear myself reciting it at the top of my lungs, yelling to the world that…"life for me ain't been no crystal stair…"

Miss Daisy's voice slices into my thoughts. "Now back to what we were talking about. My question is, just how far are any of you willing to go to do what you *gotta do* to take care of your families? Would you risk your life? Your freedom?"

I blink, glancing around the group.

Nelson raises his brow. "It's whatever. I'm not afraid of death. Death's been around me all my life."

"Word," Lenny and Westley cosign.

I wonder if I am really afraid of death. *I will fucking kill you!* The answer comes in a thunderous growl. Its likelihood causes an aching in me. I feel my chest tightening. I clutch the sides of my seat, inhale deep breaths.

I am not afraid of my own death.

I am afraid of my mother's.

I will fucking kill you!

"But that doesn't have to be you," she counters. Her voice dips with concern. "You don't have to become that life. That doesn't have to be your way of being."

Nelson stares at her. "It's too late. It already is."

"I understand your need to want to help, but quitting school or going out to do illegal things, risking your life and freedom, to get that *bread*, as Westley so eloquently put it, isn't a wise choice. Notice I said *choice*. Because we always have choices."

"Yeah, but when you're in that situation," Westley interjects, leaning forward in his seat, "and the lights are about to be shut off, or there's no heat, or no food in the house—or you're about to be evicted from ya spot, you get out there to do what you gotta do. Yeah, it might be an unwise choice but, in that moment, it's the only choice most of us have. Don't nobody really give a fuck about you bein' thrown out on the streets or goin' hungry. And ain't nobody givin' out handouts. So what we supposed to do, Miss Dee? Go hungry? See our fam out on the streets? Nah, we gotta step up and handle our responsibilities."

Miss Daisy gives Westley a look that seems filled with sadness. Or maybe it's something else. "How many of you feel like it's your responsibility to take care of your families? Or at the very least, protect them?"

Everyone in the group raises their hands. I sit on mine. But in my mind's eye, I am raising mine, too.

Missy Daisy looks around the circle; takes everyone in. I shift my eyes before her gaze falls on me. She knows my charges. Knows why I am here.

I'm going to keep her safe.

I hold my breath and wait for her to call me out. I am relieved when she doesn't.

"And where did this belief that you were responsible for your family's well-being come from?"

From me. I mull the question over in my head until I can find an answer that makes sense. Protecting my mother isn't something that was asked of me, or anything that was expected of me. It's what I had to do.

Aesop, Jackson and Jarrod all say, "My moms."

Lenny says, "My pops was never around. That nigg...my bad," he says, putting his hands up, "was too busy out gettin' high to look out for us, so my two older brothers had to hold it down. Then when they got locked up, it fell on me. You just did it 'cause that's how it is. That's what's expected."

"That's real talk, man," Jackson says. "If you have to choose between going hungry or doin' what you gotta do to put food in your mouth, you're gonna choose door number A over door number B. Period; point blank. You become the man of the house."

"My moms told me when I was eight years old," Aesop states, "that I was the man of the house when my pops got knocked. She put a pack in my hand and told me I had to get out there and make money. So I got on my grind and handled my business. No questions asked."

"I am the man of this house and what I say goes."

I feel a headache shooting to the front of my head. This is not my life. It isn't my story. I don't wanna hear any of this. I stare out of the window and try to think of something, anything, other than what's being said. But my mind draws a blank.

Miss Daisy shifts in her seat. "It's unfortunate so many of you have had to be put into positions to take on adult responsibilities. Those roles shouldn't have been yours to bear."

"It is what it is, Miss Dee," Nelson says, shrugging. He leans his chair back on its back legs. Miss Daisy tells him to put his chair down. He does. "My pops told me I had to be the man of the house until he got out. And that's what I've done. But now I'm here."

He hangs his head. Defeat wrapping its big, ugly hand around his spirit.

Miss Daisy takes him in. The room is quiet. For a moment, I see understanding and concern and disgust all wrapped up in one tiny ball as she looks at him. "What does that mean, 'but now I'm here?'"

He slowly shakes his head, clutching his eyes shut as if he's fighting back something ugly. He finally looks up. "That I'ma failure. My moms is out there struggling and I can't do shit to help her. And now she's gonna end up on the streets."

I feel his pain.

Share in his sentiment.

I'm a failure!

Miss Daisy folds her hands in her lap. "You're not a failure," she reassures him. But I know she's talking to me, too. At least, that's what I am thinking. *You're not a failure.* I repeat it in my head several times. *Then what am I?*

"If anything, it's very noble of you,"—she looks around the circle—"for all of you, to want to take care of your families; to feel the need to protect them. But the truth is it's not your fault. You should not have to shoulder the blame for your family's circumstances. None of you should. I'll say it a thousand times over, that shouldn't be your role. It's the adults who should be protecting *you*, and providing for *you*, and taking responsibility for what happens to their families. Not the other way around. But, I realize the latter is many of your realities."

"Sometimes, Miss Dee, I'm just so fuckin' tired, yo," Jarrod says out of nowhere. He's been quiet the whole group, listening and fidgeting in his seat. His voice cracks as he speaks. "It's like no matter what you do, it's still never, ever, enough. Someone is still looking for something more from you."

"And how has that made you feel?" Miss Daisy asks. Her voice is calm and filled with a caring she is known for.

He sighs. "Like I've been stuck in a dark hole, tryna scratch my way out of it." He puts his face in his hands, then runs them over his shaved head. "Man, I'm tired. I'm tired of always being there for everyone else, but no one is ever there for me. It's like eff me, know what I'm sayin'?"

"*Light cannot exist without darkness. And if there is a purpose to my darkness maybe it's to bring some balance to the world.*" I repeat the words in my head. Try to remember where I've heard it, or read it.

A balance between good and evil; love and hate.

Stabbing him, to save my mother!

Miss Daisy nods her head. "Yes. I definitely know what you're saying. But there is always a light somewhere, whether it's at the end of a long, winding tunnel or up from a deep, dark hole. You just have to believe."

Jarrod stares at Miss Daisy long and hard. I am watching him.

It looks as if he is holding back a buncha tears. I don't know him. And I don't know his struggles, or anyone else's at this place, for that matter. But I know my own. And I know what it's like to fight back tears. I know what it's like to be tired of living a lie, of living in fear, of hearing excuses that make no damn sense. And I know what it's like to pretend.

Jarrod pinches the insides of his eyes to keep what appear to be tears from falling. He sighs. "What if you have nothin' to believe in?"

Miss Daisy shifts in her seat, crosses her ankles. I try not to stare at her feet. But I can't help myself. She is wearing a pair of black ballet flats. I catch Jackson looking at them, too, and wonder if he is thinking the same thing. That her shoes make her long feet look like flippers.

"You have *you* to believe in," she says, eyeing him, then glancing around the room. "All of you have to believe in yourselves. I can believe in you. Your families can believe in you. But none of that matters if *you* don't believe in you."

Everyone in group looks at her as if what she's said has gone way over their heads. For many I'm sure it has. Jarrod looks over at me. His eyes lock on mine. I do not shift my stare from his; not this time. He shifts his gaze instead, looking back at Miss Daisy. He hangs his head. "Not when you're told all your life you ain't shit. That'll you'll never be shit."

"You're worthless."

I try to ignore the voice in my head, menacing and mean. But it plays over and over, like a scratched disc.

"You're worthless."

"You're worthless."

"You're worthless."

And then a chorus of screams floats its way to the surface.

"Randy, please don't do this…"

Fourteen

O nce again, the cafeteria is a cacophony of chatter. I try to block out all the loud talking and laughing and name-calling going on around me to no avail. And now I have a headache. Tonight the noise is unbearable and I am surprised the dining hall aides/attendants are allowing this level of ruckus. I glance around the large room and spot the reason for the chaos. There are two new attendants on duty. One is a pale, older-looking white man with a really big head and wide body. He looks like he used to play football waaaaay back in the day. The other aide is a really tall, brown-skinned guy with cornrows. He has also has big eyes and a long neck.

"Yo, Kenny," Aesop yells over to the table I am sitting at. He is sitting at another table on the right of me with three of his so-called boys. Kenny is sitting five seats down from me. And is another one of the annoying ones here. Always saying and doing what everyone else does. The seats at all the other tables were taken so that leaves me sitting here. "Check out dude over there. That nigga looks like a giraffe; word is bond. And wassup wit' the old white dude wit' that big-ass globe head."

Everyone laughs.

Since being here I have come to learn that ignorance is more common than not. Even though I don't share in the laughter, I am no different from Aesop for thinking exactly what he's so boldly saying. Nor am I any different from everyone who is laughing, even though I do not laugh with them.

I lower my eyes. Stare at my half-eaten plate—sweet potato fries, a cheeseburger and garden salad, feeling bad.

"There's been an accident."

"She is badly hurt, the car she was driving flipped over."

Mom's image, bandaged and medicated, slips its way into my mind's eye. I see her, black and blue; bruised and swollen. Her body is lying perfectly still under a crisp, white sheet. With the exception of the slight rise and fall of her chest, she looks dead. In my mind, at that very moment she is dead. I convince myself that she is never coming back as I am staring at her. My small hand reaches out and touches hers. My eyes are burning from tears that I refuse to allow to fall.

Aunt Janie is standing by her bed—one arm wrapped around me. The other wrapped around Kyle. She pulls us into her, kisses us both on our heads.

He is sitting in a chair on the other side of Mom's bed, holding her limp hand, crying and apologizing. He blames himself. And so he should.

I stare at him. Anger builds up in me like a raging sea. I want to scream and yell at him the way he yelled and screamed at her. I refuse to believe he is sorry for anything that has happened. He never is. How can he be when he keeps doing it over and over and over again? The same ole crap!

Insulting her.

Putting her down.

Threatening her.

It is his fault she is in a hospital bed.

It is his fault that she ran out of the house, upset. She wanted to leave the house with us. He wouldn't let her.

"You're not taking my sons."

"You can't stop me. They're my sons, too," she says back to him.

"I can! And I will! You want out of this marriage, then get out of it. But you are not taking my sons. I will drag your ass into court and take them from you. Do you hear me, Syreeta? You will never see them again."

I blink. My mom's lifeless body is cold beneath my touch.

"I want my mommy," Kyle cries out.

"I know you do, Sweetheart," Aunt Janie says, *trying to calm him. "Your mommy needs you to be strong for her, okay?"*

He sniffles and nods.

"She has to rest so she can get better. You have to be a big boy for her, okay?"

He nods again, swiping at his tears with his hand. "When is Mommy gonna come home?" She has been in the hospital for the last two days, fighting for her life.

"I don't know, sweetheart," Aunt Janie says, *lifting her arm from around my shoulder to wipe tears from her face. She has dropped everything—her life and family in North Carolina—to be by her sister's side; to console and look after her sister's children.*

Grandma Miriam is home with the triplets, who are babies. She has also placed her life on hold for us, her daughter's children. "Soon, I hope," Aunt Janie says. *"Your mommy has been in a really bad car accident. She needs to heal and get better, first, before she can come home."*

"Is she gonna be okay?" he asks, *wiping his own tears.*

He gets up, paces the room. He runs his hands over his face, then locks them in back of his neck, pacing and pacing and pacing. I stare at him. My eyes are on fire. He should be the one laid up and bandaged up in that hospital bed. Not her.

"Janie, I'm going to step out for some air for a bit, then stop to speak with the doctor."

She eyes him. "Okay. Take your time."

I watch him as he walks out of the room. It should be him in that hospital bed; not her.

"*He did this to her,*" I blurt out. "*I hate him!*"

"*Who are you talking about, sweetheart? Who did this to her?*"

I point toward the door. "*Him!*"

"Yo, man…" A finger snaps in my face.

I blink. *Huh?*

It's Ja'Meer. I don't know when he got here, but he's sitting across from me with his tray of food. "I asked if you were gonna eat the rest of them fries?" He's pointing at the pile of fries on my plate. I hand him my plate and watch as he uses his plastic fork to dump them onto his plate. "Yo, good lookin' out, son. You must have been sitting there in some deep thought. You didn't hear a word I said." He shovels four fries into his mouth and continues talking, "Man, you don't know what you're missin'. These things are good as hell; for real, yo."

Dang, he can eat. I stare at him as he shovels another mouthful of fries into his mouth. He keeps talking as he chews and I have to wonder if his mom ever told him about talking while he's eating.

"You up for gettin' spanked on the chess board tonight?" I shake my head at him. Aside from table tennis, he thinks he can beat me at every board game here as well. If only he knew. I am—well, was—a member of the chess club at my school. And 2010 and 2011 summer chess camp champion. But none of that matters here. So, like with ping-pong, I allow him to win.

"Nah, man," he says, taking a swig of his chocolate milk. "Don't punk out on me, either, yo, 'cause you know how you do. You be mad funny stylin' it sometimes, especially when you know I'ma 'bout to whoop that ass." He laughs and chews.

I glance down the other end of the table. Lenny has come over and is talking to Kenny. He shoots me a look. I eye him back. "What the fuck you lookin' at?" he snaps loud enough for everyone at the table to look over in my direction. I shift my eyes. Stare back down at my plate.

I don't know why that boy is always giving me a hard time. I'm getting sick of it!

"Yo, don't worry 'bout that nigga, man," Ja'Meer says, looking over at them. "That punk-ass don't want it. But, for real for real, I meant what I said earlier. If he fucks with you, I'ma knock his block off; real shit. I got you, kid. You don't talk for shit, but you still a cool-ass little dude. Ain't no one up in here gonna fuck with you while I'm here, yo."

I wanna ask him why he would wanna look out for someone who has not said a word to him since being here. Still, I appreciate the kind gesture. Even if the truth is I can handle myself. That's the one thing *he* taught me how to do. Defend myself. Too bad I wasn't able to defend Mom all those times *he* was beating her. I shoulda stabbed him a long time ago.

I swallow back my anger before it rises and spills out.

"You remind me of my little brother," Ja'Meer offers, staring at me. "He was real quiet like you, always in thought. He stayed to himself and didn't fuck with no one, either. I miss that little nigga; for real, yo."

If I were able to will the words out of my mouth, I would ask him where his brother is/was. I'd ask what happened to him. I stare at him. He gives me an intense look that almost seems filled with sadness. For a moment, I see his eyes brimming with tears. He puts the carton of milk to his lips and swallows it back. He plops the empty carton on his tray, then opens another carton. He guzzles that one down, then belches.

"Aiiight, yo, enough of all the mushy shit," he says, pushing back in his seat, then standing. "Seven o'clock sharp. Bring ya A-game, son, 'cause I'ma whoop the dog crap outta ya." He looks over at Lenny and mumbles, "Punk-ass muhfucka."

Lenny eyes him as he walks off, but doesn't say anything. Instead, he waits until he's out of view, then ice-grills me. I'm not interested in getting into a staring match with this fool. I get up and snake through the room to dump my trash. I walk over to the dishwashing window, then slide my tray in. The brown-skinned, rubber-gloved lady with high-cheekbones and squinty eyes smiles at me. She's all teeth and gums. I shift my eyes from her. There is nothing here to smile about.

I gotta get outta here!

Fifteen

I wait until I have the room to myself, then open my mail. I have another letter from my mom and my guidance counselor, Mr. Crenshaw, has sent me another card. At least once a month he sends me one. I open the envelope. On the front of the card it says: YOUNG, GIFTED & BLACK

On the inside he has written in cursive a note in dark ink:

K'wan,

Nina Simone once sang, "Oh but my joy of today/ is that we can all be proud to say/ to be young gifted and black/is where it's at…" I say this to say that, in spite of all that has happened, we here at Prep High are proud of you. You are an intelligent young man; a rising star with a very promising and bright future ahead of you. Do not be discouraged. The trials and hurdles that you are facing right now will strengthen you. Do not give up hope. Do not despair. This dark moment in your life is preparing you for something greater. You are a fearless and courageous young man, K'wan. You are the cultivator of your own journey. Continue to reach for the heavens. And we will continue to believe in you. We are waiting for you at the finish line, cheering you on.

Regards,

Mr. Crenshaw, your guidance counselor

"Wow," is all I can think to say at his kindness. I am touched by his card. He always has cool things to say. I reread it, then slide it back into its envelope, wishing I were back at school sitting in his office. Mr. Crenshaw is the coolest guidance counselor ever.

Next I open the letter my mom has sent. I pull it out and breathe in the folded white sheets of paper, closing my eyes. This is the first letter that I have actually opened, and will read. I don't know what makes this one so special from all of the others that were either sent back, or refused, or thrown in the trash unopened. My hands shake as I unfold the letter and start to read:

My dearest K'wan,

I hope you have found it in your heart to open this letter. If you have, then my prayers have been answered. If not, then I will keep writing to you and visiting you and letting you know how much I love you. I will do whatever I need/have to do until you are ready. I am filled with so many emotions as I write this. Some days are better than others. Most nights I cry myself to sleep. Other nights, I am awakened by the emptiness that tugs at my heart with you not being here. You are missed so very much. And you are loved even deeper.

I miss your smile and laughter and the way your sparkling eyes dance with mischief when you are about to get caught doing something you know you shouldn't be doing. I miss hearing you fussing with your brothers about going into your room and taking something of yours without permission and you doing the same to them. I miss you coming home from school sharing your day with me. I miss taking you to practices and meets. I miss hearing your music coming from your room. I miss watching you from the window as you play basketball by yourself or with your brothers and friends. I miss you, K'wan, so, so very much.

I can still remember the day I learned that I was pregnant with you, my firstborn, my prince. Your father and I were so very happy. It was one of the greatest moments in my life. And, I'd like to believe his as well. There was this life growing inside of me that depended on me. And I was determined to always be there for you every step of the way. I was determined to love you unconditionally, to wipe your tears away, to kiss away your bumps and bruises. I promised to mother you without smothering you; to give you room to explore and experience and expand so that you would learn about the world around you.

No matter what has happened between your father and me, K'wan, I want you to know that you were conceived out of love. You were not a mistake. You were (and are) a blessing, K'wan. My blessing, my beautiful son.

From the moment I felt you grow inside of me, I loved you more with each passing day. Your every kick, your every turn, was a constant reminder of my love for you. From the moment I learned of my pregnancy, I made a vow to cherish you forever; to never, ever, have you doubt how much you mean to me; and to always protect you, something I did not do. I am still fighting myself over that. I am still struggling to not let my failures consume me.

You, my handsome prince, have always been my pride and joy. And my greatest hope, prayer, wish, has always been for you to one day flourish into the king you were born to be; strong-willed, proud and determined. That you would evolve into a man eager to learn and face new challenges with an open mind and loving heart.

My greatest fear has been that my choices to stay with your father would become the gateway to you becoming lost in a world of uncertainty. That your personality and reality about life would become hardened by bitterness. That rage would one day consume you.

I continue to hope and pray that you will one day become the man you are destined to be in spite of your father and me. That you will develop into the kind of consciousness that allows you to become a loving and respectful man. Despite our mistakes, I continue to pray that God's grace continues to lift you and guide you so that you may land on higher ground.

I am here for you, K'wan, always. My love for you is infinite, my son.

With all that is in me,

Love,

Mom

My eyes are burning and blurry from tears. I cannot stop myself from crying. I don't know why I am so emotional. But I am. I am constantly crying like a big baby. Sometimes, it makes me feel better. Other times, I feel worse. Right at this moment, I don't know what I feel. No, I do. I am overwhelmed. I hurry into the bathroom and shut the door behind me, in case Ja'Meer walks into the room. I don't want him seeing me like this. Weak.

I keep the light off. I do not want to see my reflection. Do not want to see the hurt and sadness and shame that floods my eyes. I slide down to the floor, clutch Mom's letter, letting all of my fears and apprehensions stain the pages of her words.

I must have been in the bathroom for what feels like hours, but when I finally come out, I am glad to see that Ja'Meer is still not in the room. I am exhausted. The only thing I wanna do is sleep. I climb into bed with my clothes on, placing my mom's letter underneath my pillow and closing my eyes.

When I awaken, it is after two in the morning. Ja'Meer is snoring as usual. Tonight he is being real belligerent with it. I can't help but to think that all that noise he's making can't be normal for a boy his age.

All that snoring is ridiculous, I think, slipping outta bed and walking over to my desk. I flip on the lamp, mindful not to wake Ja'Meer. I pull out the composition book Mrs. Morgan has given me, then open it. On the first page, top line, she has written: RALPH WALDO EMERSON, "LIFE IS A JOURNEY, NOT A DESTINATION!"

The next line, she has written: WHAT YOU LOOK BACK ON, AND WHAT YOU LOOK FORWARD TO IS TOTALLY UP TO YOU. HERE ARE THREE VERY IMPORTANT QUESTIONS I WANT YOU TO ANSWER. TAKE YOUR TIME. THINK ABOUT HOW YOU WISH TO ANSWER. THERE ARE NO JUDGMENTS, NO RIGHT OR WRONG ANSWERS. THESE ARE SIMPLY SOME OF THE PIECES OF YOUR LIFE, LIKE A JIGSAW PUZZLE ONE PIECE AT A TIME.

1). WHO ARE YOU?

2). WHAT ARE YOU?

3). WHAT DO YOU BELIEVE IS YOUR PURPOSE HERE ON EARTH?

I look at each question, frowning. *I'm not doing this mess. What does she think answering these dumb questions are gonna do for me?* On the bottom of the page, last line, Mrs. Morgan has written another Ralph Emerson quote: "BE NOT THE SLAVE OF YOUR OWN PAST…"

I close the book, shut off the lamp and climb back into bed. *Be not the slave of your own past; what the heck is that supposed to mean? Doesn't she know that I am already enslaved to it? I have already been whipped by it!*

The next morning I awaken, glad that I was not harassed by nightmares. I jump into the shower, then quickly dress. I only have fifteen minutes before the start of school. I grab my schoolbooks, glad that I have my own classwork to do instead of those busy dittos the teachers give to the kids whose schools haven't sent them their work.

I spend the most part of the day daydreaming, counting the time in my head. I want to know more about the quote Mrs. Morgan wrote in that composition book. Fortunately, the day finally ends without any stress or aggravation and I am able to make my way into the library during study period.

The library is the only place we are allowed to access a computer, or the Internet. I want to know the rest of that Emerson quote. I walk up to the counselor's desk in the hallway, then fill out a slip for the library. Mr. Lee, a senior counselor signs off on it.

When I get to the library room, a large area with like eight huge round tables and about fifty bookcases packed with all types of books from fiction and nonfiction to poetry and religion, lining the shelves. Miss Pearl, another counselor aide, is working the library desk. She smiles at me as I hand her my slip. She's a tall—like basketball player tall, brown-skinned lady with slanted eyes and high cheekbones. She kinda reminds me of a black Eskimo, if they even exist.

She gives me a password for the computer, then another code to access the Internet. I type in RALPH WALDO EMERSON, then click on the link to his quotes. I write out the rest of his quote in the composition book: PLUNGE INTO THE SUBLIME SEAS, DIVE AND SWIM FAR, SO YOU SHALL COME BACK WITH SELF-RESPECT, WITH NEW POWER, WITH AN ADVANCED EXPERIENCE THAT SHALL EXPLAIN AND OVERLOOK THE OLD.

I read it to myself. Think about the quote for a moment, then close my eyes. Like what they are trying to do to me here, I try to dissect its meaning, then put it back together. But I cannot. My brain is crammed with too many other things to give any extra thoughts to this. I log off the computer, close the book, deciding not to put anymore thought or effort into any of this. I get up from the computer, then walk back over and wait for Miss Pearl to sign my pass. I decide that going back to my room and studying for a Spanish test, then reading my Physics book, is much more exciting than trying to figure out the thoughts of a dead poet—for now, anyway.

⊕

It is five in the morning. I am sitting at my desk, staring at the closed composition book. Mrs. Morgan's questions have been swimming around in my head. Who am I? What am I? What is my purpose in life? No one has ever really asked me this.

For a moment, I think about Mom's letter, about the part where she says she continues to hope and pray that I become the man that I am destined to be. What if this is my destiny? To be resentful and bitter and filled with hate. I am aware of my feelings. I do not deny them. But what if that, this, is all there will be for me. A life of misery and sadness and a trunk load of nightmares. What if all that I have been through was supposed to shape me to be what I already am, angry?

I open the book, stare at the questions, then reach for a pen. I take a deep breath, then write under the first question: I DON'T KNOW WHO I AM. I MEAN, I KNOW THE OBVIOUS. I AM A SON AND A BROTHER. I AM A STRAIGHT-A GIFTED AND TALENTED HONOR STUDENT. I AM A LACROSSE PLAYER. I AM A CHESS CHAMPION. AND A MATH TUTOR AND BOY SCOUT. I DON'T KNOW WHAT ELSE TO TELL YOU. IS THERE SOMETHING MORE YOU'RE LOOKING FOR?

Under the second question, I write: I AM ANGRY, THAT'S WHAT I AM!

The third question I want to leave blank, but I don't. I write instead: I AM ONLY FOURTEEN. I HAVE NO PURPOSE!

I am surprised when I get up from the desk and start rummaging through the trash basket, looking for the other piece of the puzzle that's been folded on paper. For some strange reason, I am relieved when I find it. I sit on the edge of my chair and open the crumpled sheet of paper.

K'wan,

I know I've hurt you, and I'm truly sorry. All I'm asking is that you give me a chance to explain, to apologize to you, and hopefully try to make it up to you. When you're ready, I will be here. I don't care how many times you refuse to see me. I am not going to stop coming up here. I don't care how long it takes until you are willing to let me back in your life, or at least willing to speak to me. I am never going to stop trying. I will never stop loving you.

Dad

When I am done, I stare at the sheet of paper, then crumple it up as anger washes over me. *Yeah, right. You don't love me!* I flip open the composition book and glance down at the Ralph Emerson quote again. *Yeah, life is a journey all right. It's been one big roller-coaster ride straight to hell for me. At least, that's how it feels.*

Sixteen

"Good morning, K'wan," Mrs. Morgan says the next morning as I walk into her office. Today she is wearing some kinda knit blouse that clings to her boobs. I really see why a lot of the guys here wish they had her for a counselor. She always gives a good show. I overheard some of them saying they thought she was easy in the sheets. Well, that's not how they said it. They used the F-word and called her nasty names and said she probably was having sex with some of the residents. They were even calling her Superhead. I didn't like that. I don't think that was a nice thing to say about an adult, but I guess they are entitled to their opinions. I'd just wish they'd learned to keep them to themselves. I wanna tell Mrs. Morgan that maybe she should tone it down some. You know. Stop with all the tight clothes and heavy makeup and lip glosses. But for some reason, I think Mrs. Morgan doesn't really care what people say about her. I kinda like that about her.

She glances at the composition book in my hand and smiles. "Please, sit. I see you brought the notebook with you. Very good. So I take it that means you wrote your answers in it for me, right." She eyes me questioningly. I nod. "May I have a look?"

I shrug, then lean up in my seat and hand her the book. I watch as she flips it open and reads my answers. She looks up at me and I realize that today her eyes are green. Wow. She's a woman of many faces. She changes her look from one extreme to the other and I wonder why. Does she not like herself? I wonder what it is she sees when she looks at herself in the mirror. Or does she do like I do and avoid looking into the mirror altogether. Is she easily bored or something? I wonder who is really hiding behind all of that makeup and masks and colored lenses.

She closes the book, looking up at me. "I want you to dig beyond the obvious. Those things you listed about who you are, they're things other people already know about you. Tell me something that no one else would know. Step outside of yourself, K'wan, and dig a little deeper."

I hear myself screaming at her, "I'm only fourteen, lady! What the heck you mean, dig deeper? I haven't even experienced life yet. Geesh!"

I blink, waiting for her to light candles, close her eyes, then start humming and chanting. She rests her forearms up on her wood desk, then fold her hands. I stare at her hands. Count the number of gold rings she has on each finger: five on her right—a diamond ring on her ring finger and one on her pointer, then a diamond band on her thumb finger. She has three rings on her left hand. I am really starting to think Mrs. Morgan likes drawing attention to herself. But why? Oh, well.

"I understand your father visited the other day and you are still refusing to see him. Yet, every week he still continues to drive up here. I'd like for you to write in your composition book why you won't visit with him. Tell me what it is you are afraid of. Will you do that for me?"

I pull in my bottom lip. I feel myself ready to go off. I am not disrespectful to adults, but I feel my temper flaring. Why is she sitting here asking me the obvious? I do not want to see him, or be anywhere around him, because of what he did to my mom and for what he has put me through. I'm not afraid of anything. He can't do anything worse than what he's already done. He can't hurt me. He's already done that. Why is she acting like she doesn't have a clue?

"K'wan, whether you want to or not, at some point, you are going to have to deal with your feelings toward your father. He will eventually be called in for family session."

I frown. I'm not doing that mess! What's the point? I am already dealing with how I feel about him. I'm ignoring him. Okay, and yes, avoiding him.

Besides, did you even talk to my mom about this? How will he be able to be in the same room with her if there's a restraining order in place?

"Given the circumstances of your case, these sessions will be with you and your dad, only. And your family sessions with your mom will be scheduled separately."

What do I have to have family sessions for? What are we going to do, sit and stare at each other? I am not talking!

Or has she forgotten that, too?

Geesh!

I raise my brow.

"The purpose for these sessions is to allow you the opportunity to hear what each of your parents has to say, then hopefully allow you to find your voice so that you can finally be heard. I believe it will not only be therapeutic for you to be heard, but for your parents as well. Everyone is hurting. And the goal of these sessions is to help everyone find a way to heal; particularly you, K'wan. You deserve to be heard. Would you like that? To have a chance for your parents to finally hear how what you've lived through has affected you?"

What good would it do now?

I shrug.

"I believe somewhere deep down there is a young man who wants to be heard. One day, K'wan, you will want to break your silence. It'll be on your terms, in your time. Not mine or your parents'. I don't believe you will ever be able to fully forgive your parents, particularly your father, until you allow yourself the opportunity to hear him out."

There goes that word again, forgiveness!

I mean no disrespect, but Mrs. Morgan should just record everything on a recorder, then give it to me to play at my convenience. This way, it'd save her time and energy from having to repeat herself over and over. Every session it's the same thing. Forgiveness, letting go, opening up; she goes on and on. For what? I'm not interested!

She is only doing her job, but still, it gets annoying sometimes.

"As I said a few sessions back, forgiveness isn't about forgetting or overlooking what was done. It isn't about letting anyone off the hook. Forgiveness is not about repressing your hurt, anger or hate."

I shift in my seat, taking a deep breath.

"It is all in your eyes, K'wan. You hate what your father did to your mother, don't you? Every time you think about it, it enrages you, doesn't it?"

I do not look at her. I stare at the posters in back of her and slowly nod.

"I want you to write about it in your composition book. Don't put any thought into it, simply right how that anger, how that rage, makes you feel. I want to know what triggers it. The more you write about it, the more you release. The more you release, the less angry you will become. You will find that writing can be very cathartic."

I scroll through my mental Rolodex to see if I am familiar with that term: cathartic. I am not. I make a note to commit its definition to memory.

Mrs. Morgan explains, "It is an experience that cleanses the emotions. For instance, for some, crying can be a very cathartic experience, especially for someone who holds in their feelings. The same thing goes for writing, releasing your emotions through pen and paper."

I am looking at her as if she is speaking a foreign language, but I think I get it. She wants to manipulate me. Yup, that's what it is. Since the lab rat won't talk, she thinks getting me to write it out is going to help her with her experiment. Mrs. Morgan can't fix me. I'm not the one in need of repair. Okay, maybe I am. But, still, I'm the only one who can change anything about me. That's what they all tell me.

"Expressive writing," she continues as if she's trying to sell the idea to me as if it were a new Xbox game, "can offer healing and promote a healthy well-being. I know the therapeutic power of writing. It's not about writing what you already know. It's about writing about things that trouble you, confuse you, or pains you. It is in the depths of that writing that allows for healing. I'd like for you to give it some thought, okay?"

Maybe.

I shrug, standing. My time is up.

Seventeen

There's another new kid in group today. Miss Daisy introduces him to the group. Tells us his name is Aiden. Not that race matters—well, not that it should—still, I secretly let out a sigh of relief that it isn't another face like mine. He's white.

There are only eight of us in group today. Aesop, Jackson, Jarrod, Corey. Westley, Nicholas—this kid from Paterson, Lenny, and me. Oh, and now Aiden, makes nine. He looks around the circle and gives everyone a head nod. Most of the guys say, "Wassup," to him. He has on a tight-fitting, white long-sleeved T-shirt with the words BORN LOSER written across his muscled chest and a pair of ripped blue jeans. I stare at his thick neck and short limbs. He's a stocky kid who reminds me of a wrestler.

Miss Daisy tells him to take the seat next to Lenny. Lenny eyes him, sizing up his next target as he cuts through the circle and takes his seat. I imagine Thick Neck putting Lenny in a chokehold, then snapping his neck. It would serve him right for thinking he's such a Billy Badass.

Miss Daisy wants us to go around the room to introduce ourselves. Everyone says their names, except me—as usual. He stares at me, waiting. "And that's K'wan," Miss Daisy says for me, extending her hand in my direction. He gives me a head nod. I surprise myself and nod back, quickly shifting my eyes. Even that's more than what I intended on doing.

"Yeah, pretty boy's real special," Lenny sneers. "He gets to sit up in here like his tongue is cut out while the rest of us have to talk. That's some real bullshit."

Miss Daisy shoots him a look. "That's enough, Leonard. Every week it's something with you. I've had enough."

Every day, I have to remind myself to not take his hate and nasty attitude toward me personally. Some days are easier than others. I understand he really hates himself. I am not the source of his misery. He is.

He sucks his teeth. "Yo, my name is Lenny. Don't call me that."

"And my name isn't 'Yo'," she snaps back, "so don't refer to me as your 'yo'." She says this with more attitude than I'm sure she intended to. But I bet she's just as sick of him and his bull as I am.

Aesop and Jackson snicker.

"Man," Corey groans. "You done got her started. Damn."

Miss Daisy continues, glancing around the room. "Damn is right. Everyone in here should focus on their own stuff and not worry about what you think others should or shouldn't be doing in this group. Everyone here will eventually share. But for those who are not ready, they can sit and listen. Active participation is more than simply sharing. It's also about listening. And listening is a skill many of you in this room can benefit from. Now, I don't want to hear another word out of you about it."

Lenny/Leonard huffs, folding his arms tightly across his chest and pushing back in his seat; he's clearly pissed that Miss Daisy has called him out by his real name. One he seems to despise.

She folds her hands in her lap. "Okay, so now that we've gotten that out of the way." She turns back to the new kid. "Aiden, why don't you share with the group a little something about yourself."

He tells us the usual stuff. That he's seventeen, from Bergen County. That he has four brothers. Most guys don't offer more than that unless they're asked to.

"So why are you here at Healing Souls?" she inquires, but of course she knows. She only asks to see how honest they'll be.

He pushes up the sleeves of his shirt, showing off a tattoo of a black dragon on his forearm. Its bright, angry flames swirl around his wrist. "The judge said this is where I had to come or go to prison for two years."

"Whatchu do?" Westley inquires, leaning forward in his seat.

"Kicked in my girl's parents' house door," Thick Neck says, nonchalantly.

We all look at him.

"And why did you kick in their door?" Miss Daisy wants to know.

"Because they wouldn't let me see my son. And I got pissed."

A few guys groan.

"Daaaaaaaaamn, yo, you was wildin'," Aesop says, shaking his head.

He shrugs. "They shoulda let me see my son."

"Man, that's effed up," Jackson says, shaking his head.

"What's effed up, him kicking in the door?" Miss Daisy asks Jackson.

"Nah, them not lettin' him see his seed. I'd probably woulda did the same thing."

"And you'd still be sitting right here; not seeing your child. So how would kicking in someone's door really benefit you?"

He shrugs, looking stupid.

I feel myself frowning and rolling my eyes up in my head at the same time. Some of these guys say some of the dumbest crap ever.

"How old is your son?" Miss Daisy asks Thick Neck, leaving Jackson stuck on stupid.

"Six months," he says, shifting his eyes.

"So, why wouldn't they let you see him?" she wants to know.

He shrugs again. "I don't know. They're real assholes."

She shakes her head. "That's a matter of opinion."

"No," he shoots back. "It's a fact."

"Okay, so again, why?"

"Why what?"

"Why were they keeping you from your son? There has to be a reason other than because they were being *assholes*, as you so eloquently put it, for them to want to keep you from seeing him. As a father, you have rights, legally. So would you like to share the real reason why they would deny you?"

He shifts in his chair. "I just did."

She raises her arched brows. "No. What you did was call them names. You told us what you want us to believe because that's how you see it. And that's how you want us to see it. And that's fine—for now. One of the things we teach in group is accountability; holding residents responsible for their own choices. And part of accountability is owning your behaviors. You're not there yet. How old is your child's mother?"

"Fifteen."

"I see. So how did kicking in her parents' front door benefit you?"

In my head, I hear myself asking my mom the same question. "How did moving *him* back in benefit *you?* Us?"

I stare at the new kid. Pretend that whatever answer he gives will be hers as well. I hold my breath.

"It didn't."

I silently exhale.

"Then how did it affect you?"

"I'm here."

"Is that all?"

He looks down at his hands, then starts fidgeting with the sleeve of his shirt. "Now they won't let me talk to my girl. And I still can't see my son."

"And how does that make you feel?"

He frowns. Looks at Miss Daisy as if she has three heads and four arms. "Angry. What you think? How would you like it if you couldn't see your kid?"

"I wouldn't," she says. "I would be very upset about it. But I would also take a look at what it is about me—what I might have done or said that may have contributed to someone trying to keep me from my child."

"Yo, that's real effed up," Jackson says, shaking his head. "I feel your pain, man. My girl's parents did the same thing to me."

Miss Daisy eyes him. "Yes, they did. But how about you share with Aiden what it was that *you* did for them to do that to you? Tell him how *you* injured your child."

He squirms in his seat. Embarrassment washes over his face as he lowers his head. "Nah, forget it. I'm good."

"No, you're not," Miss Daisy pushes. "You were quick to side with Aiden, who hasn't yet told the truth as to why he can't see his son. You were emphatic toward him because you can't see your son either and you wanna blame his mother and her parents for something you did. So no, you're not good. And we're not going to forget it. You opened the door, now man up, take responsibility, and walk through it."

Wow, she really dug into him. Good.

"Damn, son, she went in, hard, on you," Corey says. Miss Daisy shoots him a look. He eases back in his seat.

"My bad, Miss Dee," Jackson says. "It bothers me. I know what I did was effed up. But he's still my son and I should be allowed to see him."

"You are," she reminds him, "one hour a week supervised. And why do you have to be supervised, Jackson?"

Miss Daisy has turned the heat up on him and now he's sweating in his seat. He scratches his forehead, then rubs his face. "'C-c-cause they think I'ma danger to him.'"

"Now tell Aiden what happened," she pushes.

Jackson looks like he's about to either pass out or throw up. "We were beefin', and my BM kept poppin' shit. You know, runnin' her mouth nonstop, talkin' real slick. And I yoked her up while she was holding him. And he…"—he swallows—"got hurt."

This is the first time I am hearing this. I feel judgment and anger welling up inside of me. How could he do that to her? To his baby? What gave him the right to put his hands on her?

I glance over at him. He looks like he's about to cry. He turns his head away from the group, then covers his eyes with a hand.

The group waits for him to get himself together. I notice they do that a lot when someone gets upset or emotional in group. They wait for them to get it together, then start back up. Sometimes Miss Daisy will move onto something else. Another topic less painful. Today she does not. She waits with everyone else. I am curious myself, so instead of turning to the window and looking out, I wait, too.

Jackson turns back to the group. In my mind's eye, I see him counting nine sets of staring eyes, waiting. "I didn't mean to hit him. She hooked off on me first. And I didn't think. I just reacted."

"Damn, man," Jarrod says. "How'd ya lil' man get hurt?"

"When I hit her, she tried to fight me back and he fell out of her arms and hit the floor."

"Oh, damn" and "Wow" echo throughout the room.

Miss Daisy gets up from her seat. We watch as she walks over to a desk and shuffles through a stack of pamphlets. "And how does that make you feel, knowing your son was hurt?"

"I feel effed up," Jackson says, his voice cracking. "I would never hurt my seed."

"Maybe not intentionally," she says, returning to the circle holding a handful of pamphlets in her hand. She hands them to Jackson and tells him to take one and then pass them around. "But your actions did, in fact, hurt him. And they hurt his mother. And they hurt you. So who wins?" Her eyes scan the circle.

No one!

"No one," Jackson and Jarrod say.

She nods. "Exactly. Everyone loses where violence is concerned. What message do you think an abuser conveys to his or her victims when they become violent?"

That they deserve it!

"That it's their fault," Aesop states. "That they deserved it."

When the pamphlets come to me, I take one and flip through it. The first thing that catches my eye is: UP TO TEN MILLION CHILDREN WITNESS SOME FORM OF DOMESTIC VIOLENCE ANNUALLY

I am one of them!

I read another caption: ONE WOMAN IS BEATEN BY HER HUSBAND OR PARTNER EVERY FIFTEEN SECONDS IN THE UNITED STATES

I am stunned.

The next caption states: ONE IN EVERY FOUR WOMEN WILL EXPERIENCE DOMESTIC VIOLENCE IN HER LIFETIME

That's like millions of women. My mom being one of them.

I look up from the pamphlet when Miss Daisy says, "Abusers want his or her victims to believe that they are the cause of their abuse. That they are somehow responsible for their abusers mood and the way they get treated."

"See, you must want me to put my hands on you, Syreeta. I don't know why you like to test me...you must like getting your ass beat..."

"Or they'll try to excuse their abuse away by saying they just lost it, just flipped, or saw red and blacked out. Truth is, there is no moment of insanity going on with an abuser. They know exactly what it is that they are doing and why they're doing it. It's all about control." Miss Daisy pauses, glancing around the room.

"Abusers choose to manipulate situations so that it appears that they've lost control when, in fact, they've really chosen how to abuse their victims. They control where they hit them, how hard and for how long. They choose to control who they do it in front of and they choose when to stop. And he/she is in control of what type of violence they will use, whether it's a slap and not a punch, or a punch instead of a strangling—they always know. Even when they stab their victim or shoot them, they know exactly what it is they're doing. They've given thought about it, they've obsessed over it. They know exactly what the outcome is going to be and they don't give a damn about the consequences."

I am surprised to hear her use the word "damn." Miss Daisy never curses in group. Not that damn is really a curse word, but still, it isn't a word she uses. I can tell she takes this kinda stuff very serious. I do, too.

"So don't ever believe an abuser when they say they do not know why they do what they do, because it is a bold-face lie. They always know."

"Then why do they do it?" I hear myself asking her. Not because the words have fallen from my mouth, but because the question is beating up against my brain. "Why does it keep happening?"

"First, so that we're all clear. Abuse doesn't just happen. Like I said, an abuser doesn't lose control of anything. If anything, he has the most control because his victim has unsuspectingly and, most times unwillingly, given into him. Victims give up their power and their control over their own lives and minds when they acquiesce to their abuser, when they make excuses for them and cover up for them.

"Abuse happens because an abuser wants something from their

victim. Who can tell me what they think an abuser might want?"

"Sex," the kid Nicholas says.

"Sex isn't necessarily what an abuser is interested in," Miss Daisy explains. "Exerting his power over his victim is. Anyone else want to share?"

"To shut her trap up," Lenny says. He's been sitting here pouting, or whatever it is bullies do, for the most part of the group.

Miss Daisy smiles at him, as if she's pleased that he has chosen to participate in the discussion. "Yes, Lenny. Shutting her up can definitely be what he wanted to do by abusing her." She glances at her watch. "If an abuser is completely honest with himself and others, he'll be able to tell you exactly what is going on for him. He might have wanted her to stop doing something that he didn't agree with, punish her for doing something he didn't like, or for hurting his feelings, to win an argument, get his way, or like Lenny said, to get her to shut up. It's all about trying to control his victim."

"I'm warning you. Don't open your mouth to say another word..."

"Man, that's crazy," Nicholas says, shaking his head, "letting someone control you like that."

Miss Daisy shuffles some papers she has in her lap, then crosses her legs. I stare at her feet, wondering what size shoe she wears. *I bet a size twelve women's, easy.* I shift my eyes. "No one gets involved with someone who they want to be controlled by."

Then why do they stay?

That question still looms around in my head. I mean, if that's not what you want, then why put up with it. I can't understand the logic. I want to, but it makes no sense to me. It has to be more than love that makes a person want to stay with someone who beats their face in or calls them names. It has to be.

"When a woman or girl—and yes, we already know that young

girls are also being abused in relationships, don't we?" She eyes Aiden, then the rest of us. "Women don't seek out abusive men. Abusive men seek them out. She doesn't know he's abusive. If she did, nine times out of ten, she wouldn't stay."

I don't know if I believe her. A lot of them would stay. They'd stay because they'd be too busy trying find ways to change him, or fantasizing that he'd never do it to her. That's what I think.

"When a woman meets a man, she is looking for a partner. She is assessing, to the best of her ability, his potential in being a good partner. The abuser is assessing his potential to control her. He is looking for a slave, so to speak. He wants someone he can dump his burdens on, and have them become responsible for his behavior so that he doesn't have to look at himself, so that he doesn't have to see himself as the problem. Abusers manipulate and lie so much that many of them are unable to see the truth. And that's where the problems lie. He believes his own lies. And somehow he finds a way for his victim to believe them, too."

"And then she turns around and does something to piss him off," Jarrod says.

Miss Daisy shakes her head. "Domestic violence is always about power and control. It's never about anger. Yes, anger is a symptom of abuse, but it is definitely not the cause of it."

"Syreeta, you like pissing me off."

I have to admit, even though I don't always like sitting in here for two hours, Miss Daisy helps me understand different things, like abuse, a little better. And listening to what comes out of some of these guys' mouths makes me happy to be nothing like them.

"So, then, when will peeps ever stop beatin' each other up?" Aesop wants to know.

"When chicks learn to stop poppin' off at the mouth and gettin' up in a man's face," Jackson says.

I'm frowning at him in my head. He's doing exactly what Miss Daisy said abusers do, blaming. I'm starting to really believe he thinks that it's okay to hit on girls. No, I'm actually convinced of it. And judging by the look on Miss Daisy's face, she is as well.

"So, Jackson, let me get this straight. You're saying that it's a woman's fault that she gets beat on; is that what I hear you saying?"

He gives her an incredulous look, like she should already know the answer. "Well, yeah. Chicks gotta learn when to fall back so that they don't get knocked back. They really need to take a look at what they do to get yoked up."

The Bully and Corey seem to agree. I am not surprised that The Bully agrees. But just a few weeks ago, Corey claimed he didn't think it was right for a guy to put his hands on a girl. Now he's sitting here agreeing with Jackson. If you ask me, he shouldn't be agreeing with anything since he seems to like getting smacked up on, too. Not unless he's talking about himself.

I blink.

"Syreeta, you can't do anything right, then you wonder why I go upside your head. You do stupid shit."

"Yes, women play a role in their relationships. Yes, women need to be accountable for their role in exacerbating an already volatile situation. Yes, they should not be antagonistic. But to say that she is responsible for a man's behavior toward her is wrong. She is responsible for her behaviors. And he is responsible for his reactions to them. His behaviors are his choice."

Aesop twists his lips up. "Yeah, okay. Keep it Gee, Miss Dee. How many chicks really take responsibility for what they do in the relationship? How many chicks you know who don't think it's cool to do what they do, but do it anyway because they think they can get away with it because they're chicks? I hear you always talking about accountability and taking responsibility for what we do, okay, cool. But when are chicks gonna be held accountable, too?"

Probably never, I think, waiting to hear what Miss Daisy says. Personally, I can't speak about anyone else, but I know my mom wasn't the type to be nasty or mean to him. She never cursed. And if she did, I never heard her. I never even heard her raise her voice to him or heard her talk down to him or jump in his face. If anything, she was always trying to keep peace in our house. Always running around trying to keep him happy as if that—his happiness—was her mission in life. That's what I saw with my own two eyes. That's what I hated to see; Mom running around like she was a puppet—his puppet, and him being the puppeteer, yanking her strings however he wanted. I shouldn't hate my mom for that, but I do. I'm angry with her for letting him do that to her. For letting him treat her any kind of way.

"I'll admit. Women should be held to the same standard when it comes to their behaviors and their choices to engage in violence. Still, we have to first change social beliefs, behaviors, and attitudes that perpetuate the use of violence, starting with each one of you." Miss Daisy says this as her eyes sweep around the circle. "Each of us has a social responsibility to treat each other with respect and dignity."

"Man, forget that," Westley huffs. "I'm not respectin' anyone who can't respect me. You come at me ill, then you gotta catch it; period, point blank. I don't care who it is."

Miss Daisy leans over in her seat and glances over at him. "So you'd rather spend your life fighting someone you feel has disrespected you; is that what you're saying?"

He shrugs. "It's whatever."

"And it's that kind of attitude that will keep you in trouble. Change has to start with you, first."

Westley shakes his head. "Nah, I'm not beat. You try 'n play me, it's gonna be bubble wrap time for you."

Bubble wrap time? WTH?

I glance over at Westley, wondering how many times he's gotten into a fistfight with someone over something stupid.

"Westley, all that kind of attitude is going to get you is either prison or death. Nothing good will ever come out of you fighting every time you feel you've been wronged by someone. Hopefully, with time and maturity, you will change that mindset."

Yeah, good luck with that, I think as she tells us our time is up. "Make sure you look over the pamphlet I handed out," she says as everyone races out the door. "We'll talk about them in next group."

I have already decided to go to the library tonight and look more stuff up about domestic violence. I want to read more, know more. After all, it's been my life.

Eighteen

Two days have gone by, and I am still thinking about some of the stuff that I've read in that pamphlet Miss Daisy gave us. Like how 25% to 45% of all women who are beaten up on are abused while they are pregnant. I am bothered by that. What kind of man would beat on a pregnant woman; on any woman, pregnant or not?

He would. Now I wonder if he ever hit Mom while she was pregnant with one of us. Or if he stored up his anger until after she gave birth to us, then beat her. The more I learn, the more confused I become. I mean, I know what I am hearing and reading about abuse, but I still don't get it. If an abuser thinks his wife or girlfriend is such a bad person, why does he stay with her? If he is so much better than she is, so much smarter than she is, or so much more competent in life than she is, why does he stay with someone like that? Someone who he thinks is beneath him. It makes no sense to me. And even though I am slowly starting to get why a woman might stay, it still seems crazy to me.

I don't wanna be like him. And yet, I'm afraid that I already am. Then what happens? I wish there was a way I could see into my future, wish there was a way I could see what my life will be like when I become an adult. They say abuse and violence are generational. Will it stop with me? Or will I perpetuate its ugliness? That's what seeing my mom being abused has been like for me—ugly. And scary.

A counselor aide who I am not familiar with comes to the door and tells me I have mail, then walks off. I push back from the desk and get up from my seat, then walk down to the counselors' station.

"Looks like someone has lots of love today," Mrs. Knottingham says. She's another counselor here who seems really nice. She's a brown-skinned lady with big, round brown eyes and short hair that she wears in a natural 'fro-type style. Some of the kids here call her Mrs. Knottyhead because her hair is real thick and kinda knotty looking. But that's none of my business.

I give her a half-smile as she hands me my mail. I have a box from my aunt Janie and a letter from my mom. This time I don't refuse the letter. I open it in front of Mrs. Knottingham, shake the letter out, then slip it back into its envelope. The box has already been opened. Inside there's a card and three books: *A Long Way Gone: Memoirs of a Boy Soldier*, *They Poured Fire On Us From The Sky: The Story of Three Lost Boys from Sudan*, and *Monster*.

I take the books and card out, handing Mrs. Knottingham the empty box, then practically speed walk back to my room. For the first in a long time, I am anxious and excited. But I am not sure why. I mean, it's not like they haven't written me before. Mom writes me every week, sometimes twice a week in between her weekly visits. I just never open any of them. But this time I will. And Aunt Janie has sent me cards and books at least every month since I've been away from home—for almost a year. But today, I kinda want, no, I need pieces of them. I miss my family. I miss my mom. I wanna go home. I just don't know how to get there.

I feel so empty.

I clutch the books tightly beneath my arm while holding my mom's letter in my hand as I walk back to my room. "Yo, Green Eyes," Ja'Meer says as I walk into the room. He is slipping a Seton Hall Jersey on over a white tee. "I'm headin' to the rec room. You wanna get in a chess game tonight, or are you gonna stay locked up in here, studyin'? We all know you a brainiac." He laughs. "You gonna end up bein' the next Einstein so you might as well let me house your king real quick. You down or what? You need a life outta this room, man."

I shrug, setting the books on top of my desk. I wanna tell him that I lost my life somewhere between black eyes and the blade of a knife. I wanna tell him that there is no life outta this room, outta this shell of who I am. Because I am gone. That I am here physically, but I am not here emotionally. That this place is an ugly means to an end for me; that I'm just not sure what I will find, or who I will be, when I finally get to the other side. My mouth opens, but none of these things come out. He stares at me, waiting.

He walks over to me, holding his fist out. "One of these days, I'ma get ya little ass talkin', yo. Watch and see." I extend a balled hand out to him, and he gives me a pound. "Now meet me in the rec room so I can whoop that ass one good time."

I don't wanna smile. But, against my will, I do. And he shakes his head. "Aiight, yo. I'm out." He heads for the door, shooting me a peace sign.

I wait for the door to close behind him, then bring my attention to the card and letter in my hand. I am not sure why I am still clutching the letter and card tightly in one hand, while standing and staring at the closed door as if I am waiting for something or someone to appear. I take a deep breath. I am more nervous now than I've ever been. The moment of truth—hers, maybe mine—is held on the pages of my mom's letter to me.

I sit on the edge of my bed. No, this is not my life. My life is in this letter. I open Aunt Janie's card first. On the front it says: Strength, Courage & Resilience. On the inside she has written a note:

To my handsome nephew, K'wan:

I hope and pray that this note finds you doing well. I know you are going through a very difficult time right now. But I want you to know that you will get through this. You are a strong, courageous, resilient young man with the wisdom of young men twice your age. You have had to endure more than I would wish on anyone. But you will overcome. You will get through this. You are a fighter. We are all praying for you, and missing you, terribly. Don't give up, sweetheart. Your Uncle Rodney, and cousins, Simone and Eddie, all say hello and send their love. They want you to know that they are thinking about you. We all are. Hope you enjoy the books. I will be up soon to see you.

Love always,

Aunt Janie

I place the card back into its envelope, then open my mom's letter next. I scoot up on my bed, pressing my back up against the wall. Then slowly unfold the letter open.

Dear K'wan,

It hurts me knowing that you are hurting and that your father and I have caused you this pain. It hurts knowing that there is nothing that I can physically do to help ease your hurt. I want to be there for you, sweetheart, if you'd let me. I have cried and cried. I have agonized a lifetime over all that has happened since that night. I am so, so, sorry, that you had to witness any of that. That you and your brothers had to live through it, the violence, for as long as you did.

I knew from my own counseling that domestic violence affected children as well. I knew in my heart that you, in particular, had heard and seen more than you should have.

I have always said you were much more perceptive and wiser than kids your own age, yet I tried to hide so many truths from you. I tried to deny them. Tried to excuse away the bruises. But you'd always see right through me. I saw the slow burning fire in your eyes and knew how deeply affected you were by it. Yet, I tried to pretend you wouldn't be. I tried to act as if you would be able to tuck everything you ever saw or heard in the back of your mind and everything would be okay. I didn't want to acknowledge how much of an impact my own choices would have on your life. And for that I am so very sorry.

Sweetheart, I know you are angry and hurt. I am, too. I am angry at myself for not being able to protect you. It was my job, my responsibility, as your mother to keep you safe, emotionally and physically. It hurts knowing that I failed you. It hurts knowing that you felt you needed to protect me when it should have been the other way around.

I am so sorry, K'wan, for not being able to put your needs—what was most important, your safety, before my own. You may not ever understand this, but I thought letting your father move back home was what was best for all of us. In my heart, letting your father back home wasn't about you or your brothers. It was about me. I felt even if things didn't work out between your father and me that I had to give him another chance. I wanted, needed, to believe in him. I hoped and prayed he had really changed; that he would never put his hands on me again. I wanted for us to be a family.

I wanted you and your brothers to have both of your parents under the same roof without the silent treatments or the threats of violence. Instead of trusting my own instincts, I wanted to trust your father's words. It was my hope that he would get it right. That he would treat me right. That he would be the positive role model that you and your brothers needed. I needed those things, sweetheart, because I loved your father. I still do.

The painful truth is, sweetheart, I wanted your father back. I wanted the man that I had married back. The difference now is I will not ever take him back. I won't ever allow him to hurt me, or you and your brothers. Not after all that has happened over the last year. I will not live like that. I do not want you and your brothers to live like that. I know that a lot of damage has already been done. But I refuse to believe, or accept, that it is too late. I refuse to think that this is something that we cannot get through together. I am here for you, sweetheart. You are not alone in this.

The restraining order against your father stays this time. Not because I am afraid of what he might do to me. But because I am afraid of what I might do to **him** if he were to ever try to hurt or disrespect me again. I will never allow anyone else to disrespect me, or allow you and your brothers to be subjected to (or witness to) any kind of abuse again. I failed you once, K'wan. I will not fail you or your brothers twice. And I will not fail myself, not again. All that I ask is that you find it in your heart to open up. Let the professionals there help you through this. Let **me** help you through this. You are my son, my firstborn. And I have loved you from the moment you were conceived. I would give my life for you, sweetheart.

There is not a day that goes by that I am not blaming myself for what has happened. You shouldn't be there, away from your family. You are not to blame for any of this. It is not your fault. It's not your cross to bear. It is mine. It is your father's. We created this mess.

With all that is in me, I wish I could rewind the clock and erase every time you saw me cry, or heard your father call me names. I wish I could wipe away every black eye, bloody nose, or swollen lip you had to see. I know they haunt you. They haunt me. I am fighting back tears as I write this, knowing that I have helped cause this. It hurts me down to my core every time I have to leave you there. I know you are in good hands, but I know home is where you should be; home with your brothers and me, surrounded by the love of your family.

Your brothers miss you. I miss you. We all love you, K'wan, so very much. Please know, always know, you are not alone, ever.

Love Always,
Mom

I read the letter a second time, then a third until the words become blurred and the blue ink begins to smear from my tears falling onto its pages. I neatly fold it back into the envelope, lying back on my bed. I do not wipe my tears. I allow them to slowly roll out of the corners of my eyes, holding Mom's letter against my chest. I know she loves me. And I love her. Yet, her letter has not made me feel any better or worse. I still feel like I am sinking. Yet my hand grasps the letter tightly, as if it were a lifeline.

Nineteen

I don't know why I decide to leave my room, but I do. I choose to be around guys I do not speak to, connect with, or even like over being alone reading a book or studying. I do not know if that is good or bad. But it is different.

I glance around the large room. Jarrod and Jake are sitting at one of the several round board game tables situated in the room, playing backgammon. At another table, Anthony and Nelson are playing checkers, while Jackson, Aesop, Corey and Lance seem engrossed in a game of spades at another table. The Bully is sitting in one of the chairs with his long legs stretched out and his arms folded across his chest, watching the movie *21 Jump Street*. He cranes his neck. He sees me and scowls.

For some reason, I feel like giving him the finger, just once. But I pretend he is invisible instead. Two other residents are playing a game of ping-pong over in the corner.

When I don't see Ja'Meer, I turn to leave but Mr. Cee, the rec attendant on duty, calls out to me. He's a short, stocky man with brown skin who kinda reminds me of that actor/comedian dude Joe Torry; just not as funny, though. Still he's kinda cool. Actually, if I'm really honest about it, most of the staff here are cool in one way or another, unless you give them reason not to be. And since I don't talk, or break any of the rules, I don't have any problems with them.

"Silent Night; just the young man I wanna see," he says to me, waving me over to him. Silent Night is what he calls me because I don't talk. I get the *silent* part but *night* makes no sense to me. Sometimes I want to ask him how the word *night* fits into his nickname of me. "C'mon over here and let me rap to you for a minute."

I did say Mr. Cee was cool, right? But I forgot to mention he's also a motor mouth. I don't mean to be disrespectful, but it's true. He talks nonstop. And he doesn't ever seem to mind that I never say anything back. Ja'Meer says he likes to hear himself talk. "You ready for a rematch. I let you beat me last round 'cause I felt generous, but tonight I'm showing no mercy."

Inside I am laughing at him. He wins because I let him.

"Hey, Cee-Dawg," Ja'Meer calls out, walking into the day-room. For some reason, I let out a sigh of relief when I see him. I am not up for listening to Mr. Cee talk on and on about his relationship woes or his never-ending financial problems. I have enough of my own problems. But I always end up thinking if he stayed outta the casinos in Atlantic City and stopped blowing his money on lottery tickets and scratch-offs that maybe he wouldn't be in the mess he's in. Adults, I don't understand them some-times. Still, I don't need to be listening to his problems. Besides, I don't think he should be telling me any of his personal business like that anyway. "You can get at Green Eyes after I'm done with him 'cause I'ma 'bout to put the whooptie wham on him real quick."

Mr. Cee laughs as Ja'Meer walks over to the table. "Yeah, okay, okay it's all good. I have a butt whipping with your name on it, too. So you go on and handle my light work, then get ready to man up and take your lumps."

Ja'Meer and Mr. Cee give each other a pound. "So what's good, my dude?" he says, looking over at me. "You ready to get your clock spun back."

I smile it off, deciding to show him no mercy on the board tonight. Mr. Cee slides Ja'Meer the clipboard to sign out the chess pieces, then hands him a box. "Aiight, Silent Night, don't let this knucklehead beat you too bad."

I shake my head, following Ja'Meer over to a table in the center of the room. We set up our pieces. "Yo, so what's good? You aiight?"

I look up from the board.

"You looked kinda outta it earlier today. I wanna make sure you good so I won't have'ta feel bad when I whoop ya ass and house ya king."

I make a snorting sound, shaking my head. *I'm gonna have to shut him up real quick, I see.* I study the board, map out a game plan in my head, then make my move. There's a Chinese proverb that says life is like a game of chess, changing with every move. I kinda believe this to be true. I mean, in chess—like now, you try to predict what your opponent is going to do, with each move having a consequence. That's kinda the same thing in life. I kinda think the problem is not too many people, especially adults—'cause most kids aren't really taught how to plan their future moves. But grownups, if they thought ahead, if they were able to predict what would happen in the future when they did certain things and how their actions would affect everything and everyone around them, maybe we wouldn't have so many bad things happening in the world. Maybe my mom wouldn't have been beaten on. Maybe she wouldn't have stayed. And maybe I wouldn't be sitting here. Maybe…

Still, everything is about control. In chess, a player must try to control the center of the board. To lose control, means to possibly lose the game. In life, people try to control each other. Like Miss Daisy always says in group, "abuse is about power and control." To lose control, could possibly mean losing the ones you love. That's how I see it. I don't plan on losing control in this game. But I hope and pray I don't ever try to control my girlfriend, or wife—whenever I get one. Or lose control of my temper and hurt someone I love. I don't want to grow up being that kinda man. Heck, I don't want to be that kinda kid, fighting on his girlfriend, kicking in her parents' doors and whatnot. That's crazy.

Ja'Meer moves one of his bishops. I grin as I strategize to take control of the board and hem up his king. It takes me exactly thirty-two minutes to seal his fate. No words needed. He already knows. Checkmate.

"Aww, damn, yo. Aiight-aiight. You got that. Let's go another game." I give him a pitiful look. Dude hates to lose, which is why I usually let him win. But tonight, I am not feeling so generous, especially since he is always talking about beating me. Even winners have to lose, sometimes.

I shake my head.

"Yo, is that headshake a no? Or one of those poor-you kinda things?"

Both.

"C'mon, man. One more game." I shake my head again, but I don't get up from my seat. He takes that as a sign and starts setting up his pieces, again.

Mr. Cee comes over to us, laughing. "Okay, Mouth Almighty, let me find out Silent Night done put the whoopty-wham on ya trash-talking behind."

"Nah, man," Ja'Meer defends. "I let him win."

Yeah right. You wish. I raise a brow.

He laughs. "Aiight, aiight. I ain't gonna front. He got that off.

But that was warm-up practice for me. This time I'ma take it to his neck."

"Oh, so this time you gonna stomp the yard on 'im, is that right?" Mr. Cee jokes. "You gonna whoop him so bad 'til he starts to talk, huh? You gonna straight up bum-rush his king. Yeah, okay. I wanna see this."

"Aww, man. You always tryna clown someone, looking like Uncle Ruckus." I hold back a snicker, remembering a *Boondocks* episode. Although we weren't allowed to watch stuff like that at home because of all the racist and inappropriate stuff said, I would sometimes sneak and watch clips on YouTube, like the episode when a white guy is coming outta the bathroom stall from taking a dump and Uncle Ruckus told the guy that his poop smelled like sparkling ice water with a twist of lime. And when the guy didn't go to the sink and wash his hands, he said that the man didn't have to wash his hands because he had impeccable hygiene. I thought that was hilarious. Like who doesn't wash their hands after using the bathroom?

"Oh, I know you not tryna clown me, Stewie," Mr. Cee says, laughing. "With your football head."

The two of them go back and forth cracking jokes until Lenny gets pissed and starts going off. "Damn, why the fuck y'all muh-fuckas gotta be so loud? I'm tryna watch fuckin' TV."

Mr. Cee walks over and shuts the TV off. "And now the TV's watching you, so you can take your disrespectful butt on to your room for the rest of the night."

Lenny burrows his brows, staring Mr. Cee down.

"What, you have a problem you wanna solve?" Mr. Cee questions. "I said, take it on to your room. You have one minute to digest what I've said and get up or get helped up."

The Bully stands up and starts walking. "Man, I don't give a fuck about being restrained. Do what you gotta do." He says this, but he can't really mean it since he's already walking on his own. I don't look at him as he walks by. Yet he still finds a way to bump into my chair. I bite down on my bottom lip.

I am really getting sick of him.

Mr. Cee notices what he's done and confronts him, telling him he now has two days loss of rec and TV privileges for being antagonistic. He mumbles something slick under his breath as Mr. Cee radios for assistance. Two orderlies appear at the door, escorting him to his room. I don't know how they do that. Appear outta nowhere like that.

"Man, let's get back to me housing your king. You ready to play?"

I respond by moving one of my pawns.

Ja'Meer thinks for a moment, then moves his own pawn. He looks up from the board. "Yo, for real. That nigga needs his top rocked for always fuckin' with you." His jaw tightens. "That shit gets me heated, yo. I can't stand fuckin' bullies. I'm tellin' you, man"—he eyes me—"don't let that nigga keep fuckin' with you like that. Niggas like that you gotta take down real quick. Fuck him up real good one good time and he'll leave you the fuck alone, yo."

I shrug. I know he means well, but I am not in the mood for this. I never had to deal with bullies in my neighborhood. I mean, they were there, they're everywhere, still, no one ever picked with me, or Kyle. Not in our neighborhood, or at school. So this whole bullying thing is new for me. And, no, I don't like it. But I keep reminding myself that unless he actually hits me there is no need to fight him. He can keep running his mouth and calling me names all he wants. Nothing he says about me makes me who I am. He doesn't know me, so his words don't have any power over me. I have to keep repeating that in my head. That's something my mom always told Kyle and me whenever someone would say we acted white, or thought we were better than them. She'd say, "Let them talk. What they say about you doesn't add value to your life or validate who you are. As long as you know who you are, that's all that matters."

I know she's right when she says that. Nothing The Bully or anyone else like him says matters. Still, it's annoying as heck.

"If we were on the bricks, I woulda been took his head off for you, for real for real. That nigga better hope I don't ever run into his ass." I am glad when he decides to let it go, changing the subject. "Do you ever think you'll talk again?"

I wanna tell him that this isn't something I made a conscious decision to do. It happened on its own. And I've allowed myself to stay wrapped in it—this loss for words.

I shrug.

He makes another move. "Man, I don't know how you do it. I like talkin' to my girl at night, and hollerin' at my peeps too much to not talk."

We both keep our eyes on the board. For some reason I think he thinks talking to me is gonna disrupt my concentration long enough to give him the advantage over me. It doesn't. Another ten minutes, and he's lost again.

Ja'Meer gets up from his seat. "Damn, man. I'm all off my game tonight. I need to whoop someone in table tennis real quick to get my mojo back. I'ma be back for a rematch in a minute, yo."

I shake my head as he calls Mr. Cee over to play next. Mr. Cee waits until another aide comes in, then comes over to the table. "Now I'ma tell you right now, Silent Night, I'm not playing no games with you tonight. I'ma put this smack down on you, then send you to ya room, aiight."

I smirk. I allow him to make the first move. It takes forty minutes for the game to end, but when it does, I stand in victory. His king checked and his jaw dropped once again.

Next time I'll finish him off much quicker, I think, standing up. And for the first time tonight, I am smiling on my way back to my room.

Twenty

"**Y**o, Green Eyes, Green Eyes, wake up, man." For a moment, I am dazed and have forgotten where I am. It was another bad dream. That night—the night he was strangling Mom and I stabbed him. In my dream I kept stabbing him over and over and over and he was laughing at me, telling me stabbing him wasn't going to stop him from killing her. And I kept on stabbing him, yelling for him to die. But he wouldn't.

I blink, then squint my eyes, tryna adjust to the light. Ja'Meer's standing over me with a concerned look on his face. "Yo, man. You aiight?" He sits on the edge of my bed. "I don't know what's really good with you and I'm no shrink, but whatever's happened, man, it's really fuckin' with you."

I shift my eyes around the room.

"You not talkin' isn't gonna help shit get better. You gotta let that shit out, man. Trust me, I know. I used to hold a buncha shit in; especially after my brother..." He looks off for a quick moment, taking a deep breath. "Man, I was really fucked up when my brother killed himself."

My eyes widen. *Oh wow. How did he kill himself?*

"That lil nigga was my heart, yo." He pauses, pulling in his bottom lip. I can tell this is hurtful for him. If something happened to one of my brothers, I'd be hurt, too. "Muhfuckas twice his size were fuckin' with him, beatin' him up and shit. That's why I fuckin' can't stand bullies, yo. Every time I see shit like that, it makes me think about my brother, and how I wasn't there for him. It pisses me the fuck off. Fuckin' punk-ass niggas. I shoulda been there to look after him, feel me?"

I nod, feeling sadness sweep through me. Ja'Meer turns his head so I can't see the tears forming in his eyes, but when he turns back, I see a few have already fallen. He tells me his brother's name was Jayden. That he was only twelve when he jumped off a bridge two years ago. My heart sinks.

"Man, I don't know what kinda beefs you have with your fam that has you not talkin' to them, but I'd give anything to be able to talk to my brother again. Anything. This shit you doin' is crazy, man. Not talkin', especially to your brothers. Whatever's goin' on, man, you gotta work that shit through. How long you plan on bein' like this, yo, fuckin' mute?"

I pull in my bottom lip. I wanna tell him that this crap isn't easy for me. That not talking is what's keeping me sane right now. But I don't think he'd understand that. No one does.

"You gotta talk to someone, man. What you want, something to happen to someone in ya fam, like one of ya brothers or moms, and you still not talkin' to 'em? Man, once they're gone, they're gone. And there's nothing you can say or do, after the fact, to bring 'em back. I was locked up down at the Burg, man, when my brother killed himself. And I wasn't talkin' to anyone in my fam 'cause my moms called the police on me for havin' drugs and a loaded gun in the crib. I felt like she turned on me, like they all had turned on me, including my brother for finding the gun and drugs, then giving them to her. But they didn't turn on me. I turned on them." He lowers his head and holds his face in his hands. When he turns back to me, his face is wet with tears. I feel my chest tightening. I'm not used to seeing him like this—sad and hurting, like me. And I can't stand it. "My brother's gone, man…" His voice trails off. I can tell, from my own pain, that he is fighting back his emotions. But they will eventually come. Like mine, they always do.

"He'd still be alive right now if them muthafuckin' niggas weren't fuckin' with him. He'd still be alive, yo, if I'da been there for him when he needed me the most. Maybe he woulda told me what was up. And I coulda stepped to those niggas and handled that shit. Or maybe I'da showed him how to handle it on his own. I don't know. Now I won't ever know. All I know is he's gone, man. You gotta get ya mind right, man. Open ya mouth and talk." He gives me a pained, sorrowful look. "Get ya mind right, Green Eyes, before it's too late."

He gets up from my bed and walks into the bathroom, shutting the door behind him. I hold my breath and listen. I can hear the muffled sounds of crying. Sounds I am familiar with, from listening to my mom.

Twenty minutes later, he walks outta the bathroom. I am already lying back in bed. I can't help thinking that my problems aren't as big as his right now. He has shown me another side of who he is. Behind his laughter and bravado, he's just as broken as I am.

He clicks off the lights.

I roll over on my side, then whisper, "Sorry to hear about your brother, man."

Closing my eyes, hoping the nightmares stay at bay. All I see is Ja'Meer crying. And all I keep thinking about is his twelve-year-old brother jumping off that bridge, feeling helpless and hopeless, having no one he felt he could turn to. He killed him-self to end his own suffering. And now, after seeing the hurt in

Ja'Meer's eyes and hearing it in his voice, I do not know if killing yourself is a good thing or a bad thing. But I do know that it now feels like a selfish thing to do. I make a promise to not ever put my mom and brothers through that. *No matter what happens, or what I am going through, I'm not gonna do that to them.*

⊕

The next morning, Ja'Meer is sitting on his bed when I come outta the bathroom. I can tell he's been waiting on me. "Yo, man. I apologize for dumpin' all that shit on you last night; my bad. I don't know what happened. I guess I got kinda caught up tryna get you to see that ignorin' ya fam ain't worth it. You feel me?"

I nod.

"I know you gotta go through whatever it is you're going through; however you need to go through it." He gets up from his bed and starts fidgeting with some papers on his desk. "I'm cool with it, if you don't ever wanna talk to me, aiight?" He looks over at me. "But, you gotta promise me, man. That one day you will talk to someone, aiight? That you'll let that shit out."

I stare at him and wonder if this is what it would be like having an older brother; someone to look out for me the way I should be looking out for my own brothers. A sudden sadness comes over me for not being home with them. Seems like every time I try to stay lost in my own misery, something, or someone—Ja'Meer, Miss Daisy, Mrs. Morgan, my Mom—comes along and tries to find a way to remind me that I am not the only one going through stuff.

I think about his brother, then think about my own, trying to imagine his loss; the pain he, and his mom, must feel.

With my friends at home and school, we talk about things like sports and girls, about summer camps and vacation plans and hopes for college. We talk about the kinda cars we're gonna get when we turn seventeen and get our driver's licenses, about trust funds, and learning how to invest. The only secrets we tell are the ones about the girls who might show us their boobs on the back of the bus or kiss us behind the school's bleachers. There is no talk about feelings and fears. No one ever lets you see their hurts and tears, or the fact that their lives are not as perfect as we all pretend them to be. Maybe some of my friends do have perfect lives; maybe they don't. Either way, I am constantly reminded that even in the most perfect situations, nothing's ever really perfect. There's always a crack hidden somewhere in the seams. All it takes is the right moment for someone else to notice that it's there, before they start pulling and picking at it until they uncover secrets you try to keep hidden; until they find a way to tear down your little house of lies and expose your naked truths. Nothing is ever what it seems.

Ja'Meer gives me a real serious look as if he is trying to see into my soul. "Yo, man, promise me that you won't do no stupid shit like tryna kill ya'self, aiight?"

You don't have to worry about that. I'm done with thinking about stuff like that. Well, okay, it might still come to my mind from time to time, but I am not gonna entertain it for long. And if I do, I'll think about his little brother and those tears I saw (and heard) him shed last night, then dismiss any thoughts of ever hurting myself from outta my head.

I nod, following him out the room.

"Yo, man," he says in a hushed tone. "I ain't say nuthin', but I heard what you said last night. Thanks." I give him a blank look. He laughs. "Aiight, play stupid if you want, yo. I know what I heard. Yeah, you mighta whispered it, but I still heard that shit." I stare down at the freshly waxed floor. The floors almost look like glass. I shift my eyes when I start to see my reflection in them. "It's all good. I'm not gonna repeat that shit. You can trust me, man, for real."

I nod, believingly, as we walk into the cafeteria. There are two counselor aides sitting at the door; they check off our names. It's French toast and home fries day so it's crowded. I grab a tray, then go down the serving line. Ja'Meer is now back to being his chatterbox self. Whatever moment he mighta had last night is now a thing of the past. And I'm cool with that. We all have our moments.

He taps me on the shoulder. "Yo, Green Eyes, you gonna let me get ya potatoes, right?"

I shake my head, keeping myself from laughing at his greedy self. No matter how many helpings they give us here, he'll still try to eat whatever's on my plate.

Twenty-One

"Oh, K'wan, honey," Mom says, hugging and kissing me. "It's so good to see you." At first my body stiffens, but it relaxes when she hugs me again. I hug her back. It's Saturday visiting time and it's packed. I catch a few guys gawking at my mom, and I narrow my eyes at them. I don't like the way they look at her. The Bully also eyes her. I frown and he scowls at me.

Today, Mom is here by herself. Well, at least that's what I assume when I only see one empty chair next to her. Then I think that maybe Kyle has come with her until she drowns out my hopes with, "Your brothers are with your father." This causes the hairs on the back of my neck to rise. I am disappointed. No, pissed. He probably took my brothers on spite so I couldn't see them today. His way of paying me back for not wanting to see him. "But I have a surprise for you." I am not interested in any surprises; only seeing my brothers. She looks over my shoulder at something, then quickly shifts her eyes back to me. "You look tired, sweetheart. Are you sleeping at night?" I turn my eyes, glancing around the visiting room. "K'wan, I wish you'd talk to the people here. You'd feel so much better if you'd just let it out, sweetheart. I know you're angry at me; at your father."

I shift in my seat, staring at my hands in my lap. Mom reaches over and takes my hand into hers. "Have you read my letters? They haven't come back returned so I've taken that to mean you've opened them."

I nod and she smiles; relief seems to fill her eyes. "I knew if I kept writing you that one day you'd finally open them. I meant everything I said, K'wan. I'm so sorry, sweetheart; for everything. If I could take all that has happened back, I would. But I know I can't change the shoulda, coulda, wouldas or even the maybes if I had of..." She scoots her chair up closer to me, our knees practically touch. She leans forward. "The only thing I can do is try to fix this mess I helped put you in. This isn't the life I had planned for you. This isn't your life; not here. Your life is home with your family. I want you home. You are"—her voice catches in her throat—"missed so much."

She places a hand up to her neck, shaking her head as if she's trying to sift through her thoughts, or maybe her emotions. "There is so much I want to tell you. So much I want you to understand. This is not what I dreamed of. Being a wife and mother was a part of my life plan, not losing my voice and being beaten. Your father wasn't always like that. Abusive." My body stiffens. "That's not the man I fell in love with."

There goes that word again, *love*. I know it is a verb. An action word. I know how it is defined in the dictionary; its definition subjective and ever-changing depending on moods and experiences and whatever else. Love seems to have too many rules or maybe none at all. Still, the more I hear it used, the more I hear people profess it, the more certain I am that it's overrated. And that maybe I'm not missing anything spectacular. Maybe I should stay single and avoid all of the trappings of what people claim it to be.

Love is what love does.

Yeah, right!

Love is what slapped, punched and kicked her. Love is what strangled her half to death. Love is what almost got her killed.

"In spite of everything he has done, your father is a good man.

And there was a time when he was good to me. Then something changed. No, maybe it didn't. Maybe I finally saw him and *it* for what it was. But by then it was too late. I had five kids, no career, no life outside of the one that your father provided me, us. Somehow, in wanting the perfect life, I created a way to block out anything unhappy. Sweetheart, I would have never stayed for as long as I did had I been able to walk away. But love wouldn't let me. Hope wouldn't let me."

I stare at her.

Love can be blinding.

No, it can be stupid!

"I know you might not understand what I'm saying right now, but one day, when you meet someone and fall in love, you will."

I'm never falling in love.

"You'll see that life and love isn't always black and white. Everything isn't cut and dry. There are grey areas that sometimes cloud our judgment and become confusing. And just when you have a moment of clarity and can finally see things clearly for what they are, something comes along and blocks your vision. Something changes your mind. And you stay. And before you know it, you're right back where you started. Yet, you make a conscious decision to give it another try, then another, and another. Then before you know it, you've found yourself in too deep, stuck in half-truths and false hopes, trying to hold onto something you know can't ever be fixed or saved. Still, you try. That's what happened to me, K'wan. I wanted to keep my marriage. I wanted to keep my family. I didn't know how to not be a wife. I didn't know how to simply be me. Not at first. And your father knew that. He knew how much I loved him and I allowed him to use it against me. I allowed him to turn my feelings inside out and turn something good ugly."

She lets go of my hand and reaches into her pocket, pulling out a travel pack of tissues. She dabs at her eyes, then wipes her tear-streaked face. "I'm not blaming him. Your father only did what I allowed him to do."

Why? Why'd you let him do that to you?

I want to push the questions out, but they won't come. There's a thick knot in my throat. I try to swallow it back.

I am left to blink, then narrow my eyes. I am trying to push back images of her swollen face. Trying to erase bruises from around her neck, handprints, and fists marks. Things he did to her.

Mom blows her nose, temporarily pulling me back into the moment; the here and now. She squeezes my hand, and I squeeze it back, looking up at her. "I've talked to Dr. Curtis. You remember who he is, right?"

Of course I do. He's the reason I'm here instead of rotting away in some prison. Pieces of Mrs. Morgan's session float in my head. "The executive director of Healing Souls has taken a special interest in you. You'll be in good hands. He's one of the best."

I meet Mom's gaze, shaking the session with Mrs. Morgan from my head—for now, at least.

"I have asked if he'd be willing to see you; at least a few times while you're here."

She had to have called him for him to be interested in seeing me. But why? *It's not like seeing Dr. Curtis stopped you from letting him move back in with us.*

"Believe it or not, Dr. Curtis saved me. He's the one who helped me find my voice and realize that I didn't have to settle. That I could still love your father and love me more. And even though I did let your father move back in with us, I did it on my terms. Not his."

Yeah and you see where that got us. You almost killed. And me here.

My mind drifts back. Back to when I am ten again. It's like nine o'clock at night. Mom is downstairs in the family room. I am sitting at the counter eating ice cream; Kyle and the triplets are already in bed. He walks into the kitchen. His tie hangs loosely around his neck. "What are you still doing up, kiddo?" he asks, rubbing my head. "It's past your bedtime."

"Mommy said I could have ice cream." For some reason, I wish I wouldn't have said anything. Wish I would have hidden somewhere. I can see the veins in his neck stretch, then pulse. Something changes, his mood, his face, his eyes. And now I am frightened that Mom will get into trouble.

"Is that so? Well, finish up and get in bed. You have school in the morning."

"Okay," I say, cautiously, eying him over the rim of my bowl as I scoop ice cream into my mouth. I watch as he heads downstairs. My heart is pounding in my chest. I hurriedly finish the rest of my ice cream, rinse out my bowl and stick it, along with my spoon, into the dishwasher, then inch down the stairs. I hear them, no him, talking.

"So, once again, you sat on your fat behind all day doing nothing..."

"No, Randy, I have been up since six o'clock in the morning, as I am every morning. As you can see, the house is quiet and clean as always..."

"Ever since you started going to that shrink of yours, you've been getting real mouthy."

"No, Randy. I'm just slowly starting to see life through a different set of eyes."

I inch my way closer down the stairs, then tiptoe. Before I know it, I am peeking into the family room. Certain he is going to hit her. I see him snatch the book she is reading outta her hand, then sling it across the room. I watch him point his finger in her face. His hand opens and closes into a tight fist. I hold my breath, waiting.

"I'm telling you right now. I'm not in the mood for your damn mouth. You say one more thing, and I'm gonna shove something down it. Do you understand me?"

"Yes, Randy." Mom's voice is low. "I understand."

I let out a sigh of relief when he doesn't hit her, quickly moving away from the door and running into the game room, hiding until he has gone upstairs. I wait a few minutes more, then sneak back upstairs to my room.

I climb into bed, staring up at the ceiling; wishing him dead. I roll over on my side, pretending to be asleep when Mom comes in to check on me as she always does before she goes to her own room. I lie perfectly still. She touches the side of my head, then plants a kiss on me. I hold my breath. I do not exhale until I hear her closing my door shut.

"Sweetheart," Mom says, reaching up all the way over and touching the side of my face. I look at her. Her hands are so soft. When she looks into my eyes, I see her love for me. I feel it. I don't wanna be mad at her anymore. But I don't know how not to be. I mean, I know it's not her fault what he did to her. Sitting in group has made me see that. But there are times when I still blame her. "I know in my heart that Dr. Curtis can help you get through this. No matter how long it takes, I'm going to be right here with you. Whatever you need to know to understand, I'll tell you."

I don't wanna listen to this anymore. I want her to change the subject. Talk about the triplets or work or Kyle's games; anything but this. I am getting restless. I twist in my chair, stretch my right leg out, then look around the room. "Your surprise is here," she says, smiling as she stands.

A surprise doesn't sound so bad after all now. I turn in the direction of her smile. It is my Aunt Janie. She practically walk-runs over to us; she is wearing a toothy white smile on her face. I stand up and she wraps her arms around me. I breathe in her peachy scent, happy to see her. She steps back, taking me in. "Look at you, handsome as ever. And I can't get over how tall you've gotten. Ohmygod, I am so happy to see you, handsome nephew with them gorgeous eyes." I blush as she fusses over me, drawing attention over to us. She is very pretty, like my mom. I feel lots of eyes on us, on them. She gives me another hug, then she and Mom hug.

"I didn't think you were going to make it," Mom says as she sits back down. "Glad you made it safe."

Aunt Janie sits in the chair next to her. "Girl, I didn't think I was going to make it either. I can't stand flying into Newark. I can't ever remember how to get out of there. Had me going around in circles until I finally got it right. Anyway, I'm here."

Mom rubs her back. "Well, you're here now. That's all that matters; safe and sound. I'm glad to see you."

"Me, too." Mom pulls her into her. I watch as they kiss each other on the cheeks. I smile inside, admiring their resemblance. At first glance, if Aunt Janie wasn't like four years older than Mom, they could almost pass for twins. That's how much they look alike. Aunt Janie has slanted gray eyes, too. Compared to theirs, mine do almost look green. Aunt Janie reaches over and grabs my hand. "And I'm glad to see my handsome nephew even more. Did you get the books I sent you, sweetheart?"

I nod. I wanna thank her. I had meant to write her to say it, but I get up from my seat and give her another hug, then kiss her on the cheek. It's the best I can do for now.

She is smiling. "I know you have a lot on your mind, sweetheart, so don't you worry about writing back. You just worry about getting better and getting out of here, okay?"

I nod.

"Your uncle Rodney and the kids send their love, as always." I smile.

"How's everyone doing?" Mom wants to know.

Aunt Janie waves her on. "Girl, Eddie's talking about going into the Marines next year. And Simone has decided to go to law school. First, she was going to apply to medical schools in the fall, then it was applying for doctorate programs in education, now it's law school. I told Rodney, we'll know when it's time to write the tuition checks what her plans are. Oh, before I forget," Aunt Janie says, looking at me. "Your grandmother gave me a check to give to you. I'm going to give it to your mom, okay?"

I nod. She tells me it's for four hundred dollars. *Wow!* Grandma Liz is always sending money to me and my brothers. Aunt Janie tells me she is staying for two weeks and will be here to visit me every visit. "Lord knows I'd stay longer if I could. It tears me up to see you in here like this, sweetheart. You are loved so very much, K'wan." I smile, knowingly. "We are all here for you. You understand?"

I nod. And for the rest of the visit I enjoy my visit with my mom and aunt, listening to them share stories, feed me words of encouragement, and plant seeds of hope. Today has turned out to be a really good day. No, better than good...great!

Twenty-Two

Sunday afternoon, I am back in the library searching the Internet, reading more stuff on domestic violence. Reading the articles on why women stay, replaying things Miss Daisy has said in group, things my mom has said, is all helping me piece together a level of understanding that doesn't have me so angry with her. Not today, anyway. Today, I accept that my mom isn't to blame for what he did. Tomorrow, I can't be so sure I will feel the same way. I have to learn to do what Mr. Jacobs—one of the social workers at the detention center—used to always say: "Learn to live in the moment. Stay in the present." I don't know how to do that yet. I'd like to try. For some reason, Mrs. Morgan finds her way into my head. "Guilt and worry are two very useless emotions. Guilt keeps you stuck in the past. Worry keeps you obsessing about the future. Things you have no control over. The present, the here and now, is where change happens. It is the only thing you have any control over."

I scroll through a domestic violence fact sheet I have found online. Most of it is stuff I have already heard, or read. "A battering incident is never an isolated event...battering tends to increase and become more violent over time...many batterers learned violent behavior growing up in an abusive family. Domestic violence does not end with separation. Over 70% of the women injured in domestic violence cases are injured after separation."

This information frightens me, but I keep reading. My mom has always told me and Kyle that knowledge is power. I'm thinking knowing this kinda stuff could also save someone's life. Maybe. Understanding it so that I don't ever become him might be what saves me from myself. I hope.

Still, I can't stop thinking how boys who witness domestic violence are twice as likely to abuse their own partners and children when they become adults. This knowing worries me. I know the potential for that to be me is real. I can say I don't wanna ever be violent with my family, but what's to stop me if I feel cornered or pressured or whatever it is that triggers abusers?

"Every day, three women die as a result of abuse."

Every time this plays in my head, I feel myself getting choked up, knowing that that could have been my mom. She could have easily been one of those women killed. And the scary part is she still could. I don't trust him not to hurt my mom.

My head is hurting. There are hundreds and hundreds of thousands of articles and blogs and websites and links on domestic violence. It is overwhelming. How many people are affected by it, how many children are exposed to it, how many women have been killed by it, and children caught in the crossfire of violence. It is depressing.

I decide I've had enough, logging off the computer. I walk up to the desk, handing the counselor aide my pass. She signs it, smiling at me. I am too drained to acknowledge her. The only thing I am aware of is that she is new. I walk out to the counselor's desk to hand in my library pass, then head for my room.

As I'm walking by the dayroom, a ping pong ball rolls out into the hall. Instead of stepping over it, I pick it up, then toss it to Jarrod, who's playing a game with some other kid. As I turn to leave, The Bully bumps into me, causing me to stumble a bit. No excuse me, nothing.

"Yo, watch the fuck where you're going," he growls, heading into the dayroom. I bite the inside of my lip and start to walk off when Miss Pat—another counselor here—calls me over to the counselor's station.

"Did I see what I think I saw?" she asks, knowing she's not gonna get a response from me. "Did Leonard push you?" I shake my head. She narrows her eyes as if she doesn't believe me. Well, it's not a lie and it's really not the truth either. He didn't push me. Still, I can tell she doesn't believe me. "I didn't expect you to admit it, which is why I'm glad we have cameras all over this place. In the meantime…" She picks up the phone, then presses an extension. "Can you rewind a tape for me? Yes, corridor three from the last twenty minutes, near the door of the rec room. Uh-huh, that's it…tell me what you see. Okay, thanks, just what I thought." She hangs up the phone, then walks around the station. "I'm going to have a little conversation with Mister Man. This mess with him has been going on for far too long." She looks around to see who else is around, then leans in and whispers. "Now I didn't tell you this, but if I were your mother, I'd tell you that the next time he does something like that, you kick his ass up and down these halls. But you didn't hear that from me." She walks off toward the rec room, and I head back to my room.

For some reason, I stop in front of the pay phones. No, I know the reason. I wanna hear my mom's voice, or one of my brothers'. I miss my family. I take a deep breath, and make a collect call home. This is the fourth time since being here that I have done this, called collect just to hear someone's voice. I usually hang up as soon as they answer.

My mom's voice drifts through the receiver. "Hello? Hello? K'wan, sweetheart?"

I do not respond. I close my eyes. Try to picture what everyone is doing right now. What they had for dinner. It's almost eight at night. The triplets are probably already in bed. Kyle is probably playing videogames or just getting home from practice. Mom is probably reading a book. She likes reading books by African American authors. She always says it's a good escape from her own life. I agree. I can read a book in two days if I really enjoy it.

I hang up before she can say anything else, then head to my room feeling like I am dragging around a heart full of bricks. I spend the rest of the day in my room, avoiding the other kids, listening to music and replaying what I've read online about domestic violence over and over in my head. Knowing that there are millions of kids like me who have lived through some kinda violence, it confirms that I am not alone, even though I feel like I am. Truth is, I am sorta. I mean, I tried to find stories of other kids who stabbed their fathers or tried to kill them for abusing their moms, but I didn't find any. I saw a few where the fathers were killed because he was repeatedly abusive to the kids. Mine wasn't like that. There was another story of a twelve-year-old boy who stabbed his father with a knife during an argument. Mine never argued with me. But I suspect he was being abused too. I don't think any kid would just stab their father over an argument unless he was either abusive, or the kid was kinda off his rocker. Then again, I don't know. It seemed like there was more to the story, but I didn't have time to research. I honestly was not that interested. I only wanted to find something more specific to me and my situation. So far nothing, but I'm sure something's out there; I'll keep looking. Then again, maybe I won't. Maybe I am the only one.

Twenty-Three

"Hello, K'wan," Mrs. Morgan says as I am walking into her office. Today she is wearing some kinda red lace blouse thingy over a black shirt. Her lips are painted bright red and real shiny as if she's slathered a ton of lip gloss on. I do not understand why she wears this kinda stuff to work. I blink, trying not to stare. I do not want to frown but it is hard not to so I shift my eyes. I am not disrespectful so I try not to think disrespectful things, but they should have rules or a handbook on how (and when) to wear different shades of lipstick. I shouldn't have to sit through an hour-and-a-half of counseling looking at her shiny red lips. "How are you doing this morning?" I turn to look at her as she closes a file she has open, then slides it over to her left.

I shrug.

Mrs. Morgan's glossy lips turn up into a slight smile. I shift in my seat. She extends her hands out in front of her, then clasps them together. She eyes me cautiously, or maybe there are a buncha questions behind her stare. "K'wan, I know about your nightmares."

My eyes widen. I cannot believe Ja'Meer betrayed me like that. He swore he'd never tell anyone anything. He said I could trust him. Now I see he's two-faced. I should have known it was all a lie. He's no different from anyone else. Say one thing, then turn around and do another. He's a liar, too. I take a deep breath, gripping the sides of my seat. I want to get up and walk out of here, then find him so I can punch him in the mouth.

Before all that has happened, I was never like this—wanting to fight. I would rather walk away, then fight with someone. But, Ja'Meer, I guess I kinda wanted to believe him. Because I thought he was cool.

My jaw clenches.

"Don't be upset with him," Mrs. Morgan says as if she's in my head. "I promise you, he didn't mean any harm. Believe it or not, that young man, Ja'Meer, right?" I nod. "He's your friend, a real one. And everyone needs at least one of those while they're here. He talks a lot to his therapist about you."

Why in the heck is he using up his counseling time talking about me?

I frown.

"Nothing specific," she quickly assures me, "but enough for his counselor to know that he's very concerned about you. She's the one who told me about your nightmares. That young man really wants to help you, K'wan. He actually asked her for counseling tips. Wanted to know what kinds of things he could do himself to get you to open up and talk about what's going on with you until you were ready to talk to a professional. I think that's real noble of him for wanting to help you. He sounds like someone who really cares about what happens to you."

I lower my head, feeling bad for thinking unkindly of him.

"See," she says, getting up from her seat. She walks around her desk and sits in the chair next to me. "You are surrounded by people who care about you; even those you don't know. All you have to do now is let those same people help you get through this."

I look over at her and think maybe I should have brought Mom's letter with me. I'm not sure why, but I feel like I should have.

"So these bad dreams you're having. Are you having them every night?"

I stare at her. *Shouldn't you already know all of this since Ja'Meer's ran off and blabbed his mouth to his therapist?*

I don't want to be mad at him. But I am. I feel like he should have asked me, first. He should have allowed me to tell him if it was okay to talk about me to his counselor. I know why he didn't. He knows I woulda probably said no. And if the shoe was on the other foot, I'm sure I'd do the same thing.

She is staring at me, waiting for me to respond.

I shake my head.

"When you wake up from these nightmares, do you remember all or most of them?"

Yes. There is always yelling and screaming. And threats. There is always crying, tears of fear and sadness. Mine.

I grimace, closing my eyes and shaking my head. I think, try to remember. No, on second thought, I don't remember every detail in any of my dreams. But I do remember most of everything. The graveyard, my mom's tombstone, her empty grave—waiting for her, the pitch blackness of the night, those things are inked into my brain. I can't shake them. I can't run from them. They find me.

"K'wan, I'd really like for you to see Doctor Singh again." I shake my head. *No! I don't want to see that shrink again. He was creepy! And I don't wanna be on medication. I am not crazy.*

She nods, understandingly. "K'wan, what you've been through has been extremely traumatic. And sometimes people who have experienced traumatic events suffer from nightmares. And sometimes these nightmares are linked to what's referred to PTSD. Nightmares are one of seventeen possible symptoms related to PTSD. Do you know what that is?"

I slowly shake my head.

"It stands for Post Traumatic Stress Disorder. It's an anxiety disorder that can affect adults as well as young children and teens. It manifests itself after someone has been through a traumatic event, whether it's something horrible and scary that you've witnessed or something that has happened to you. Events that could have caused someone or someone they know to be killed or badly hurt. You may think that your life or others' lives are in danger."

Like my moms.

"You may feel afraid, or feel as if you have no control over what is happening. It can have you feeling scared, angry, or confused."

And hopeless, right?

"Have you had these nightmares for more than three months?"

I nod my head.

"Nightmares are considered complex dreams that cause high levels of anxiety or terror. The content of these dreams revolving around danger or imminent harm that involves the frightening set of circumstances that were involved during the trauma."

I lower my head, closing my eyes. Mrs. Morgan's voice starts to fade out.

"I'm going to kill you, Syreeta. Is that what you want? Me to fucking kill you?"

Mom is clawing at his hands, his face, trying to get him off of her. But he is too strong.

He is shaking her, his hands around her neck. Mom is gasping. I see her eyes bulging from out of their sockets. The knife is in my hand. I stab him. Over and over and over, I keep stabbing him; blood gushing out everywhere.

"I hate you, I hate you, I hate you," I repeat over and over as I am stabbing him.

I drop the knife.

"PTSD is a disorder that some people get, and others do not. And it's unclear as to why. But what we do know is that many people who develop Post Traumatic Stress Disorder get better at some point. And even if they continue to have some symptoms, there is very effective treatment to help them cope."

I blink. Swallow back the lump in my throat. Mrs. Morgan reaches for the box of tissue on her desk, then slides it over to me as tears drop, making little dark, wet circles on my shirt. I'm so mad at him; at her, Mom. I don't wanna be mad at my mom. I don't wanna blame her. But I do. I blame her. I blame him. And I blame myself. I know what everybody says, that they did this. They chose this. I know what Miss Daisy says. That adults choose partners; adults choose to become parents; and adults choose to hurt each other. I know I don't have control over who my parents are. And I don't even know—after being here and listening to all these other kids talk about their parents—if I would want to choose to have different parents. I only wish that *he* could have been different to Mom, to us.

Mrs. Morgan places her hand over mine, causing me to glance over at her. "PTSD can disrupt your life if it goes untreated, but it doesn't have to disrupt yours. We can help you get through this, K'wan. And I think somewhere deep down inside of you, you want help. Am I right?"

I lower my head and shrug. I think she takes that as a sign that I don't know. But, she's wrong. I do know. I know that I wanna go home. That I don't wanna keep holding onto all of this stuff. It gives me headaches. I don't wanna keep having bad dreams. I don't wanna keep worrying that something is going to happen to my mom. But as long as he's alive, as long as I think there is a chance that my mom will change her mind and take him back, I am always going to be worried that he will hurt her.

"The difference is I will not ever take him back. I won't ever allow him to hurt me, or you and your brother…. I failed you once, K'wan. I will not fail you or your brothers twice."

How can I trust what she says? I want to. I can't go back to that house if she goes back on her word and allows him back in. I won't. I know, I feel, it in my bones that the next time I *will* finish what I failed to do the last time. I will kill him. I don't wanna think like this. And I don't want this to be my life—locked away and angry.

But for now it is.

Mrs. Morgan waits for my answer.

I hear a buncha voices in my head—my mom's, my aunt Janie's, my grandma Ellen's, Miss Daisy's, Mrs. Morgan's, the social worker's at the detention center, all telling me, encouraging me, to open up. To let them help me. Telling me that I am loved. That I am not alone; that I do not have to go through any of this by myself.

I hear Ja'Meer saying, "You gotta talk to someone, man…"

I reach for more tissue, wipe my eyes, then blow my nose. "Will you let us help you?" she asks again. I roll the ball of wet tissue into my hands, not bothering to wipe my tears as they fall.

Right now I wish I were invisible. I wish I could close my eyes and literally disappear. I am tired of counselors looking at me like I'm some wounded animal. Maybe that's not what she's doing. But that's what it feels like. That's how I feel, like I am some lab rat. I don't wanna keep thinking about what happened. But I can't help it. It—the memories, won't leave me alone. They won't let me forget. But, I don't know if I really wanna forget. Remembering keeps me hating *him* for doing what he did—to my mom, to me, to my brothers. I am afraid to forget. I don't wanna forget. I can't forget. Forgetting would mean letting him back into my life. I can't.

I just wanna be able to remember without feeling like I'm being controlled by my thoughts. I don't wanna be a prisoner to nightmares anymore.

Mrs. Morgan stares at me, patiently waiting.

I hear Ja'Meer in my head. *"You not talkin' isn't gonna help shit get better...how long you plan on bein like this, yo, fuckin' mute?"*

My mom's voice follows, *"K'wan, please open up. Let the professionals help you."*

I take a deep breath, then slowly nod.

Yes.

Mrs. Morgan smiles as she pats my hand. "Good. I promise you. In the long run, you will feel much better."

I hope so. I nod. I wanna tell her that I am scared, nervous, but I don't. I still can't seem to find my voice, or the strength to push the words out of me. She glances at her watch, standing up. My time is up. I stand up as well, feeling relieved.

"I will share in our next treatment team meeting your decision, then schedule you to see Dr. Curtis. In the meantime, you and I will continue to chip away at those walls, one session at a time, until we are able to get to the center of all that troubles you, okay?"

I nod. Mrs. Morgan calls out to me as I reach the door.

I turn to her.

"I'm very proud of you, K'wan." And this time when she smiles at me, her brightly painted lips are no longer a painful distraction.

Twenty-Four

m I going to end up being an abuser, like him?

The question keeps nagging at me. For some reason, my IPC session with Mrs. Morgan this morning has my mind racing in a thousand different directions. Right after leaving her office, I went straight to the library and logged onto one of the computers. I needed to know more about this PTSD stuff she was talking about. I want to understand it better. To see how it applies to me. After reading some of the articles and fact sheets, I think it does. This knowing bothers me. I am a label. PTSD. Those four letters, an acronym that now describes me. And now I worry that it will define me; that those letters will somehow be stamped on my forehead for everyone else to see. I am over-reacting, allowing my imagination to get the best of me, but still it bothers me.

I read on one site that kids can get PTSD by the events caused by war, a friend's suicide, or seeing violence in the area in which they live, including family violence. The article stated that there were at least 3-10 million children who witness family violence each year.

I take a deep breath. I don't wanna live with labels. I don't wanna keep having those bad dreams, either. I am tired.

Pieces of my mom's letter play in my head. *"I tried to act as if you would be able to tuck everything you ever saw or heard in the back of your mind and everything would be okay. Letting your father back home wasn't about you or your brothers. It was about me. It is not your fault. You are not to blame. I love you so much..."*

I am glad I finally decided to open her letter and read it. But I am still sad, still angry, and still confused. She wants me to open up, but she doesn't understand. It's not that easy. I told Mrs. Morgan that I wanted help, but now I am not so sure. I have held in so much, for so long. And the truth is I wouldn't know where to start, or even how to start. I don't know how to get this stuff out of me. I'm not even sure if I really wanna let it out. I am scared. If I open up, I am afraid of how it will all come out. I am afraid of what might come out. I feel like an overstuffed pressure cooker that is about to explode. Sometimes I feel like I am about to really lose it—whatever *it* is. I mean, I want to scream at her, at him. And if I could look myself in the mirror long enough, I'd yell at myself, too.

"I knew from my own counseling that domestic violence affected children as well...."

I feel like she chose him over me and my brothers. I don't know if I should feel that way or not, but I do. And I do not wanna apologize for feeling that way. I told her over and over and over again that I hated him. That I did not like him, and she didn't listen to me. All she ever said were things like: "That's not nice" or "Don't say that about your father." I feel like she brushed me off. That she didn't take my feelings seriously. That I hate him. That I will kill him. I told her I was scared that he was going to hurt her. And she promised me she wouldn't let him; just like she's promised in her letter. But I do not know if I can trust her. Those were words that she said once before, and she did not keep them. How can I ever trust her not to break her promise again?

I can't.

Mom says it's not my fault—what happened. Mrs. Morgan and Miss Daisy say I am not to blame. The social worker at the youth detention center told me that I could heal from everything that has happened. How when I don't believe any of them? No matter how hard I try, I can't let go of the fact that I feel like I am the cause of all of this. That I do blame myself. That the damage is already done. I am already him.

"Boys who witness their fathers' abuse of their mothers are more likely to inflict severe violence as adults," Miss Daisy says this as if she is in my head. She confirms my biggest fear. Validates what I already know. I shift in my seat as she hands a stack of papers to Jarrod and asks him to take one, then pass them around. She continues, "Studies also suggests that girls who witness their mothers being abused may in fact tolerate abuse as adults more than girls who do not. Statistics state children who witness the abuse of their mothers are more likely to be abused themselves."

Sitting here, I wish I could blink my eyes and somehow disappear. That I could rewind a clock and be ten again, back at Disney World, laughing and playing with my brothers, splashing around in the pool, going on all the roller coasters and water rides. It was the most fun I can remember us having—as a family. *He* was nice to Mom. And he did things with us, fun things. And Mom was smiling. She looked happy. And they were holding hands and kissing and joking around. It was different. I wasn't afraid that he was going to hurt her. I could simply be a ten-year-old kid, eating tons of ice cream, candy, and hotdogs. And I could sleep at night. For a whole week, I could sleep!

I turn my gaze back to the window as Miss Daisy asks the group how many of us were ever physically abused in our homes or somewhere else by another adult. There are only eight of us in group today: Nelson Aesop, Corey, Jackson, Jarrod, Anthony, Westley, and me.

I was not. But they say emotional abuse is worse.

Jackson and Jarrod shift in their seats. Westley is the only one who raises his hand. Maybe he is the only one brave enough to admit it in front of everyone else. He shares how he and his two sisters were placed in foster care because his mom would beat them with anything she could get her hands on when she was angry; that she would also leave them home alone for two and three days to use drugs. "She was getting high real bad back then," he adds. "But she went to rehab and cleaned herself up, then got us back."

"And she's stayed clean?" Miss Daisy wants to know.

"Well, yeah, sorta. She still likes to get her drink on, but she's not doing coke anymore. And she blazes every now and then, but she's not doing that other sh…I mean stuff anymore."

"So she smokes weed and drinks," Miss Daisy inquires. It sounds like a statement as if she wants to be clear that she's heard him right. Her face is expressionless when she asks/says this. It dawns on me that anytime I've seen her face like this—emotionless—it's usually when someone is sharing something that sounds crazy—well, crazy to me. But I believe she thinks the same thing, but can't show it or say it because she's supposed to be nonjudgmental.

"Yeah," Westley says. "I'm cool with it as long as she isn't tryna smoke my stash."

Smoke his stash? I turn my head toward the window and frown. *Wow*, I think, thankful my parents didn't do drugs. I don't know much about drug use or stuff like that since I am not around them like that. But I have read stuff online and in books and magazines about them. And I have seen what it has done to celebrities' lives to know enough that drugs aren't anything I want to ever try or do. I don't even think I'd want to be friends with anyone who used them. Maybe if they only smoke weed, I would. But the stuff I have read about it says that that is the gateway drug to other things. I look over at Westley and wonder if that's how it all happened for his mom. Smoking weed first, then going onto other kinds of drugs. I don't know what it's like to live with drug addicts or alcoholics. And I wish that I didn't have to know what it was like to live with someone who beat up on my mom, either. But I have. So in that sense, I guess an abuser is an abuser no matter what it is they abuse, right? I mean, whether it's drugs or people, it still affects the people who are around them in some way. Isn't that why we're all here?

"I don't care if she drinks or smokes as long as she doesn't mess up again. I turn back to the group. Glance over at Westley.

"That's wassup, man," Nelson says. "Them drugs ain't no joke."

"For real, yo," Jarrod agrees.

"I don't think I was abused," Jackson blurts out, taking a ditto, then handing them to me. He leans back on the legs of his chair. Miss Daisy eyes him, and he sits his chair back down. "I mean, my moms used to kick my lil ass when I was mad young, but that's 'cause I was bad as hell. She used to yoke me up and be ready to go with the fists real quick. But I stayed doin' stuff, so I deserved it."

Miss Daisy takes it all in. She folds her hands in her lap. "So you think you deserved to get beat with fists; that that kind of disciplining is okay?"

He shakes his head. "Nah, I'm not saying that. But, that's how my moms got it in. Or she'd have one of my uncles hit me with a few body shots if I was giving her a hard time."

I blink. I've never gotten beatings from my mom. She's never even yelled at me.

"Yeah, my moms used to tear me and my sister up with this thin leather strap that used to feel like it a razor, especially if she got me coming outta the shower or didn't have on a shirt. It would cut into my skin. And if we really pissed her off she'd beat us with extension cords or whatever else she could get her hands on. Or wait until we were asleep."

I cringe.

Next Jarrod and Nelson share how their fathers would beat them. How they would get punched up like grown men on the streets. I shift in my chair. Getting beatings isn't an experience I share with any of them. *He* beat on my mom, not us. Being yelled at or called names isn't something he did to me and my brothers, either. Those things were reserved for my mom.

I feel lost, like I really don't belong here with any of them. Not listening to how they were beat up by their parents. Still, as I sit here and listen to everyone share their stories of whippings and what sounds to me like modern day flogging, I wonder why he only did those things to my mom. Wonder why he never beat or screamed at me and my brothers. Why was his anger directed only at her?

I shift my eyes and stare out the window, wondering if things would have turned out different if I'd been the one he beat up on instead of my mom. Would I have still stabbed him? Still wanted him dead? Or hated him as much as I do?

"Family violence has very devastating effects on children," Miss Daisy states, looking around the circle. I look over at her, wondering if she's somehow snuck into my room and read my mom's letter. "Who can tell me what children need growing up?"

"A place to sleep," Jackson offers. Jarrod says kids need food and clothes, followed by Nelson, who says they need someone to love them.

I agree with them. But add my own to the list in my head. *To feel safe. To feel special. To feel loved.*

Miss Daisy nods her head. "All of you are correct. Absolutely, children need their basic human needs met; food, clothing and shelter. But, most importantly, they need a safe and secure home—violence free. And they need adults, parents, caretakers, that love and protect them. No matter what is happening in the world around them, children need a sense of stability. They need structure and routine."

Aesop leans forward in his seat, resting his elbows on his knees. "Yeah, but don't you think a parent can love their kids, but not be able to give them all those things you're talkin' about? I mean, they might want it for them, but don't know how to give it to them."

Miss Daisy nods. "Yes, I do believe a parent can love their children deeply. But if they are not making it their priority to ensure their children's emotional and physical safety, then they have still failed them in some way. Adults can make choices, but up until a certain age, children can't. They have to rely on the adults around them to hopefully make healthy, safe choices for them. Raising your own children is a privilege these days. It is no longer a right. Rights get taken away, right along with privileges, every day. And when there is violence in the home, children are denied their right to a safe and stable environment."

"The sheet I have passed around to you," Miss Daisy says, flipping through a booklet, "is a 2010 Uniform Crime Report prepared by the New Jersey State Police every year for the preceding year. I want you to take a look at it." Everyone eyes the sheet of paper. For some reason, my hand shakes. "Who wants to read the first half of the first bullet for me?"

Anthony raises his hand. "There were seventy-four-thousand, two-hundred and forty-four domestic violence offenses reported by police in two-thousand-and-ten."

I blink when I skim down to the next bullet and read that there were 38 domestic violence murders in New Jersey. *Thirty-eight?* My heart thumps in my chest, knowing that my mom could have been one of those who had been murdered.

The next line says that there were 31,234 assaults and 32,598 harassment offenses reported. It says 13,371 wives were the reported victims. I feel sick, knowing my mom was one of them. She is a statistic. I am a statistic. Seeing this stuff doesn't make me feel any better. If anything, it makes me angrier that he did this to us. That she let him. And because of it, we have become a part of a statistical summary report.

Miss Daisy reads from another sheet that lists domestic violence offenses and arrests by counties. When she says four of the thirty-eight murders committed in New Jersey were in Bergen County, where I live, I close my eyes, wondering whose mom was killed. I feel guilty for feeling relieved that it wasn't my mom. But I am. Miss Daisy goes down the list of counties. When she finishes, I have a massive headache.

Why do they have to kill them? What makes them want to go to that extreme? A dozen whys are slowly starting to stir in my head.

"I will fucking kill you..."

If he really wanted to kill Mom, wouldn't he have just killed her? Wouldn't he have waited until she was asleep and then ended it? Or did he just wanna torture her? Beat her, then make her beg for her life. I want to know if these kinda men are crazy. I mean, like psychiatric cuckoo-crazy. I glance over at Miss Daisy, hoping she will say something that helps make sense—if at all possible—out of it. It all seems sick to me. It has me wondering if this is like a disease. Is it hereditary?

Miss Daisy says, "Domestic violence is learned behavior. It is generational. Not genetic. It is not a disease. It is a choice. It is a cycle that can be broken. But it has to start with you. You young men don't have to become men who are abusive to the women and children in your lives."

"But do people like that really change?" Nelson asks.

I hold my breath.

Miss Daisy nods her head. "Abusers will not change their behaviors unless they are willing to change. They have to recognize and acknowledge their abusive behavior and have a full understanding of the effect it has had on their partners, their children, their relationships, and themselves."

I swallow. *But what if they have said all those things and made their families believe them, then go back to abusing them, like he did to my mom?*

"Yo, them nig…my bad, Miss Dee," Jarrod says. "Them dudes don't care about changing. My mom's boyfriend used to always tell her how he knows what he did was wrong. He used to apologize to her and me and my sisters. Promise that he'd never do it again. Then a few months, or weeks, later he'd go right back to doing the same shit all over again. And she'd keep taking him back."

Miss Daisy looks at him with understanding eyes. Or maybe it's sympathy. "He definitely doesn't sound like someone who was invested in making any real change. Change doesn't happen overnight. It is a process. And abusers have to have their awareness raised. They need to understand their feelings, where they originate, what triggers them. But they have to want to get completely honest about it. And they have to be open to wanting to learn alternative ways to express themselves as opposed to using violence. They need to recognize when they are acting abusively. And that requires work. It requires commitment. And it requires taking one hundred percent responsibility for everything they say and do."

She looks around the room, making sure we understand what she has said, then glances down at her watch. "Okay, gentlemen, before we wrap up, let me say this. Every day is a choice. What you do this very moment can affect you for the rest of your lives. Think before you act. Challenge negative self-talk; replace it with positive thinking. There are consequences and rewards for everything we do. That's all for today. We'll pick back up next group."

Everyone scrambles out of the room, except me. Today, I am lingering. But I do not know why. Miss Daisy looks up from her notes, sitting her pen down on a chart. She takes me in. She looks worried. "K'wan, is everything okay?"

I swallow, then shrug.

"Is there something you would like to say?"

I shake my head. But, I do not know if that's true or not. There has to be a reason why I am still standing here. She gets up from her seat and walks over to me. "If there's something you want to talk about, I am here for you. We all are. Whenever you're ready, we'll listen, okay?" I nod. She reaches out and touches my arm. "I'm worried about you, K'wan. You are holding onto so much toxic energy that it is weighing you down. If you don't find a way to release it, it will slowly eat away at you."

I want to tell her that it already has eaten away at me. I feel like there are a thousand moths gnawing holes in me. And I am slowly unraveling; slowly falling apart.

Her eyes are kind as she gives me a smile. "K'wan, we can help you, if you let us. If only you would start to open up. I promise you, you'd start to feel so much better. Don't let unresolved anger boil over into hate. It will become self-destructive to you."

You're two years too late. It already has. I walk out the door.

Twenty-Five

Ever since my IPC session last week with Mrs. Morgan this whole PTSD stuff has been playing in my head. I really wanna understand it. I went online again and read more about how kids can witness violence in different ways. Like being in the same room and getting caught in the middle of a fight, trying to stop it; or by being in another room but hearing the abuse, or seeing the bruises following a violent incident. Kyle and I witnessed plenty of that—the bruises! Then Mom trying to hide them or lie about them. I think Kyle always believed her when she'd say she tripped and fell up the stairs, or slipped in the tub. I never did believe her. I knew she wasn't telling the truth. And that used to piss me off; her lying for him. At least that's how it felt, like she was protecting him or something. Okay, maybe she wasn't lying for him; maybe it was for herself. Maybe because she was embarrassed or ashamed or filled with guilt, like I have been. Not embarrassed or ashamed, but filled with guilt. *What was it Mrs. Morgan said in IPC about guilt?*

Was it a waste of time? No, that wasn't it.

Anyway, that article I read online also stated how kids can be forced to take part in verbally abusing the victim. That's mean and crazy. I can't imagine being forced to beat up on my own mom, or being forced to say mean things to her or call her names. I suppose I should be thankful he wasn't like that.

"Guilt and worry are two useless emotions."

Yeah, that's it!

I read kids react in different ways to living in a home with violence. But all kids witnessing it are being emotionally abused. They say if kids do not feel safe in their own homes—like I didn't—it can have severe emotional and physical effects on them. This knowing has me wondering if victims who choose to stay in those kinda situations shouldn't let their kids live somewhere else. Why should kids have to stay in that kinda craziness? It makes no sense to me. Actually, nothing adults do makes any sense to me.

I knock on Mrs. Morgan's door; she greets me with a big, toothy smile as she waves me in. "Hello, K'wan," she says, sounding extra chipper this morning. Today she is wearing hot pink—hot pink lipstick, eye shadow, nail polish, blouse and skirt. I can't see her shoes, but I bet she has on hot pink heels, too. I hope this getup she has on isn't her way of letting out her inner Nicki Minaj. In my mind's eye, I am shaking my head at this sight. Mrs. Morgan is really, really nice, but this right here is downright horrid. That's not a nice thing to say, but, *Wow*. I can't believe she's really overdosed on all this pink. She looks like a big swirl of cotton candy.

"Is everything okay with you?"

Uh, no. I feel dizzy looking at all that pink.

I blink, blink again, then slowly nod.

"Good. In our last session we, I mean I, talked to you a little about PTSD and what that meant. And we talked about you doing some journaling as well. I don't see your composition book today, so I take it that means you aren't up for writing out your feelings, are you?"

She's probably wearing hot pink underwear, too, knowing her, I think feeling guilty for that kinda thought even crossing my mind. I can't look at her. But I can't stop but wonder who picks out her clothes for her. Does she, or one of her teenaged granddaughters?

"It's fine if you're not ready to journal. It's not something we typically require of our residents, still…" She pauses, giving me an intense stare as if she is trying to figure something out. She folds her hands in front of her. "I believe it would be extremely beneficial to you; particularly with you being non-communicative, verbally."

She opens a folder, mine I guess, and starts writing. "K'wan, I'd really like to talk about the violence you witnessed in your home over the years. Many women and children who have experienced abuse use silence or denial to try to cope with the violence. Silence is an abuser's best friend. It keeps him hidden. If no one talks about it, the abuse, then the abuser can go unnoticed. He can keep his behaviors secret, and he can continue to abuse without consequence."

Yeah, like he did for all those years.

I think back to his consequences. The first time the police were called, he walked out in handcuffs. The second time, he was led out on a stretcher. The next time, I am certain—unless I am still locked away at this place—will be in a body bag. Hopefully, for everyone's sake, there is no next time.

"I will never, ever, let your father hurt me again…"

I want to believe her. I want to trust that she means it this time. But I don't know if I can. My mom has promised many times in the past to not let him hurt her again, then he does.

"K'wan, it's obvious you've been using silence as a way to cope with the abuse you've witnessed over the years."

I look at her. No, what's *obvious* is my mom didn't listen to me 'cause if she had maybe none of us would be in this mess. At least he wouldn't have been back in our house. Why did she really need him there? He was still paying the bills. He was still providing for us, and for her. So why did she have to take him back? I mean, I know what she said in the two letters of hers I read, that she wanted to give him another chance. That she wanted to keep the family together. That it was for her; not for us. And none of that still makes any sense to me. Not after everything he did.

"K'wan, using silent treatment is an unhealthy coping skill that can be used to gain control, manipulate, or emotionally blackmail."

Like what he did to us!

I'm not tryna control or manipulate or blackmail anyone. He *was!*

I shift in my seat.

She obviously doesn't know what she's talking about.

"It's a common behavior in not only abusers, but children as well—especially teens. For you, K'wan, after everything you've been through, being silent is the one thing you can control. It is a power play. Similar to what happens in domestic violence, it's about trying to have power and control in a relationship. The difference here is I don't believe that you are trying to control or manipulate anyone, are you?"

I slowly shake my head.

"I know. We all know. And I'm sure you wish we'd all simply disappear. Go away and leave you alone in your silence. Is that right? You want us to leave you alone, and go on with our days ignoring you, not bothering you, not trying to get you to talk."

Finally she gets it. Yes, leave me alone.

I nod.

She gives me a faint smile. I don't know if it's one that is dipped in kindness or pity, but she smiles and her eyes seem to swallow me in whole. *"Using silent treatment is an unhealthy coping skill that can be used to gain control, manipulate, or emotionally blackmail."*

I shift in my seat.

That isn't me. But it's something in how she said that that makes me uncomfortable. She's saying without really saying it that I am no different from him. That I am being abusive, too!

But I'm not! I'm not talking because the words won't come out. Not because I am trying to punish anyone. Not because I am trying to control anyone. I am trying to stay in control of me.

But maybe I am trying to punish them. I am angry at them. I am hurt by them. I am sad because of them. I already admitted this. Well, not to her, but to myself.

I swallow, then take a deep breath.

The one who's trying to manipulate is her. She's trying to manipulate me into talking about what I've lived through. All that talking about it is gonna to do is piss me off, then make it difficult for me to go to sleep tonight. While she's home in her bed sound asleep, I'll be tossing and turning through the night. I am the one who'll be fighting back sleep, fighting back nightmares. I'll be the one exhausted in the morning. So, no, there's nothing I wanna talk about. It happened. He tried to kill my mom. I stabbed him. And now I'm here.

I know I said I'm broken. But what I don't think I told you is that I have all these pieces of me that need to be put back in their place, but I don't know when, where, or how to start putting them back together. Heck, I don't even know if I really wanna be put back together. I mean, what if I don't like the end result, then what?

I turn my head toward the window, staring out. Off in the distance, I see a stray cat aimlessly wandering the grounds, probably looking for food, or for something to kill and toy with. I don't like cats, but this one looks like I feel…lonely and lost.

"We are not going to leave you alone, K'wan," Mrs. Morgan says, causing me to look back at her. "Every last one of us here will continue to talk to you. Your family will continue to talk to you. No one will give up on you. No matter how much you might want us to leave you alone. We're not going to give you want you want. We're going to give you what you need. Support, encouragement, and yes, space. But not a lot of it—so don't get excited. We're only giving you enough for you to sort out your feelings. Do you understand?"

I blink, nodding.

"You do not have to suffer in silence, K'wan. The abuse wasn't your fault. What your father did to your mother isn't your fault."

I turn away from her. I wanna get up and walk out, but something keeps me chained to my seat. It is my fault. Maybe for not what he did to her, but maybe I coulda said more to her; maybe if I woulda begged her to not take him back, maybe if I woulda cried more, she woulda heard me. Maybe she woulda listened. She woulda believed me when I said I was scared—for her, for me, for my brother…maybe.

Mrs. Morgan gets up from her desk and walks around to me. She sits in the chair next to me, handing me a box of tissue. "It wasn't your fault," she says softly. "You're not to blame for anything he did to her. You are not to blame for your father's choices or your mother's, K'wan."

The tears are falling, slowly at first, but the more she talks, the faster they fall. He coulda killed her. I hold my head down, covering my face with my hand. I see the blood. And the bruises. And her swollen face. Why couldn't she listen to me? I told her how I felt. That I was scared. That I didn't like him. He promised he would never hurt her again, but he did. She promised to never let him, but she did. I can't trust either one of them. I can't even trust myself.

She repeats herself, "It wasn't your fault. I know you feel guilty for what happened to your mom. But that guilt isn't yours to bear."

But it is! I couldn't keep her safe.

"Protecting your mother wasn't your job, K'wan."

Then why do I feel like it was?

Mrs. Morgan keeps saying it over and over and over, that it wasn't my fault, that I am not to blame, then finally she says nothing at all. She sits still. Allows me to drown in my tears of guilt.

I can't stop the tears. I am trying hard to shut them off, but they keep falling. And now I am no longer for sure if I am crying for me or if I am crying for my mom and my brothers, or if my tears are for Ja'Meer and his brother. All I know is I am really a broken mess.

I am not sure how long I am sitting here crying, but I know that we have gone over our time. But Mrs. Morgan doesn't seem to mind. She gives me a chance to finally get myself together. I am hiccupping now.

"K'wa...let us help you get through this. You are not alone in this, okay?"

I nod. As I'm getting up from my seat, I glance down at Mrs. Morgan's feet. If I weren't so sad, I'd probably smile. *I knew it. Pink shoes, too!* They are strappy heels that wrap up around her calves and her shiny pink toes are peeking out through the openings of her shoe.

I head for the door. I don't care if she looks like cotton candy or bag of Skittles, I like Mrs. Morgan. I really, really do!

Twenty-Six

oday, there are eight other residents in group besides me: Aesop, Anthony, Corey, Nelson, Jackson, Westley, Marco, and The Bully. I glance around the circle. Miss Daisy greets us, then asks if anyone has anything they'd like to share in group. As usual no one does. I feel her eyes on me as I turn toward the window. I breathe out a quiet sigh of relief that she has not called on me for anything.

"Well, since no one has anything they'd like to talk about, today I want to talk about physical abuse in relationships. Who can tell me what that is?"

"It's yokin' somebody up or stompin' them out," Westley says, raising his hand.

"Yes, physical abuse is any physical contact between you and another person, particularly your partner. It is any violent behavior, including hitting, biting, slapping, punching, burning, shoving or kicking..."

"Damn, my girl bit me once," Jackson says, lifting his arm and showing a bite mark on his forearm.

"And what did you do when she bit you?" Miss Daisy asks.

"I laughed. She was wildin' hard that night. We were both kinda drunk."

"Yo, that's effen bananas, yo," Jarrod says, shaking his head. "Looks like your girl tried to take a chunk of your arm off."

"Yeah, I had to get stitches"—he raises his forearm and shows the room his tattoo. Permanent teeth marks—"but it's all good. She's still my boo-thang."

Miss Daisy keeps her face expressionless. But I know she has to be thinking what I'm thinking: This boy's nuts!

Aesop shakes his head. "Damn, man. And you ain't knock her teeth out?"

"Nah. I mean, we wrestled around for a minute. I had to squeeze her nose shut to finally get her off a me. But I didn't wanna go in on her 'cause I know how she is when she drinks."

That's crazy. Maybe y'all shouldn't drink.

Nelson says, "You must really love that girl to let her get that off like that."

"Word, son, you good," Aesop says. "'Cause had it been me, I'da knocked her fronts out; for real for real. Girl or not, she woulda been coughing out her teeth."

"Yeah, I ain't gonna front. She's my heart. She's the only one that holds it down for me. She's good until she starts drinkin', then she's ready to go with the hands at the drop of a hat. I told her she gotta cut back some on her drinkin'."

You think?

In my mind's eye, I'm sitting here rolling my eyes up in my head listening to all of this craziness. If this is the kinda stuff love makes you do, then I am more and more convinced I don't want any part of it. Listening to these guys, I have to wonder if they even know what love is. People say we are born to love and taught to hate, but we still have to be shown love. We still have to be taught how to love. If we're not taught it, how can we show it? How can we even know what it is if we haven't experienced it? I don't know. It all seems so complicated. Love, that is. And it seems to either make some people do crazy things, or makes them crazier than what they already are.

"Yo, one time me and my BM was beefin' and she spit on me. Yo, real talk. I spazzed out on her lil as...My bad, Miss Dee..."

See, what I tell you?

"No problem. Tell us what you did when she spit on you, which is also assault; just so you all know."

"I was like, 'yo, you wanna spit, then let's do this. I'll show you how to do it. And I hawked up a buncha spit and gave it to her dead in her face."

I cringe. *Craziness! And I bet they're still together, too.*

"Yo, what the hell?" Jackson says, sounding disgusted. "Yo, man, that's some straight up nastiness. I'da probably taken her face off after that."

A few guys grumble and side with Jackson.

"Man, I wanted to. But I checked myself real quick and spun off on her. I mean, we peaced it up a few days after that, but still, I was really feelin' some kinda way about that."

Wow, spitting must be the new way to show love. This is all crazy-nuts.com for me.

Miss Daisy shifts in her seat. "So when is it ever okay to assault someone?"

It's not; at least not in my opinion.

"When they put their hands on you first," Nelson states. "My moms always said if someone hits you first then you have the right to eff 'em up. She said when someone hits you, they automatically give you permission to take it to their head."

"For real, for real," Aesop concurs, shaking his head. "Real talk, if someone comes at you first, then it's gloves off, lights out. Straight knuckle up and take it to their ribcage."

I blink.

Corey jumps in. "Nah, if it's another ni...my bad, I mean, another cat tryna bring it to you, then yeah, no doubt. Go in on his ass. But I don't think you should ever put ya hands on a female."

"So, Corey," Miss Daisy inquires, leaning up in her seat. "Are you saying that it's okay for a female to hit a male?"

"Nah, but it's no big deal if she does. Chicks can't physically hurt you like a guy can."

What planet is this guy from?

"That's a misconception," Miss Daisy states. "A woman may not be physically as strong as a man, but she can still hurt him if she hits him. And in some cases, kill him if she hits him in the right spot. Society has brainwashed us into believing that it's more acceptable for a woman to hit a man than a man hitting a woman. We have to teach kids early on that hitting each other is not acceptable, and when they do it—whether it's a girl or not—she needs to have consequences. Assault is assault, no matter how you try to sugarcoat it."

Aesop leans forward in his chair. "So Miss Dee, when my girl starts spazzin' and smacks me up, what should I do?"

"Well, honestly. The first time I would have a talk with her, letting her know what the boundaries are; what types of behaviors will be acceptable or not. Second time, I'd call the police." Everyone laughs as if she's said the funniest thing since Kevin Hart.

Strings of, "Yo, I ain't no snitch…yeah, right, picture that…I ain't no punk…" whip around the room.

"And if she continues to put her hands on you and you are bothered by it, then she may not be the one for you. Loving someone doesn't mean you have to stay with them or continue to put up with abuse from them. Someone may have plenty of good qualities and be really nice people out in public, but if he or she is mistreating you, disrespecting you, or assaulting you, then they are not the ones for you."

I can't believe there are kids my age who are in abusive relationships and think it's cool. I listen to Aesop, Jackson, Corey and whoever else chimes in go back and forth with Miss Daisy about how their girlfriends have hit them, cut them and even tried to stab them and how they have either restrained them, hit them or both, then ended up making up. And no one learns anything from it.

Wow...

I'm not even allowed to date until I'm sixteen. And I can't imagine being with, or liking, a girl who hits me or spits on me. I'd be too afraid that I might beat her up. And that's something I don't ever wanna do. So, I'm thinking, no...it's best that I stay away from girls like that. But these guys don't seem to get it. They are already doing a lot of things that only grownups should be doing, or not doing. Fighting and cursing each other. It's all crazy to me. And now my head hurts from listening to all of this madness.

"Sounds like there is a lot of mutual disrespect and abuse going on in many of your relationships," Miss Daisy states. She seems sad with this revelation. Maybe it's not as much of a revelation as it is a reality. Still, it's disturbing. Well, at least for me it is. I can only imagine what some of their kids are gonna go through. I mean, I know what I lived through. I know what I heard and saw. And I know how it has bothered me. How it has frightened me. How it all haunts me.

"Man, chicks are crazy out there," Marco says. "And they can get away with it, but let a dude wile out and it's about to be a problem."

The Bully agrees. "That's real talk. That's why I don't be beat for a buncha broads. They only good for three things..."

Sex, I bet, is the first thing.

Missy Daisy tilts her head in his direction. "And what might those three things be?"

"Pen palin' it up to help make time go by when I'm locked up or in programs, sex, and keepin' my gear up when I'm out on the bricks. Other than that, I ain't beat for nuthin' else."

Wow. *So he's also a user, along with being a hater.* I keep from making a face.

Several guys laugh. Tell him he's nuts. But Miss Daisy praises him for his honesty. Tells the group that he's entitled to his opinions and his beliefs, then she tells him that she hopes one day his attitudes and beliefs about women change. Otherwise, he will always find himself in unfulfilling relationships with them.

He shrugs. "I already told you what they're good for, so I'm good."

She stares at him for a moment, then moves on. I guess she decides to leave him stuck in his stupidity. "Anyway, back to the topic. In response to what Marco said about what happens to men as opposed to women who are aggressive in relationships, he's correct. Men are arrested and charged with domestic violence much quicker than women are. Part of that has to do with men not wanting to call the police on their partners, which would hold them accountable. Another part of that has to do with police officers' and judges' biases about what domestic violence and abuse is or isn't. A lot of people refuse to believe women, young and old, can be aggressive in their relationships. And a third part of this problem in my opinion is that some—being the operative word—women know how to work the system to their advantage. I'm a woman, and, yes. I'm saying it. I've seen it happen. Some women know how to turn on the tears and get sympathy from the police and judges. I'm not saying it's right, but it does happen."

"So they manipulate," Marco states.

"Yes, sadly, they manipulate. Men and women both manipulate situations and people to get what they want."

"Not to change the subject or nothing, Miss Dee," Nelson says. "But I wanted to tell you before I forgot that my moms found another job, and the mortgage people are helping her get into some kinda program so we don't lose our house."

Miss Daisy smiles, tells him that's great news. "I'm really glad to hear that. See, things always have a way with working out when you least expect them to." She glances at her watch. "Okay, gentlemen, it's that time. Remember, nothing changes if nothing changes. See you next group."

Twenty-Seven

am called down to the staff desk after breakfast. Mrs. Lyons, a thin salon-tanned lady with really big boobs and big red hair, is at the desk today. She's one of the counselor aides here. And one of the females the guys here say crude things about. I try not to listen to the stuff they say they'd like to do to her because it's disrespectful and nasty. Being here has me realizing that a lot of guys are really horny and desperate for sex. Like, who thinks about doing nasty things to someone old enough to be their mother, or grandma?

Ja'Meer says, "It's every guy's dream to get laid by a cougar." Then he shared, "Man, I'd like to put my dick in between her titties and bust my jizz in her face."

Yuck!

He laughed. But I didn't see anything funny. My mom would kill me if I ever talked like that. Maybe I'll think differently about cougars and boobs and doing things with them when I'm sixteen. But right now, that's nasty!

Mrs. Lyons smiles at me when she sees me approaching the desk. "Good morning, handsome. How's my favorite resident this morning?"

I'm only your favorite resident because I don't talk. I smile back at her. I glance up at the white board that has every resident's name on it and the wings they are on. I am on 3 West. I see my name.

I blink.

W/Dr. Curtis @ 10AM is written in one of the boxes next to my name.

I am surprised at first, then nervous. It's not that I did not realize that this day would come. I just didn't expect it to be today. I wonder why Mrs. Morgan didn't tell me my appointment with him was so soon.

Mrs. Lyons hands me a pass. Tells me she is going to have to walk me over to the other side of the building

⊕

Dr. Curtis's office is nothing like Mrs. Morgan's. It's huge. And there are a bunch of tropical plants around the room and statues of African Warriors in glass cases. He has a bookcase that lines the length of one wall and it is filled with all kinds of books.

He stands up and walks around his dark wood desk when I walk into the room. "K'wan, thanks for coming." He briskly walks toward me, looking me in the eyes as he extends his hand out to me. "I'm glad we're finally getting a chance to talk again. Please, have a seat." I shake his hand. He has a strong handshake.

I find myself comparing notes. Unlike Mrs. Morgan, who sits behind her desk during my IPC's, Dr. Curtis is sitting in a leather chair across from me. And, unlike the hard chairs in Mrs. Morgan's office, the one I am sitting in is buttery soft leather. My whole body sinks into its cushions.

I try not to stare at him. But I still can't believe he's a doctor. He looks kinda young to be one. He actually doesn't even look like one. That's what I remember thinking the first time he came to the detention center to see me. He reminds me of one of those male models I see on the covers of magazines like *Details*, *Esquire*, and *GQ*.

"Before we get started," Dr. Curtis says. "I want to tell that I understand what it is you are going through."

I eye him. *Yeah, right. How would you understand what I've been through? You probably say that same crap to everyone who comes in here to see you.*

"Experiencing any level of trauma can be very frightening. It can have you feeling very numb, and-or-experiencing feelings of helplessness. Things I'm sure you've been experiencing."

I swallow.

"I want you to know that I have talked in great length with both of your parents. And as you already know, I have worked with your mother individually over the last two years."

I shift in my seat. For some reason, I feel sweat rolling down my back and the palms of my hands are getting sweaty. Dr. Curtis seems nice enough. I know when Mrs. Morgan asked me if I was willing to let them help me, I said, well nodded, yes. Still, I am not sure what it is that Dr. Curtis can do for me. It's not like he can erase what's already happened.

"I say all this to say, we have all taken a special interest in you here."

Why, because I'm everyone's lab project? Let's see who can get the mute kid to speak. Is that the treatment goal? I stare at him.

He continues, "You've been through a lot over the last year. There's been a lot for you to try to absorb and understand. This year alone I'm sure has been extremely hard for you. Mrs. Morgan indicates that you are ready to let us help you. Is that still the case?"

I shrug. Truth is I thought I did. But now I don't know. All I wanna do is be able to sleep through the night, every night, without tossing and turning, without waking up drenched in sweat and tears. I don't wanna have to be forced to talk about it. Maybe he can give me some kinda pills to help me sleep at night.

"I am aware of the nightmares you are experiencing. I would

like to, at some point, explore these dreams with you. To help you sort them out so that they don't have so much power over you. Are they every night?"

I shake my head.

"How often?"

I close my eyes, then open them.

Four or five times a week, sometimes more.

"I know Mrs. Morgan talked a little about PTSD with you; am I correct?"

I nod.

"That is what we believe you are suffering from. Although the violence you witnessed in your home wasn't directed at you, you were still very affected by it. Like secondhand smoke, second-hand violence is just as devastating emotionally and psychologically. What you witnessed the night of your arrest was an extremely traumatic event."

I shift my eyes.

"There are studies that indicate children who grow up witnessing domestic violence in their homes tend to be, on average, more aggressive and fearful, and more often suffer from anxiety, depression, and other trauma-related symptoms. I am sure you have heard that boys who witness domestic violence are more likely to abuse as adults."

He pauses, waits for me to respond. I nod.

"And I'm sure knowing that can be frightening, especially when you swear to yourself that is not who you want to ever be; am I right?"

I swallow. *Yes, this, along with something happening to my mom or brothers, really scares me. But something inside me tells me that I am already him.*

I look at him and nod, again.

Dr. Curtis leans forward in his seat. He rests his elbows up on his knees, then steeples his hands together. "I know. I was scared, too. It's frightening for anyone witnessing violence. So I know what you're going through, what you went through..."

I give him a "yeah right" look.

"When I was ten and eleven, I would sit in my room and hear my parents fighting, then I'd hear my mother scream and I'd know that my father had hit her again. But I also knew that every morning at exactly five forty-five, she would get up, make his breakfast, prepare his lunch, then see him off to work. Then she would wake me and my two sisters up, make sure we were fed, then see us off to school. Not once did I see her shed a tear, or hear her complain. She went through life and pretended that everything was fine. And I learned to pretend, too."

Pretending...that feels like what my whole life's been about. Pretending not to know, pretending not to see, pretending around friends, pretending at school, pretending, pretending and more pretending until it started to seem real.

"What you've gone through, K'wan, what your father put you, your mother, and brothers through has been difficult for everyone. It has affected everyone in some way. It's been emotionally damaging. It has damaged relationships, yours with your father, and his with you and your mother. I know what it's like to hate your father. I know what it's like to blame your mother and be torn about it because you love her. I know what it's like to be angry. And I also know what it's like to heal."

I blink. I am surprised to hear all of this. I want to know more. Want to know what it was like for him. Did he try to protect his mother? Did he ever wanna kill his father? I want to know if he has a wife and kids. Want to know if he's ever hit them or simply ignored them.

I swallow.

What did you do?

"When I was seven or eight, I would hide under the covers and cry. Other times I would try to get in the middle of them, or try to pull my father off of her. But he was always too big and too strong. Sometimes seeing me standing there, or hearing me cry out, would jolt him back to his senses and he'd stop hitting her; other times he might not. You wanted to protect your mother. You felt you had to, right?"

I look away, nodding.

"It's normal for kids, particularly sons, to want to protect their mothers. But in many instances, the younger children who jump in to help are usually the ones who end up getting physically hurt in the process. Protecting your mother wasn't your job."

I stare at him. *Then whose was it?*

"You were not responsible for her safety."

Then who was?

"You are not to blame. None of what has happened to your family is your fault. I say all this to say, I know, firsthand, what domestic violence does to families. So when I tell you that I understand what it is you are going through, I want you to be clear that those are not simply words. They are from experience. But I want you to know that those experiences do not have to control you. Or become you. Your worry that something bad might happen to your mother doesn't have to consume you. It is okay to worry about her well-being, but it's not okay to let it rent space in your head to the point that you are obsessing over it. That isn't healthy, nor is it helpful.

"Children who witness abuse are the silent victims. They are the ones who are often forgotten. That's been you, K'wan. Many parents think, hope, that their children are not directly affected by what's going on between them. They think because they only argue or fight when the kids are in bed or out of earshot that they are not aware of what it is going on. But they are sadly mistaken. Children know. They can sense it."

I agree with him. I want to tell him how I sat up in my room countless nights, waiting. Want to tell him how the waiting was the worst part for me; the not knowing when it (the abuse) would start and end; the not knowing what to do to stop it or keep it from happening. Over and over and over, I would try to think up ways to stop it. All I ever wanted was for the fighting to stop.

And, no, he didn't come home every night and beat my mom or yell and scream at her. Weeks, even months, would go by before something would set him off and the fighting would start. And I always knew when it was starting to build up. If he slammed something—a cabinet, a door, his hand down on a table; if his jaws tightened or he spoke to my mom through clenched teeth, I knew it wouldn't take much to throw him over the edge and the fighting and name-calling would soon follow. Unless Mom was able to say or do something that would keep the ugly beast from showing up with its fists balled up and fire shooting from outta its mouth. You never knew what would set him off. He was as unpredictable as he was predictable. You knew something was gonna happen, you just didn't know when, or how, or why. You only knew. Other times, when you thought— after you anticipated and waited—there'd be fighting, there wouldn't be. He'd walk away or let it go. He'd wanna laugh and joke with me and my brothers. Shoot a game of hoops with Kyle and me, or bike ride, or whatever. He'd wanna do stuff with us. Then something would happen, some kinda switch would go off in his head, and outta nowhere he'd turn into something mean and ugly. Maybe it wasn't outta nowhere. Maybe it was already there, lurking around, waiting for a reason to show its hideous head.

I hear myself telling him all this.

"Everyone here has taken a special interest in helping you through this, K'wan, including myself. But none of us can do the work for you. Or be more invested in you and your treatment than you. So, are you ready to invest in you?"

I take a deep breath, nodding.

"Good," he says as he flashes a mouthful of straight white teeth. They are the whitest teeth I have seen in a long time. I wonder if they are real. "You're in good hands, young man. There's lots of work to do. And some days will definitely be better than others. But we'll get through it, one step at a time, all right?"

I nod again. He gets up and walks over to me, extending his hand. I stand up, grip his hand and shake it. He looks me in the eyes. "I'll have my secretary send you a slip to see me next week; same time. Okay?"

I nod, then walk toward the door, but turn back to look at him when he says to me, "By the way, nothing changes if nothing changes. If you want different results, then you're going to need to do something different. Enjoy the rest of your afternoon."

You too, I think, walking outta his office. I take a deep breath, feeling something shift inside of me. I'm not sure what, but something feels different. At least for this moment.

Twenty-Eight

don't know what makes me think of Mrs. Broward, my second-grade teacher. But I do. She was a short, older-looking lady. Well, at six, everyone looks old. And she was mean. I can remember her asking the class who they looked up to, and me standing up and saying, "My daddy..." I remember saying this with as much pride as a six-year-old can have. And when she asked why I looked up to him, I stared at her like she should have already known why and said, "Because he is big and strong. He takes my baby brother and me to the park, and buys us toys. My daddy has lots and lots of money, too. And we live in a really big house. And he built me a tree house in the backyard, too..."

I can't remember what she said after that, but I remember her kinda rolling her eyes up in her head, then moving on to the next kid. My feelings were hurt. Then another time she asked us who our favorite superheroes were. While everyone else in class raised their hands and called out comic book and TV characters, like Spiderman, Superman, Catwoman, and Storm, I raised my hand and said, "My daddy."

Again, she gave me a strange look that made me feel stupid. I remember her saying, "Your daddy isn't a superhero. Superheros have superhuman strength and a desire to save the world. So, let's try again, who is your superhero?"

"My daddy," I told her again. I remember feeling tears coming to my eyes. In my six-year-old brain, he did have superhuman strength and he could save the world, if he wanted to. And I refused to change my mind about it, or have her or anyone else try to change it for me. He wasn't a cartoon fantasy; he was real. And he was *my* superhero. Then one day I saw my superhero slap my mom and my whole world was turned upside down. He no longer could save the world, or me.

We needed saving from him.

Mrs. Morgan waves me in when she sees me at the door. Today she is wearing all red—red dress, red shoes, red nails, red lips. She looks like a big ball of fire. I hold my breath and wait for the fire alarm to go off. I exhale when it doesn't.

Her painted lips curl up into a wide smile. She has streaks of red across her teeth. I blink. "So you've met with Dr. Curtis, I heard." I nod. "And it wasn't as painful as you thought it would be, was it?"

I shrug, shaking my head. It dawns on me that Mrs. Morgan is wearing a wig today. It's like one of those wigs with the bangs, short back, and pointed ends that touch the tip of her jawline.

"You're going to do great with Dr. Curtis. He is truly one of the best psychologists in the field. And he's one of very few men of color to practice psychology in the state of New Jersey."

I nod. Truth is, I went online and Googled him. I read up on him and all of the social and civic organizations he is involved with, along with all of the stuff he does working with women and kids, and even men in domestic violence. I never thought I would care one way or the other, but I'm kinda glad I'm gonna be working with him.

"So, I thought today we'd talk a little more about resentments. How's that?"

I shrug. *See, if she started recording these sessions, all I'd have to do is pull out the tape on resentment and press* PLAY.

"When we are stuck in our resentments, K'wan, we cannot grow emotionally or spiritually. What we are potentially doing is blocking our blessings. The blessings of peace of mind and peace in our hearts. Carrying the burden of resentment usually has a negative effect on you. We spend more time focusing so much on the person we resent that we miss out on enjoying life and what's most important. The way to let go of resentments is through forgiveness..."

I sigh. She is relentless.

She smiles. "You cringe every time I bring up anything about forgiveness. Forgiveness is a big pill to swallow. And everyone is not always ready to swallow it. The thing with forgiveness is that it has to be of free will. It must be a choice you make, and you make alone. It can't be done because it's something you *think* you *should* or *must* do. No, forgiveness only works when it is something that *you* want to do."

I pull in my bottom lip.

"This is not what you want to hear, but until you start talking, until you start opening up in sessions, this—resentment and forgiveness, and letting go—is what will be talked about." She tilts her head. "Fair enough?"

I nod.

"Good. At some point, you are going to need to decide if you want to hang onto your resentment toward your father, or let it go. And the only way you can decide that is by talking things out with him." She spends the next I don't know how many minutes going on and on and on about forgiveness and acting as if I've already forgiven him until I can actually forgive him. I don't know. It wasn't making any sense to me. All I know is I've done enough pretending. And I'm doing anymore. I won't be *acting as if* about anything. There is no forgiveness and no more pretending.

She glances at her watch. And I am relieved that my time is up.

As I getting up to leave Mrs. Morgan's office, Mrs. Broward comes to mind again. This time I see her pasty face smirking at me. I can almost hear her saying, "See, I told you he wasn't a superhero."

You're right. He isn't. And he's no longer anyone I look up to, either. He is just the man who beat my mother up and tried to kill her.

Twenty-Nine

oday's group is smaller than I've known it to be since I've been here. There are only six of us here: this new kid, Lance, Elijah, Jarrod, Corey, Jackson, and me. Miss Daisy says smaller groups are more effective. They're all a waste of time if you ask me. But, whatever!

The new kid is tall. String-bean-thin from Englewood. He tells us he's sixteen. And spent one year at the Jamesburg Training School for Boys—a juvenile correctional facility in New Jersey, for aggravated assault. Everyone—with the exception of me—introduces themselves to him. Miss Daisy eyes me, before telling him who I am. He gives me a head nod. I nod back and feel a headache pushing its way into my head. Miss Daisy wants to know how he got his charges. I turn my head toward the window and stare out.

Today it is rainy and windy. I watch as the wind beats up the leaves and branches on the trees. Heavy droplets of rain ping up against the window. Far off in the distance, I see lightning. Something my ninety-one-year-old great-aunt once said to me and my brother, Kyle, when we were visiting her in North Carolina comes to mind. It was summertime, hot and sunny. We were outside playing with some of our cousins when all of a sudden it started pouring down raining and thundering while the sun was still shining. She said the Devil was beating his wife. I saw two more sun showers after that—once when we were on vacation in Hawaii and the other time in Saint Lucia. If the Devil only beat his wife during a sun shower, then who the heck was beating their wife right now?

"One in every four women will experience domestic violence in her lifetime…" The article I read it from is stuck in my head, along with everything else. Knowing my mom is one of the four women who has been beaten and abused bothers me. Its truth hurts.

The devil stays real busy, I think, watching lightning crack through the sky like an angry whip.

"Abuse and violence is a choice…"

That is something else I read, and have heard since being here. That everything one does is a choice. That there are consequences and rewards for our choices. That we don't always chose what's right, or what makes sense.

This has me thinking, wondering, if there really are consequences. I know there are consequences when we break the law, like run a red light, rob a bank, or sell drugs. But it doesn't seem like it's against the law to beat up on people. People say it's against the law, but I don't know. It seems kinda lopsided. The law, that is. I don't understand it. It all seems crazy to me.

Like when a woman calls the police on the man who beats her, then runs down to the police station to bail him out. A man beats up on his wife or girlfriend, then she takes him back. A woman gets a restraining order, then drops it, and lets the guy who beats her move back home. That's what my mom did. She's like those other women. Let him beat her, then take him back. Where's the consequence in all of that?

The answer: I stab him!

The truth: I would have paid someone to finish what I failed to do. Kill him!

I hate that man for what he did!

"Randy, please. You'll wake the kids.

"Don't try to pull the kids into this. You started this with your lies and sneakiness. So you have no one to blame but yourself."

"Randy, I don't want to fight with you…"

There's scuffling.

"Don't you fucking walk away from me when I'm talking to you… I'll break your damn face…"

Instinctively, I know Mom's being hit.

"I will kick your fucking teeth down your throat…"

I hear the stomps. I hear the cries for help. He's kicking her. I hear her screaming. Hear her begging him to stop. He doesn't. Then there is no more stomping and muffled sounds of someone being punched. There's no crying. It's become silent. And there's nothing I can do. I am frozen in place, scared.

I blink.

"My mom's husband came home drunk one night," the new kid says, slicing into my thoughts, "and started arguing with her about some dumb shit. He didn't like what she said so he punched her in the eye, then bashed her head into the glass table." I shift in my seat. Peel my eyes away from the window and the rain and look over in his direction. He shakes his head. "I got tired of him puttin' his hands on her. So I hit him with a few body shots, then knocked his ass out. My Moms kept sayin' she was gonna leave him. But…" He pauses, looking around the room until his eyes lock on mine. I turn back to the storm outside.

"Go on," Miss Daisy urges.

"She never did."

"Was he arrested?"

"Yeah. But, then she turned around and bailed him out, like she always does. Shit's crazy."

"I'm sure she has her reasons," Miss Daisy offers.

I will my eyes from rolling.

"Yeah, maybe she did. It's still a buncha BS. Don't anyone wanna keep seein' their mom's face all busted up 'cause some bum-ass muhfucka can't keep his hands to himself. That shit pissed me off. I got sick of hearing them fighting, all the time. I'm like, damn. Can they ever get along? And the only reason I never bounced outta there is because I didn't wanna leave my brother and two sisters in that craziness."

"Are they still together?" Miss Daisy asks. I don't need to look over at him to know the answer.

"Yeah," he says. "But DYFS took my brother and sisters from her. And I'm glad. At least now they're not dealin' with his drinking and them fighting all the time."

"Are they with family?" she asks. He tells her that they're living with his aunt and uncle. That they've been living with them for the last three months.

"All she has to do is get rid of him and complete some kinda counseling stuff and they can go back home. But she actin' like she wanna be stuck on stupid or sumthin'. Like she don't want 'em home. I know my moms is a grown woman so she's gonna do whatever she wants; no matter what I say, or how I feel about it. But what kinda woman puts a no-good muhfucka before her kids? That's crazy." He shakes his head. "I lost a lotta respect for her for that, for real."

"My moms used to do that same crap," Elijah says, leaning forward and resting his elbows on his knees. He's also sixteen and from somewhere down by the shore. Atlantic City, I think. He told us in group a while back, but I never really pay much attention to what most of the kids here say. And I really don't care. I don't care about any of this shit. The other guys in the group patiently wait for Elijah to continue sharing. They look on with wide eyes, anxious and eager to hear more. But I do not share in their curiosity. I want to go back to my room. I want to put on my headphones and get lost in the sounds of music. I want to listen to anything other than the soundtrack of his life, or anyone else's. I have my own troubles. I have my own story, but I am not willing to share; not here. And definitely not with them. I imagine being out in the rain barefoot, running through the puddles, chasing my little brothers.

I wanna go home!

"She stayed puttin' her nig—my bad, Miss Dee—her men, before me and my brothers.

"Man, that would piss me off, for real, yo," I hear someone say. The voice sounds like Jarrod's. "Me and my sister used to be mad scared when our pops would come home and start snappin'. Peeps always asked why my moms never called the police on him. Why would she? He was the police. His badge meant he could do whatever he wanted to her, us, and get away with it. And he did. Everyone acted like she was lyin' on him or sumthin'. He walked around the crib actin' like he was some kinda God or sumthin'." He shakes his head. "It was crazy."

"I hate the effen po-lice," Jackson says, shaking his head. "They the main ones who be doin' dumb shit, thinkin' they can get away with it."

"Word," Elijah and Corey cosign.

"All police officers aren't bad," Miss Daisy offers, shifting in her seat. "Like in any profession, there are the ones who don't ever abuse their power and positions, and can switch hats once they've left the building. Then you have those who become controlled by their positions, who think they're above the law and can do whatever they want without any consequence. They go home to their families and mistreat them because they believe they can."

"Have you ever been hit?" Corey wants to know. Everyone looks at her, waiting to see if she shares her truths.

She nods. "Yes, once. And that's all it took for me to pack my things and never look back." Elijah wants to know how long she was with him. Nelson wants to know who he was to her. "He was my husband, at the time. And I'd been with him for almost ten years."

"Why'd you leave dude, though. Didn't you love him?" Corey asks.

"Sure I did. But he slapped me in front of my children, and I couldn't let that go. That was my bottom line. I had to think about what kind of example I would be setting for my son and daughter if I stayed."

"Wow," Jackson says. "Do you wish you woulda stayed?"

She tilts her head. "What I wish is that he'd never put his hands on me, but he did. So I did what I had to do for me. And let me tell you. It wasn't easy uprooting my kids from their school and friends. And many times I wanted to give in, go back and try again. But, I didn't. I couldn't trust him. And I couldn't trust myself to not ever leave if he'd hit me again. So, no, I don't wish I would have stayed."

Miss Daisy looks over at me. And for the first time since I've been in her group, I am looking at her through a different set of eyes. I see her as a woman who saved her children. Envy creeps up in me and I shift my gaze to the floor. Why couldn't my mom do that? Pick up and leave and never look back.

I need to know, want to ask, does it take more strength and courage to stay in an abusive house or leave it? I want to know if she ever lived in fear. In my mind's eye, I see myself opening my mouth and attempting to push the words out, but they become stuck in my throat.

I swallow.

"Are you still married to him?" Jackson asks.

She shakes her head. "No, I divorced him eight years ago. But he is very much involved in our children's lives and the two of us are now friends."

"Man, I don't know if I wanna be friends with my girl if we broke up," Elijah says.

"When you're an adult and you have children together, you do what you need to do in order to get along for the sake of the children. My kids needed both their mother and father, and I wasn't about to deprive them of that. And I wasn't going to allow them to see the two of us going at each other's throats, bickering and disrespecting each other. I left him for me, and I forgave him for me.

"I accepted him back into my space for my children's sake. But believe me, everything in relationships isn't always cut and dry. There are many women who will leave a man the first time he raises a hand to her. Then there are some who might leave after the third, fourth, seventh, eighth, or more times. Then there are others will never leave, and that is their decision—to stay. They all have their stories and their reasons for why. I know I had mine. So I say all that to say, don't be so judgmental toward those who choose to stay. Sometimes staying isn't the hardest thing they'll ever have to do; leaving is.

"Your mothers, your sisters, your grandmothers, your aunts, or the neighbor down the street have made life choices. Many of them have made or will make sacrifices that you will not understand. Many of them will risk their lives for love. It is not an easy cross to bear. And, yes, many of their choices will affect their children, and the people around them. And, yes, some will be left with deep emotional wounds that may never heal. Some will be left with emotional and physical scarring. And their children will be scarred, also. Then there are those special ones who will rise about the ashes unscathed. They are a rarity."

She eyes the group, smiling. "Every last one of you has been affected in some way by what your parents have done; the choices they've made. But their mistakes shouldn't be what define you, or control you. Who they were or what they've become doesn't have to be you. If you truly want change, if you truly want to break any cycle, then you have to think different, be different, and do different. You have to be able to forgive, and let go."

I shift in my seat. She is starting to sound like Mrs. Morgan. *"Right or wrong, people who say they love us, choose to hurt us. But we still have the power to forgive them. We can choose to let go of what they've done to us. Or choose to hold onto it."*

"Yo, forget that. I'm not forgivin' jack," Jackson says. "You put ya hands on me, I'm takin' ya top off."

"Violence only begets more violence," Miss Daisy states. "And it solves nothing."

"Yeah, maybe not," he continues. "But I bet you they'll think twice before doin' it again."

"Nah, I don't think that's always true," the new kid says. "My moms used to go at it wit' that nig"—He looks over at Miss Daisy, putting his hands up—"my bad. I mean, the no good mofo she's married to. And all that did was make him wanna go in even harder on her. He'd get angrier and crazier. The last time is when I snapped."

The last time is when I snapped. I repeat that in my head. Wonder if, in fact, I did snap. I don't think so. No, I didn't snap. I remember everything happening as if it were this very moment.

For some reason, this particular night, like so many other nights, I can't sleep. I am lying in my bed, staring up at the ceiling when I hear Mom screaming. I quickly jump up out of bed and reach for the knife hidden between my mattresses. I know what I am going to do with the knife. I know what I want to do to him. Kill him. I run out of my room. They aren't in the bedroom this time, locked behind a door. The screams are coming from downstairs. My heart is in overdrive, pumping a mile a minute. It feels like my head is about to explode. He is on top of her with both of his hands wrapped around her throat, shaking her like she's a rag doll. There is a lump in my throat.

I hear him saying over and over and over, "I am going to fucking kill you!"

"Stop it!" I hear myself yelling. "Get off of her! You're hurting her!" I plunge the knife into his back, then his shoulder, then his back again. I stab him repeatedly. Blood is spurting out all over the place. "I hate you! I hope you die!"

He collapses on top of Mom, who is passed out, but I don't know this. She isn't moving so I think he has killed her. I think I have killed him. I drop the knife. Roll him off of Mom, then try to wake her up. "Mom, wake up! Mom, please!" I keep shaking her.

The triplets are screaming and crying. Kyle is holding them back. He is crying and screaming, "What have you done! You killed him! Mommy is dead!"

I start rocking her in my arms, crying. I have blood all over me. Blood is pooling out of him. I keep thinking she is gone. That he has taken her from us. And then she gasps and coughs. And I burst into tears.

I don't remember hearing or seeing Kyle on the phone with the police. I don't know exactly when they arrive. But there are paramedics and stretchers and sirens and flashing lights. And I am in handcuffs.

"My lil' sister dialed nine-one-one," the new kid says, bringing me back to what's going on in the group. "And they arrested him and me. But he got bailed out. And I had to sit in juvie. That shit's crazy." He shakes his head. "He beats her and gets to go back to his life. But I try to protect her and I'm the one who gets all effen hemmed up. It's crazy; for real. The whole system's effen crooked."

Miss Daisy taps her finger to her lips like she always does when she's thinking about what she's going to say before she says it. "Do you think there was another way you could have handled what happened that night?"

No, I didn't want to do anything different, I answer in my head.

He shakes his head. "Nah, he had it comin'. I wasn't 'bout to stand there and let him keep beatin' on her."

"The next time he hits on her, I'm gonna stab him," is what I hear myself saying. I didn't care about anything other than making him pay. I wanted him to feel my hate for him. To know how much I hurt. I agree with the new kid. I wasn't going to let him put his hands on her again.

She nods. "Or you could have called the police and let them handle the situation."

He twists his face up. "The police? Are you for real? What you think they were gonna do?"

Miss Daisy shifts in her seat. "They would have arrested him, like they did. And you'd most likely still be at home with your family." She looks around the room. Her eyes fall on me. "And a few of you sitting here definitely wouldn't be here." I shift my eyes. I know that is being directed to me. Maybe she's right. I don't know. But what I did know is I couldn't keep living like that. I couldn't sit back and do nothing.

"Again, young men," Miss Daisy continues, "it is about *your* choices and taking responsibility for them, regardless of what someone else has said or done to you, or around you."

"Yeah, well, he shoulda kept his hands to himself," the new kid says, stretching his legs out in front of him. "And I wouldn't have done what I did to him."

"So you blame him for what *you* did?" Miss Daisy asks.

Yes, I blame him. Not for what I did to him, but for what he did to me. And I blame my mom, too. I don't wanna blame her, but I do.

Sitting here is stirring up feelings in me. I am trying so hard to block out these emotions; to not deal with them. I'm scared to deal with them. But these groups are making it hard for me to ignore them. I feel myself getting angry. I grip the sides of my chair.

The new kid shifts in his seat. And so do I. "Hell, yeah, I blame him," he says. "Why shouldn't I?"

"Your stepfather is—"

He frowns. "That dude is nothin' to me."

"Okay, your mother's husband is responsible for his own behaviors. But that doesn't negate you taking responsibility for yours."

He pounds his chest with the palm of his hand. "I take responsibility for what I did. And I'd do it again. But I'm not the problem. He is. And my moms is too damn stupid to see it."

"Your mother isn't stupid," Miss Daisy says to him. "Love can sometimes be blinding. Right now, your mom, like so many other women, only sees what her heart allows her to see. And that sometimes means only seeing what we want to see."

"That sounds like stupid to me," Corey says.

He should talk, I think, biting down on my bottom lip, *when he's the one who keeps going back to a girl who goes upside his head and cuts up his stuff. If you ask me, he's the last person who should be calling anyone stupid.*

I let out a sigh of relief when Miss Daisy says, "Okay, gentlemen, that'll be all. Next group, we'll talk more about personal responsibility."

I roll my eyes up in my head. *Great. Another sermon on responsibility; just what I need!*

Thirty

"**Y**o, K'wan," Ja'Meer says, coming into the room. I'm at my desk finishing up my last Calculus problem. I look up from my notebook. "You have a visit." I knit my brows together, confused. The attendant at the desk told me earlier today that my mom called in and said she wouldn't be able to make it tonight because the triplets were sick. So I am surprised to hear someone is here to see me.

Maybe she left them home with Kyle, I think, nodding at him in acknowledgement as I get up from the desk, closing my book. I change into a Duke tee shirt, then walk out into the corridor and head down to the visiting room.

I see Kyle standing by the doorway before I reach it. He gives me a head nod, and I smile, giving him one back. I am happy to see him. It feels like I haven't seen him in months, when it's only been a few visits. We give each other a brotherly grip and hug when I reach him. "Before you go in," he says, stepping back. He's almost as tall as me. I feel like I've been away forever. "Grandma Ellen's here…and Dad."

I feel the blood rushing from my head. I haven't seen him since my last court hearing. I refused his visits while I was in the detention center. And the three times that he's come here to visit, I've turned back around and left the minute I spotted him, like now. Kyle grabs me by the arm.

"I know you don't want to see him, but please, man. You gonna have to say something to him one day. He's our father." I cringe. "C'mon, K'wan, man; do it for me. Besides, Grandma Ellen flew all the way here to see you."

My palms are suddenly sweaty.

Kyle is looking at me with pleading eyes. I can tell this is something he really wants. But it's not what I want. I want nothing to do with him. I don't want to look at him. I don't want hear his voice. I don't want to be around him, ever. But I do want to see my grandma.

I take a deep breath. Attempt to steady my racing heart.

"You can't stay mad at him forever," Kyle says, eyeing me. "Like for real. You won't even talk, man. It's crazy." He shakes his head, letting my arm go. "How do you think that makes me feel? How do you think Mom feels? She's sad. I'm sad. I want my brother home, man. But you won't even talk to us. We miss you, man; even Dad does."

I roll my eyes at the sound of him missing me.

"He does. And it's not fair that you're treating us like this. We come to see you and you won't even open your mouth. I hate even coming here. But Mom *and* Dad say I have to."

I am shocked and hurt that he has said this. That he hates coming here. Does he not know I *hate* being here? I wonder how he thinks I feel. I'm the one here. I'm the one away from my family and friends. He has his life. He gets to go to school and hang out with his friends and play sports, while I'm stuck here. I can't deal with this right now. I feel like he's blaming me for what's happened. And I don't need that when I am already blaming myself for everything else.

My chest tightens.

"I feel like I'm always in the middle of everything," Kyle continues. "So, please, don't walk out. If you don't wanna talk, then don't. But don't walk out. If you do, it'll really hurt Grandma Ellen. And you know you're her favorite."

I feel like I am being set up. Feel like Grandma Ellen coming is the bait being used to reel me in. But I know my grandma loves me. And I know if I were to turn around and go back to my room that it would upset her. I don't wanna upset her. But what about how this is going to make me feel? Uncomfortable. I turn to leave.

"Man, everything's not all about you, K'wan. Grandma flew all this way to see you, and you're just gonna go back to your room?" I start to walk away. "I don't even know why I even bother coming up here. It's like you don't even want to see us." That stops me. I stare at him. He stares back. "Don't you want us to keep coming to visit?"

I want to see everyone, except him! I scream in my head. *He has no business being here. I don't want him here!*

"Do you know Mom cries every time she leaves this place? She gets in the car and cries for almost ten minutes before she can drive off. K'wan, you gotta talk. Let these people help you or something. This isn't right, man. Do you have to be so selfish?"

Selfish? He can't be serious? I have been anything but selfish. Everything I did was to protect Mom and him and the triplets. I stopped that man from killing our mom; how is that being selfish? How can he say he isn't going to visit again?

I blink. I want to tell him how hard this is for me. I want him to know how alone I feel. And how seeing him and the triplets is what makes this hellhole bearable. I want to tell him how much I love him and don't want him to be mad at me.

I hear Mrs. Morgan's voice in my head. "*Sometimes we have to do things that make us uncomfortable. We have to push past our resistance and know that every decision we make isn't going to always be about us. It can't be when other people are involved.*"

I shut my eyes tight, then open them as I walk in the room. I see him, first. And I immediately feel the bottom of my sneakers stick to the floor. I can't look at him. I see too much of me in him. I feel sick to my stomach. That's not who I want to be.

Grandma Ellen doesn't wait for me to make it over to them before she is up out of her seat and her arms are wrapped around me. "Oh, my precious grandbaby," she says, kissing me on the cheek. She is crying. "I am so happy to see you." She steps back to get a better look at me. Her wet eyes are filled with love and worry and sadness. At least that's what I think I see. I struggle to keep my eyes on hers.

"Look at you; handsome as ever. You've gotten taller, too." She fusses over me, like she always does. Holding the sides of my face in her warm, soft hands, then pulling me into her and planting a kiss on my forehead. "You know your grandma loves you, dearly. And you know, no matter what, you'll always have a special place in my heart." I nod, knowingly. "Good. We've got to hurry up and get you out of this Godforsaken place so I can get you home and fatten you up. Put some meat on my grandbaby's bones."

Against my will, I smile. She hugs me again. "God is so good. He's going to keep you wrapped in His grace and mercy, baby. All you got to do is believe." She takes me by the hand and guides me over to where they're sitting. It's as if she knows that I am not able to walk on my own. "I know this is hard for you, baby, but I want you to do this for your grandma, okay? Your father really does love you, K'wan." My body stiffens. She stops and grabs hold of both of my hands, and squeezes them. "I'm praying for you, baby. There is nothing God can't see you through. He is right here with you. And so am I."

I am relieved she doesn't pull out a Bible and start citing scriptures. He stands up to greet me. I try not to look at him, but it's too late. I see him. And in his eyes I see sadness.

"Hey, son," he says, walking toward me. As he opens his arms to embrace me, I step out of his reach and take a seat, next to Kyle on the opposite end of where he's sitting. Though not far enough, it'll do for now. Grandma Ellen sits beside him. Kyle gives me the evil eye. I shrug.

I catch a glimpse of his big hands and, for a split second, imagine the palm of his hand landing flat on the side of Mom's face. I picture him grabbing her by the hair and slinging her to the floor before stomping on her. I see Mom gasping; struggling to get from under the soles of his size twelve shoe. I see the print of his anger etched in her face in bright colors.

I sit on my hands.

"Your grandfather sends his love," Grandma Ellen says, bringing me back to this painfully awkward moment. "He gave me some money for you. He's worried sick about you, baby. We all are." I look at her. Her bottom lip quivers as she reaches in her purse and takes out a pack of tissues. She pulls out a few sheets and dabs at her eyes. "We want you to get better so you can come home. You hear me?" I slowly nod, holding back my own tears. "It tears my heart up, seeing you here."

He extends his arm and pulls Grandma into him, giving her a shoulder to cry on.

I shift in my seat.

Grandma balls her tissue up in a ball. "Randall, you need to fix this mess. I don't like seeing my grandbaby like this."

I free my left hand from beneath me and rub my forehead. I am feeling a headache coming on.

"I will, Mom," he says as he consoles her. I am sad to see her cry. I sit in my seat with pent-up tears I refuse to shed. I glance around the visiting room, thankful that there are only three other residents in here with their families.

"Man," Kyle says, bumping a shoulder into me, shifting the

conversation. I can tell he's uncomfortable as well. "I wish you coulda been at my game last night. We slaughtered those fools on the court." He makes an imaginary shot in the air. "Swoosh, I'm all net. You gotta hurry up and get home so you can see me in action."

"Your brother will be home in no time to see you play," he says. I hear admiration in his voice as he says this to Kyle. I feel his eyes on me. "We all want you home, K'wan."

Sadness quickly washes over me. I swallow. I want to get out of here. I want to go home. I miss my family. I feel tears filling my eyes.

I need to get outta here!

"Mom has me going to a counselor," Kyle offers out of nowhere. My eyes widen. I am surprised at this revelation. I wonder why he needs a counselor. "At first I didn't wanna go talk to a stranger, but she's kinda cool. And I kinda feel better after I talk to her."

I glance at him, wondering what he talks to her about. Wonder if he says anything about me, if he talks about that night. I wish I knew if he were angry at me, if he blames me. Even though he's never said it, I sometimes feel like he does, like earlier when we were standing out in the hall.

He shifts gears again. "Guess who asked about you? She said she is going to pray for you and hopes you come home soon."

I give him a quizzical look.

"Tabitha. I think she likes you, man." He chuckles, pulling a white envelope from outta his pocket and handing it to me. Tabitha is a girl from my school. She also lives down the street from us. She's cute and really smart. She has the second highest G.P.A. in our class, behind me. And she reminds me of the actress Zoe Saldana; I like Zoe. And I really like Tabitha. All the boys do. She has really nice eyes and these deep, perfect dimples that make me wanna stick my finger in them whenever she smiles. But we're only friends. "She even blew a kiss at me, then told me to catch it and bring it to you."

I keep from making a face, shifting in my seat. I am more uncomfortable now than I was before. I take the letter from him. My heart leaps in my chest as I grip the envelope in my hand.

Grandma Ellen reaches over and pats Kyle on the hand. "Come sit next to your father so I can sit next to your brother." Kyle gets up, and they switch seats. She takes my hand in hers. "I want you to look at me, baby." I turn to her. "You are loved, you hear me?"

I nod, taking her in. Grandma's skin reminds me of cocoa beans. Deep and rich and smooth. I cut my over at him. He's wiping something out of his eye. A tear, I think. But I don't want to think about it. I shift my eyes back as Kyle gets up. He asks that man for money to get something to drink from out of the vending machine, then asks me and Grandma if we want anything. I shake my head. Grandma wants a ginger ale. He walks off.

"I promised myself I was going to keep quiet." She sniffles, then dabs the balled tissue in her hand at her eyes.

"Mom, don't," he warns. "Not here; not now."

"Yes, now, Randall," she shoots back. "I want my grandbaby out of this place." She brings her attention back to me. "I want you to do something for me, okay?" I hold my breath, slowly nodding. "Whenever they start those family meetings here, I want you to promise me that you won't get up and walk out, okay? Give your father a chance to speak; hear him out, okay? He has some things that he needs for you to hear, and only from him."

I start to feel lightheaded from holding my breath. She is asking me to be in a room alone with him—well, with a counselor, too. Still, it's unfair of her. I don't know if I can make her that kinda promise. I don't wanna make a promise I may not keep. But Grandma knows I'd never break a promise to her, ever.

I stare at her, wondering if she has any idea what it is she is asking of me. She can't possibly know how much I hate him. How much I wish he woulda died that night. She can't possibly know what he did to my mom. What he put her through. He didn't care enough about us. So why should I care about anything he has to say. No, I can't promise her that. And I won't.

I lean over and give her a hug and a kiss. She hugs me back. I stand up to leave, and she grabs me by the arm. "I am your grandmother, and I love you. Don't run from this; from us. If you want to hate your father, hate him. But love *you* enough to at least listen to what he has to say. You might hear something that will soften your heart, or ease some of your anger, or you might not, but you'll never know unless you try." She tightens her grip on my arm. "Sit, please."

Reluctantly, I do as I am told. She knows I would never be disrespectful to her, or around her. "Promise me you will do that for me, sweetheart."

"Mom, please," he says to her. "Let me handle this. He's my son."

"And he's my grandson."

"I want—"

She puts a hand up to stop him. "Not another word, Randall." I've never seen this side of her before—angry. He sits back in his seat, lets her finish. She shifts in her seat, then turns back to me. "K'wan, baby, I know you're angry. Hell, I'm angry—very." She cuts her eyes over at him. "But I am not letting my anger control me. And I am not going to let it get in the way of me loving those around me. And I don't want you to either. I love your father; he's my son. And I always will. And I love you, too, baby. You are surrounded by people who love you and who want to see you through this. And no matter how hard you try to push us away, or shut us out, we are going to be right here for you every step of the way. We're not going anywhere."

She wipes her tears. "I am so damn angry with your father. And he knows it. To see my grandbaby sitting up in this place, but I love him so very much and he knows that as well. Still, I could smack the taste out his mouth for what he's done." She looks over at him.

"Mom, please," he says again. "Don't you know how bad I already feel?"

"Tell that to this child, right here. He's the one that needs to hear it."

I bite down on my lip, fighting back tears. I want to get up and run out but something holds me down. I am stuck to my seat. My legs feel heavy, like they're being weighted down by lead.

He moves over to Kyle's seat. Grandma gets up, squeezes my shoulder, then leaves me alone with him. And I feel abandoned. "K'wan," he starts, leaning over in his seat, clasping his hands together. "I know I fucked up, son. And there aren't enough apologies in this world to ever convey how damn sorry I am for what I've done to your mother, your brothers—and most importantly, you. I know this, everything I've done, has affected you the most. I lost my family because of me. And I know you're hurt and angry with me. Everything I did has been because of *me*. Not you, or your brothers, or your mother. I hate what I did to your mother. Every day I am reminded of what I had and what I've lost. I..." He pauses, then pulls in a deep breath. He is choking up. I try to move my legs, try to stand. Try to distance myself from him, from his words. From this...this pain that rips through me like a sharp blade.

I can't move.

I feel paralyzed from the waist down.

"I was selfish and thoughtless. And I can't ever undo what's already happened. That man I was, the man I showed you, is not the man I want you to ever be. It's not the man I thought I'd ever be, but he is. I can't stop you from hating me. I hate me. But I want you to know if I could take back every nasty thing I ever said to your mother, every mean thing I ever did to her, every slap, every kick, I would. If I could have my hands chopped off and my tongue cut out, I would. I'd gladly die right now if I thought that would change things. Your mother never deserved to be treated the way I treated her. You and your brothers never deserved to witness, or overhear, any of it."

He pauses, pinching the insides of his eyes with his fingers. He is trying to keep his own emotions in check; trying to press shut the wells of his eyes. "Son, I've never in my life felt more hurt or ashamed than I do now. Seeing you here, knowing I caused this. I don't know how, or if I ever can, make it up to your mom, you, and your brothers, but I want to do whatever I can to try. I know you may not believe it, but I have changed."

You're right. I don't believe you. You're a fucking liar! A woman beater!

I can't do this. I fight to keep my emotions contained. There's a creek slowly rising inside of me and I am frightened that it will swell out of control. I shut my eyes, tight. My eyelids have become dams. But I do not believe they are strong enough to handle the spillways. I clench my fist. And rock back and forth. Waves of emotion are crashing inside of me, causing my eyes to flood with tears.

His voice cracks. "I am so disappointed and hurt."

I can't sit here and listen to him anymore. I feel like I am about to explode. I am afraid if I don't get up and get out of here now, away from him, I will lose it.

I hold my breath, hoping to calm my racing heart. I glance around the room, stare over at Grandma Ellen until her gaze meets mine. She mouths, "I love you," then presses her hands together as if she is praying. I look at her with pleading eyes to come back and rescue me. But she doesn't. She shifts her eyes back to Kyle, leaving me feeling helpless.

I am rocking. My right leg is shaking. My fists are balled. I am breathing in and out, heavy and loud. I count backward from ten in my head. Try to uncoil the cluster of knots that have formed in my stomach.

I can't take this anymore!

I jump up from my seat and bolt out the door, running out into the hallway, leaving behind everything I am, and nothing I ever want to be.

Thirty-One

My IPC session with Mrs. Morgan was cancelled this morning. And for some reason I am disappointed. She's always kept her sessions with me. Now I'm sitting here in group worried, hoping nothing has happened to her. I know she dresses kinda crazy sometimes and wears a buncha makeup and other props that make her hard to not stare at, but I still like her.

"How many times have you thought you were in love?" Miss Daisy asks, causing me to bring my attention to the group. That annoying word *love* seems to keep popping up every time I turn around. I glance around the group. There are ten of us here today: Nelson, Anthony, Jackson, The Bully, Aesop, Corey, Lance, Westley, Aiden, and me.

"Man, I'm always in love," Jackson says, smiling. "Any time I see a big booty and smile, it's love at first sight."

"Aww, man," Corey laughs. "Go 'head with that. That ain't no love at first sight. That's all lust. Love at first hump. You a horny hound."

Aesop makes howling dog sounds and the group laughs.

Miss Daisy claps her hands to get our attention. "Alright, gentlemen, settle down. Let's stay focused. Many people confuse love with lust"—She cuts her eye over at Jackson—"and vice versa."

"Well, it works for me," Jackson says, grinning. "I get what I want. They get want they want and we're all happy. I lust 'em, then love 'em."

"Yeah, and then leave 'em," Corey adds, laughing. "No wonder you stay gettin' lumped up."

"It's all good as long as I stay mackin' the honeys, I'll take my lumps. And proudly hump all of my lovin' in 'em."

The two of them go back and forth with jokes and I am surprised Miss Daisy is allowing this. Then again, I'm not. I've learned she sometimes sits back and lets the guys talk amongst themselves. She says it tells her a lot about who we are and how we think. Well, them, that is.

"Okay, Corey and Jackson, that's enough," Miss Daisy warns, eyeing them. She crosses her feet at the ankles. "Who can tell me how many types of love they think there are? I'm talking about the kind of love when you're in a relationship with someone."

When no one seems to know the answer she tells us there are three kinds of love, then explains them to us. "Relationships usually begin with romantic love, then move on to either what is called a nurturing love, which is a healthy kind of love, or into something toxic, which we call an addictive or possessive love. This type of love is extremely unhealthy."

I glance around the group and see that Miss Daisy has piqued everyone's attention, including mine. We all wanna know more. Everyone's attention is on her and she takes that as her cue to continue. "Romantic love is exciting. You find yourself thinking of only each other, and may spend lots of time together wanting to get to know each other. You enjoy spending as much time together as you can. In this stage, after awhile, you get to know each other better and decide whether or not it's something you want to continue or break off. If the relationship continues, it will either evolve into what we know as a nurturing love that allows both people in the relationship to grow and be happy. It encourages individuality and autonomy within the relationship. Both partners trust each other and our supportive of each other."

That definitely doesn't sound like anything he and Mom had...nurturing.

"Partners encourage each other and genuinely want the best for each other. They allow room for personal and professional growth as well as within the relationship. Couples in this type or relationship are comfortable and safe sharing their feelings with each other and are never afraid of each other."

Nope, that's definitely not what they had!

"Both of you can be yourself without shame or ridicule or without being demeaned or disrespected. If that's not the kind of love a couple has in their relationship, then it's definitely a red flag that something may not be right. It could mean that they are in what we call a possessive or addictive love, which isn't really love. It's a desperate need for the other. The need for the other person is more of an addiction than anything else. The thought of being alone may be frightening, and while men and women express it differently, a possessive partner will do almost anything to maintain control of the relationship. And, unfortunately, from listening to some of your relationship stories, this is the kind of love it appears many of you have."

Everyone squirms in their seats. Miss Daisy has hit a few nerves.

"How many of you feel like you can't live without your girlfriends? Or that they can't live without you?"

Everyone except The Bully and me raise their hands. I feel like a real odd ball. They all look over at me like I'm strange. Now I shift in my seat.

Miss Daisy continues, "Possessive love is rooted in jealousy and insecurities. How many of you are jealous?"

Nelson, Jackson, Westley, Aiden and Lance raise their hands.

"Why?" Miss Daisy wants to know.

"'Cause I don't want my girl up in no other guy's face," Nelson says, frowning his face up. "She knows not to play me. But I even *think* she's tryna play me, I'll snap on her real quick. Plus, I'm part Hispanic and all Hispanic men are extremely jealous."

Miss Daisy tilts her head. "Where'd you get that from; that all Hispanic men are jealous?"

"My pops and all of my uncles are mad jealous. So it has to be in my blood."

Everyone laughs. What he says sounds stupid to me. Even I know that jealousy has nothing to do with culture or race, geesh.

"Jealousy isn't solely cultural-based. Yes, there are some cultures where the men appear extremely more jealous than others. But, overall, jealousy isn't a black thing or a white thing or a Hispanic thing. It's not about race; it's about insecurity."

"My girl says being jealous lets you know how much someone loves you; is that true?" Jackson wants to know.

"I'm sorry to disappoint you," Miss Daisy says, leaning forward in her seat, "Jealousy is based in fear, not love. And it definitely doesn't prove love. What it does prove is how insecure someone is. Whether the fear is real or imagined, it still exists. The fear of losing your partner to someone else, the fear of being without them, or the fear of being alone, all contribute to one's insecurity about the relationship. And about themselves."

The Bully grunts. "Man, I'm not beat for all that. If a chick wants to start frontin', playin all kinda mind games and whatnot, then I'ma give her the axe. There's too many other broads out there to be stressin' over one. She don't wanna act right, make her the ex and move onto the next."

"Word," Aiden says. "That's wassup."

"So, Miss Dee, you saying not even a little jealousy is cool? I mean, can't someone be a little bit jealous, but not be all crazy with it?"

"Yeah, Miss Dee," Westly ways. "I know you said jealousy is not based in love and all, but a little jealousy can't hurt. At least that lets your girl know you want her."

"Whether it's a little or a lot, jealousy is still jealousy, no matter how you look at it. It's only natural that partners want to protect what they view as theirs; their relationship, that is. No one wants someone else to come in and sabotage their relationship, or for their partner to somehow become interested in someone else.

"And many people believe that it can sometimes be a good thing in a relationship because it can open the door of communication and allow people to express their concerns as long as you don't let it get the best of you. Tell me this, how many of you have demanded your girl stop talking to guys or have gone out and beat up someone you either caught your girl with, or thought she was getting too cozy with?"

Again, everyone raises their hands except for The Bully and me.

"Why?" Miss Daisy asks.

Because they're stupid!

"'Cause he disrespected my relationship and you don't do that," Jackson states.

Miss Daisy explains, "If you're in a relationship with someone and they open the door for inappropriateness, then they are the ones who disrespect your relationship, not the other party. Everyone plays a role in their relationship. And everyone needs to be responsible for who and what they allow in it."

Jackson shrugs. "I still broke his nose. And he knew to stay away from her. I bet you every time he saw me, dude broke out and ran the other way."

"And that proved what?" Miss Daisy questions.

That he's special.

"It let dude know that she's my girl so he had better step off or feel my wrath."

The Bully, Corey, and Jackson laugh at this.

These guys are older than me, but I act more mature than all of them. My mom always says maturity has nothing to do with age and now I see that.

Miss Daisy asks, "So Jackson, you don't think there was another way in which you could have handled that situation?"

He shakes his head. "Nah. I had already warned her that the next time I saw her talking to him, I was gonna handle him, so it was what it was. She wanted to keep talking to him, so I snapped his snout."

Lenny and Aesop laugh.

"And what's so funny about his violence?" Miss Daisy asks, sounding annoyed.

Lenny shifts in his seat. "Nothing. It's how he said it; that's all. Besides, dude shoulda had his snot locker wrecked if he knew he had a girl."

"Well, there's nothing funny about violence. And there's nothing sexy or cute about jealousy. Immature and insecure little boys and girls, and immature and insecure men and women run around banging on, and kicking in doors and beating up people they don't want their partners around. Insecure people attack and assault people who look at their partners or if they think their partners are looking at someone else. Insecure people allow jealousy to consume them. And somewhere, somebody kills somebody because they're jealous. Then sometimes they kill themselves. Jealousy has robbed people of their lives and sabotaged relationships. It has had people seeing and believing something that doesn't really exist because it is all in their heads because of paranoid thinking, so there is nothing cute at all about jealousy. That green-eyed monster has destroyed relationships and people."

"My girl is mad jealous," Aiden says. "But that's because she doesn't trust me."

"And why doesn't she trust you?" Miss Daisy inquires.

"She caught me cheating on her a couple of times."

"So on top of jealousy issues, you and your girlfriend have trust issues as well. That's definitely the makings for disaster."

These guys and their relationship problems are nuts.

Miss Daisy asks the group how many of them start blowing up their girlfriends' phones if they don't respond to their texts or emails within two or three minutes, how many of them want to know where they are and what they're doing and who they're doing it with 24/7, or get crazy when their girls speak to another guy.

All this stuff sounds real psycho to me.

Everyone in the circle raise their hands except me. *Wow, The Bully won't fight a guy over a girl, but he'll practically stalk and harass her. That's real priceless.*

I shake my head, glancing over at him.

He catches me. "Yo, what the fuck you looking at? I don't know what the fuck ya pussy ass shaking your head for."

"Leonard, get out, now," Miss Daisy snaps, pressing the panic button. "I've warned you more than a dozen times about your mouth and aggressive outbursts. I will not tolerate it. And you will not be allowed back in this group."

He opens his mouth to say something when the door flies open and two, no three, counselor aides—or what the residents call The Goon Squad because they're all over six feet with bulging muscles—come rushing into the room.

"Is everything all right up in here, Miss Dee?" Muscle Man One asks. They all look like professional body builders.

"No. Get Mr. Disrespectful out of my group."

He jumps up from his seat. "Bitch-ass nigga, I should punch you in—" He doesn't get the rest of his words out before he is yanked up under his arms and escorted out the door.

Miss Daisy looks around the circle. "Now, is there anyone else who needs to be dragged out of here?" When no one responds, she says, "Good. Now where were we? Oh, yes. How many of you are checking your partner's Facebook pages or go through their phones, or get mad when she won't let you?"

Everyone's hands go up again. And now I am more convinced than ever that they are all a buncha kooks.

Aesop, Lance, Westley, and Jackson say their girls do the same things to them so they don't see what the big deal is. I frown.

There are really a lot of crazy, insecure people in the world. I'm gonna give up on the idea of dating or ever getting married and become a monk or priest because this kinda stuff is sickening.

Listening to Miss Daisy really makes me think I don't ever wanna sign up for having a relationship. It's all too scary. Like how will you know if someone has a screw loose or not when you first meet them? Maybe you can tell if they say or do something, but what if they don't? Then what? In the beginning, everyone is always tryna be nice to everybody, so you might not see it. Or you might really start liking them and ignore it. Then you're stuck with them. Uh, no thank you. I'll stay single for two hundred, please.

Miss Daisy continues, "The big deal is that going through someone else's phones or emails or text messages isn't healthy for any relationship. And if you're doing it because you can't trust each other, then perhaps you don't need to be together."

"Well, I don't think it's a problem if the other person is cool with it," Lance says. "I mean, my girl used to go through my phone all the time, and it was no biggie. She'd let me go through hers, too."

"Well, that's different if that's something the both of you are open to. But most people are not. And most often than not, someone is going through their partner's things or personal space without their permission. How many of you have gotten into fights or arguments when you or your partners have refused to let the other go through their phones, emails, texts, or Facebook messages?"

Everyone raises their hands, again. Retarded.com! I can't believe they're fighting over phones and social media, like for real? Who does that?

Insecure people!

"So when you're checking each other's Facebook pages and going through each other's phones, what exactly are you looking for? And what are you going to do when you find it?"

Anthony and Aesop tell her when they do it, they're checking to see if their girls are talking to other dudes and what kinda things they're talking about behind their backs. Jackson and Nelson say the same thing. They also say that they do it to let their girls know that they're watching them. And they all justify what they do by saying that they do it because their girls do it to them.

So again, these kids are nuts!

She glances at her watch. "Well, gentlemen, it's that time. Good discussion. Hopefully, we'll finish up next group." Everyone scatters outta the room.

Thirty-Two

I am called down to Dr. Curtis' office for my second IPC. I'm kinda nervous. No, maybe nervous isn't it. Anxious, yeah, that's it. I walk into his office and he greets me. I can smell his cologne. It smells expensive.

He shakes my hand, then sits in the leather chair across from me. He crosses his ankle up over his knee. He has on a pair of expensive designer leather loafers. "How are you, K'wan?"

I shrug.

"I understand your last counseling session with Mrs. Morgan was pretty emotional for you." It sounds more like a question than a statement, so I nod. "You're carrying a lot of emotional baggage—most of it not belonging to you, and it's weighing heavy on you. Everything you are feeling, or have felt—anger, guilt, stress, insecurity, aloneness, fear, confusion—are all natural emotional responses to the abuse you've witnessed. You did not cause the abuse, nor were you the problem. Your father's belief system and distorted thinking were the problems. His choice to abuse your mother was his and his alone. None of that had anything to do with you. You did not provoke him into being abusive to your mother. And it had nothing to do with your father not being able to manage his anger. On the contrary, he knew exactly what he was doing. And he knew when, where, how and why he was doing it. Trust me. It is, and was, not your fault.

"And be very clear. Your father's choice to use violence, his choice to exert power and control in his relationship with your mother has cost him dearly. You've been severely affected by his choices. Your brothers have been affected by them. Your mother. And so has he. He has been greatly impacted by his abusive behavior."

I give him an unbelieving look. *Yeah, right!*

"Your father's behaviors have cost him his relationship with you, your mother, and I'm sure in some ways, with your brothers. And he has had to face legal consequences as a result of them. And again, his behaviors were his choices. Not yours. Anytime you might have overheard him telling your mother that she was making him violent, it was one of many abuse tactics abusers use. Just like you believed the abuse was your fault, at some point, so did your mother. It's an effective accusation that works for the abuser, especially if other people are also making her feel that perhaps it's something she's done or said to cause his abusive behaviors. He doesn't have to take responsibility or ownership for it."

Dr. Curtis leans forward in his seat. "What your father did was not your fault. And it was never your mother's fault. Unfortunately—like so many other victims of abuse—your mother believed she was not only responsible for the abuse, but responsible to keep the abuse from not happening. She tried to change her behavior in order to avoid the abuse, or to keep it from escalating. I bet you thought the same thing. That if you kept getting straight A's and you kept winning awards, that if you stayed this perfect kid, that he wouldn't abuse your mother anymore, didn't you?"

I blink, feeling my chest tighten. I nod.

"And the more abusive he was, the harder you tried. And the harder your mother tried, and still nothing changed. You know why? Because all his abusive behaviors were for him to change.

He was responsible for stopping the violence. Not you; not your mother."

I swallow. He is saying stuff that I've heard before, but that I am now really hearing for the first time. I hear him, and it is starting to make sense, sorta.

"You're suffering from the psychological effects of your father's abuse, K'wan. Feelings of anxiousness, difficulty sleeping, the nightmares and flashbacks…"

I blink.

That's me!

"There may have been times when you would complain of physical ailments like stomach aches or headache."

I did that!

"What you have done is internalize your distress and have withdrawn from others, which is another effect of domestic violence on children. You thought you should be able to stop the violence in some way, but you weren't. You couldn't. And that is eating you up inside. Am I right?"

I pull in my bottom lip. Bite down on it to keep the tears from falling. He is hitting a raw nerve. I am feeling exposed. I lower my head and nod.

"K'wan, if I know nothing else, I know your parents love you."

Then why did they put me through this?

Dr. Curtis tries to talk to me about my nightmares, but I refuse to. Maybe one day, but not today. Instead he talks about cognitive therapy. Tells me how it's a type of therapy that is short, like sixteen sessions, but I will have to do homework assignments.

I frown.

He chuckles. "Don't worry. They'll be very painless work assignments. I will give you reading materials and you'll be encouraged to practice the techniques learned."

For some reason, all of this CBT stuff is starting to sound like a lotta work.

He explains, "This is a very effective treatment approach that is particularly useful with treating post traumatic stress disorders. My role as your therapist will be to listen, teach, and encourage you. Your role is to express concerns, learn new ways of thinking and feeling, and to act on that learning. Together—collaboratively, we can help you restructure your whole thought process and hopefully change your outlook. Will it be easy? No. Not at first. It will require work on your part. You will be taught specific techniques and concepts during each session. I won't be here to teach you *what* to do. Instead, I will teach you *how* to do it for yourself."

I blink. He is losing me with all of this clinical mumbo jumbo.

"Am I losing you?" he asks, knowingly.

I nod.

"CBT—cognitive behavioral therapy—is based on the idea that thoughts cause feelings and behaviors, not external stimuli like people, situations, or events. The benefit of this is that even if the situation doesn't change, you can still change the way you think to feel and act better. The goal of CBT is to help you unlearn unwanted reactions and learn new ways of reacting. When you learn how and why you are doing well, you will eventually know what to do to continue doing well. It'll all make sense once we start it."

He explains how people with PTSD can develop fears of reminders of their traumatic experiences, like triggers. And how they can bring about thoughts and feelings connected with the trauma. He says the reminders can be in the form of nightmares, memories, or intrusive thoughts. And can bring about distress, causing a person to fear and avoid them.

"The goal is to help reduce the level of fear and anxiety connected with these reminders/triggers. This is usually done by having you confront, or be exposed to, the reminders. In your case, that would be your father. Sometimes even the thought of something we fear can bring about anxiety. For instance, your fear that something bad might happen to your mother."

I blink, feeling like he's inside my head. Then I remember what he told me in our first session. That he understands what I am going through because he went through it, too. *I wonder if he went to counseling to help him, or if he had to be put into a program.*

When our session is over, Dr. Curtis stands up and shakes my hand. He stares into my eyes and says, "K'wan, it's time for you to face your fears."

I walk out, feeling more anxious than before I walked in.

"Syreeta, I will fucking kill you."

Thirty-Three

A tray slams on the table in front of me, startling me back to the present. I look up from my own tray of now cold food. It's The Bully with a scowl on his face. And I know it's gonna be a problem. He sits in the chair directly across from me. I glance around the room. There are two empty seats where Aesop sits. And there's an empty chair down at the other end of the table where Kenny sits. Yet, he purposefully wishes to mess with me.

"Yo, you need to take ya soft-ass somewhere else. I'm not tryna look in ya face while I eat."

For some reason, Ja'Meer's brother comes to mind. An image of him jumping over that bridge flashes through my mind. This bothers me.

Then go take your bully behind somewhere else and sit. I'm about sick of you.

I stare him down without blinking.

"Don't sit there starin' at me, pussy. Get ya punk-ass up and go sit somewhere else."

The tables around us start to get quiet. I can feel all eyes on me. A hundred sets of them, watching and waiting. I glance around the room, partially to see who exactly is looking at us while hoping one of the counselor aides is paying attention to this situation and intervenes before it starts to unfold.

I run a list of the dos and don'ts I have been taught in my head. *Don't ever bully anyone. But don't you ever let anyone bully you, either. Karate is about discipline. Use it only when necessary. A true martial artist avoids unnecessary conflicts by all means necessary...you protect yourself when you need to, but don't go looking for trouble. Try to resolve your conflicts without the use of violence. Be a warrior, fight for a cause.*

I have always gone about the business of going to school, excelling in classes, and avoiding trouble. But here, with kids like The Bully, it is almost impossible. Misery loves company. Yet, no matter how many times I try not to entertain it, it doesn't, won't, take no for an answer.

He sneers. "You'se a real bitch-ass nigga."

I sit stone still, almost mannequin-like, before I take a deep breath. I am sick of this boy. Sick of his bullying and slick comments. Sick of him walking around here like he's King Kick-Ass. Sick of him thinking he can do and say whatever he wants. Sick of him thinking that I am afraid of him. Yet, as bad as I want to shut him up one good time, I don't want problems. I simply want to do my time here, and get the heck out of here, unscathed. I want to go home!

Still, this is where I sit. I make a conscious choice to not budge. Any other time I would get up. Silently walk away. But tonight I do not feel like walking away. I am tired of walking—no, running—away from him. If a fight is what he is looking for, then I will happily oblige. I will give his miserable butt the entertainment he's been looking for. But I will not, I refuse to, throw the first punch.

I narrow my eyes at him.

He gets up from his seat, plants his hands, palms down, on the table and leans up in my face. "I said. Get. The. Fuck. Up."

I keep my eyes locked on his, unblinking. Take another deep breath, and steady my nerves. I was not raised to be disrespectful or to look for trouble. I was taught to treat people how I want to be treated. To learn how to pick and choose what my battles were going to be.

I hear Ja'Meer saying, "Yo, if that nigga ever fucks with you, let me know. I got you. I can't stand that muhfucka."

I blink.

"My brother killed himself."

I blink again. This is not really worth my energy. He is not worth it. Still, it's the principle. He can't think it's cool to mess with me. If I don't stand up for myself, he will continue to think he can intimidate me. And I've had enough.

"Pussy, did you hear what the fuck I said?"

"Don't ever let anyone put their hands on you. Protect yourself."

I imagine Ja'Meer saying, "Yo, Green Eyes, fuck his ass up. Break that nigga's ass...I got you."

I swallow.

I can tell not getting up has made him look like a bigger fool than he already is. I know he will have to save face. And I am worried about what I might do if he hits me. Right now, I do not see him. It is not his voice I hear. I hear and see my father. I hear *him* yelling at Mom. I see *him* choking her. I am very afraid. And Lenny should be, too.

My breathing becomes heavy. My nostrils begin to flare. I am grinding my teeth, forcefully pressing them together to the point that I feel like they will pulverize down to my gums. I start counting backward, starting at fifty—my conscious attempt to keep myself from exploding.

"What the fuck you wanna do, *pussy*? Where's ya lil bodyguard now, punk-ass nigga? You want me to smack the shit outta you?

Better yet, how 'bout I smack my dick in ya mom's mouth, then ram it in her ass?"

Everything around me goes blank. He's disrespected my mom. And no one does that. I am no longer concerned about him hitting me first or about consequences that may follow. I am becoming someone else. And it is not my body that leaps up from the table. And it isn't my fist that punches him in his mouth, then follows it with a right hook to his nose. I am my father. He is my father. And I am fighting them both—him and my father. I punch him again as he falls backward, seemingly startled and surprised that I have hit him. Not once, not twice, but three times. Each blow more intense. He tries to regain himself and fight back, but I am light on my feet and quicker than he anticipated.

He's awakened a beast that had lain dormant. One I have kept buried deep inside of me—until now. I don't remember exactly when he hit the floor. Was it after the fifth punch or before it? Don't remember how long I stomp and punch him mercilessly, taking out on him eight months of pent-up anger and frustration that have nothing—and everything—to do with him. I beat him until I am being restrained by four aides and he is being carried out on a stretcher.

Thirty-Four

t is early morning. 8 A.M. I don't know why, but I am standing outside Dr. Curtis's office, leaning up against the wall, waiting for him. He doesn't seem surprised to see me when he finally approaches his office. Instead, he smiles, shaking my hand as he says, "Come in." I follow behind him to his office. He flips on his light. "Have a seat."

He removes his suit jacket, then takes a seat across from me. He doesn't grab a pen or pad; it dawns on me he never does. He studies me, patiently. And I can kinda see why my mom liked going to him. I can tell he's easy to talk to, even if I haven't said two words to him, yet.

The silence between us is starting to make me uncomfortable and I wonder if I made a mistake coming here. I wonder why I didn't go to Mrs. Morgan's office instead. Try to figure out why I am really sitting here. Then it dawns on me. And it must dawn on him as he sits back in his chair and says, "Let's talk."

He knows that I am ready.

I swallow.

"How about you start wherever you feel most comfortable, in the middle, at the beginning, toward the end, it doesn't matter. Take a deep breath, and tell me how it happened."

I am not sure if he is talking about the fight with Lenny, or the stabbing, but I say, "He wouldn't…" My voice sounds foreign to me. I shift in my seat as I break out into a sweat. I can feel it rolling down my armpits and back. I wonder if I've forgotten to put on deodorant. Slowly, the words start spilling outta my mouth, then I am rambling nonstop. "I-I...got sick of him bothering me. Always saying things under his breath and staring me down and purposefully bumping into me. He wouldn't stop. Every time I turned around, he'd find a way to start with me. And every time I kept ignoring him, kept tryna avoid him, but that wasn't good enough. He still had to bother me. I wanted to hurt him. And I wanted to stomp him. And break every bone in his body. I didn't snap, and I didn't lose it. I made a choice to fight him when he said he was gonna do disrespectful stuff to my mom. That was it. And yes, I could have told somebody, but I had to handle this my way. I had to." I stop for air, taking a deep breath.

Dr. Curtis sits with his back straight, his ankle resting on his knee. I glance at his designer shoe, then at him. Everything about him, the way he dresses, reminds me that he should be on the cover of a magazine instead of sitting here. He folds his hands in his lap. "Do you regret what happened?"

Again, I'm not sure which situation he is talking about. I shake my head. Tell him I do not regret doing what I did. That he got what he asked for. That he deserved it. That maybe now he'll learn that he can't go around bullying other kids. "I didn't wanna fight him. But I don't feel bad that I did. I knew what I was doing. And I knew what my intentions were. To hurt him, physically."

"Like when you stabbed your father?"

My eyes widen. I am surprised by his question, clearly not prepared for it. But I won't lie. I am aware of my truths. I nod. "Yes. I wanted to hurt him. Both of them."

He nods, knowingly. "Would you like to talk about your father?"

I cringe, shaking my head.

"Are you ready to talk about your nightmares?"

The last thing I wanna do is awaken those night demons. "No."

"Okay, then. We don't have to talk about that either. Not today. But as I told you the other day, it's time to face your fears. Did you have a nightmare last night?" I tell him no. He wants to know when the last time I had one. I think for a moment, then tell him two nights ago. "Do you remember what it was about?"

I nod, swallowing back the memory. There was blood everywhere. On the walls, all over the floor, I was soaked in it. The knife was in my hand.

"Is it a recurring dream?" I give him a confused look. "Is it a dream that you have frequently?"

I know what he is doing. Trying to get me talk about my dreams, even though I told him I didn't want to. I shift my eyes.

"I'll tell you what. Let's talk about you."

I fidget with the sleeve of my shirt. *You know all you need to know about me.* I don't wanna talk about me. And I don't wanna talk about *him*. I don't wanna talk about my nightmares. But, I have all of these questions swarming around in my head, like buzzing bees.

"K'wan, I know Mrs. Morgan has discussed with you our plan to start incorporating family sessions into your treatment plan. I'm sure you have lots of questions you'd like to have answered." He eyes me as if he already knows this. "Has Mrs. Morgan discussed with you how we've decided to work these sessions with you and your parents out?"

I shake my head.

"Your sessions with your mom will be with Mrs. Morgan. And the ones you have with your father will be with me. How does that sound?"

I shrug. "I don't wanna talk to him."

He nods, knowingly. "That's understandable given all that's happened. But it's something that has to happen. So there's no sense in prolonging the inevitable. I believe these sessions are extremely important to your healing."

"I'm not talking to him."

"That's fine. Then you can listen. Your father has a lot that he wants, needs, for you to hear. He wants to talk to you. You owe it to yourself to at least hear him out."

It's probably gonna be all lies, anyway, so who cares what he has to say. It's still not gonna change anything. He's a woman beater. And I hate him!

I feel myself getting angry. "Why did she have to let him abuse her?"

"No woman wants to be abused. On the outside looking in, it may appear that that is what she was doing—letting your father abuse her. She wasn't. It might look as if she tolerated the abuse, but she didn't. Your mother, like so many other women, had to formulate a plan in her mind, she had to weigh risk factors, and she needed to develop protective strategies that would not only help her survive in such a volatile situation, but also protect her and you and your brothers. And that sometimes meant having to minimize or deny the abuse for fear of making things worse. Sometimes that might have been to comply with or attempt to placate your father. And when there are threats—to harm and/or kill—sometimes a woman's decision to stay or leave is heavily impacted by that fear."

"Why did she take him back? Why couldn't she keep him out of the house?"

Dr. Curtis rubs his chin. "Those are questions you should ask your mother. She can best answer them for you."

I frown. "But you were her therapist, so you should know why."

"You're correct. I was her therapist. And I still am."

"Isn't this like a conflict of interest then?"

He looks thoughtfully at me. "Not unless you want it to be. But if you are uncomfortable knowing that I am still seeing your mother in counseling, then you can refuse to see me at any time. My job right now is to help you work through your nightmares, and hopefully help shed some light on those things that might not make sense to you. I know your mother spoke to you about her conversation with me. And I know you are aware that she has, in fact, given me written and verbal consent to share with you her counseling journey."

"Then tell me why she took him back!" He doesn't seem bothered at the fact that I have raised my voice at him. I apologize to him.

He gives me a head nod. "It's fine. You've been holding a lot in." He shifts in his seat. "K'wan, women stay in abusive relationships and they go back to them for many different reasons. It's all very personal and, oftentimes, an extremely painful choice. Fear is what usually keeps women stuck in abusive situations or going back to them. The fear of being alone, fear of not being able to make it on their own, fear of losing their children, fear of what others will think, and the list goes on. If you'd like me to tell you generally why women take abusers back, I'd be more than happy to do so. But to speak specifically about your mother's reasons, I'd prefer you'd ask her; preferably during your family session with her. In all fairness to you, I will say this. Your mother's choice to reconcile with your father was a very difficult decision for her to make. But it was something she had to do for her."

"Seems like you do whatever the hell that damn therapist of yours tells you to do."

I eye him. "Did you tell her to go back?"

"I'm not in the business of telling any of my patients what to do," he says, evenly. "So to answer your question, no. I encouraged your mother to not do anything based on emotion. To make her decisions based on objectivity. To simply trust her gut."

"Do you think that's what she did…trusted her gut?" I already know the answer, but I ask anyway.

Pieces of her letter to me swirl around in my head. *I thought letting your father move back home was what was best for all of us. In my heart, letting your father back home wasn't about you or your brothers. It was about me.*

He looks thoughtfully at me as is if he is trying to choose his words carefully. He gives me a saddened look. "I believe she trusted her heart."

Thirty-five

"**D**aaaaaaaaaaaaaaaaaaamn, yo. He shut my nigga Len's lights out…You see that nigga, Len, get knocked the fuck out? Yo, word is bond, that lil nigga slid his ass…he had the nigga dazed! That's what his ass gets for always poppin' shit."

This is the excitement around here over the last week—me punching out The Bully. Truth is now I feel really bad about doing it, even if he did deserve it. Now that I've thought about it more, I guess I really could have handled that situation differently. But I also know that I didn't want to. At that moment when he got in my face, I felt like I owed it to him. I owed it to Ja'Meer's brother and anyone else who's been bullied by someone to shut his mouth for once and for all. I felt like he asked for it, so I gave it to him.

I hear he has a busted lip and broken nose. Hopefully, I won't have to worry about him bothering me. Now all of a sudden, guys who barely spoke to me, or were giving me the screw face now wanna speak. But I don't acknowledge them. I don't like people like that.

Fighting usually gets you kicked out of here, but for some reason, I am still here. I think a lot of the staff spoke up on my behalf. Told the treatment team how Lenny kept antagonizing me. But everyone already knew he was a bully. They were wondering when someone was going to finally, as the kids here say, "Take it to his head."

My only consequence for knocking him out and breaking his nose is a loss of rec privileges for two weeks. That doesn't bother me since I barely go to rec anyway.

Lenny had to go to the medical unit overnight, then got sent back to his county's detention center. That's where he is now, back sitting in detention. But I overheard someone saying he might be able to come back. It doesn't bother me if he does; I don't have a problem with him. He had it with me. Hopefully now it's solved.

I walk into the cafeteria feeling like everyone is watching me and whispering. I know they're really not, but my overactive imagination is once again getting the best of me. This place isn't a psychiatric hospital or anything, but sometimes I look at some of these residents here and listen to some of their conversations and swear I am hearing cuckoo clocks ringing. This is a treatment facility for behavioral issues, but I swear sometimes it feels like a loony bin.

Tonight they are serving baked chicken, mashed potatoes and gravy, string beans and cornbread. I take two chocolate milks, then glance around the room for someplace to sit; preferably away from anyone who is trouble. I find a seat at an empty table in a corner, next to one of the counselor's desks. Nobody wants to sit next to the counselor's desk. But it doesn't bother me. Since my fight with Lenny, they now have three counselor's aides in here at all times. Not that I think it'll matter. If someone wants to fight, they're going to do it anyway.

I sit and pick at my potatoes. I don't like legs or thighs, so I won't eat the chicken. I eat the string beans, then drink the two cartons of milk, looking around to see if I spot Ja'Meer in case he wants the rest of my food. I don't see him.

"Hey, man, I know you don't talk." I glance up and it's Jarrod.

"I gotta say I didn't think you had it in you, but you really did Lenny's ass up right; that's wassup."

I blink. This guy has said nothing to me the whole time I've been here. Close to three months. Yet he's standing here now tryna make small talk with me about a fight I had with someone I really didn't wanna fight in the first place.

"I hear you're real good at chess. Maybe we can play a few rounds one of these days; maybe tonight, if you want."

I nod, but I have no intention of playing with him. I can't even if I wanted to. I am still on loss of rec privilege for the next week. He must not have gotten the memo.

"Cool. Aiight, I'm out." I watch him as he walks off, then bring my attention back to my picked over plate, wondering if they ever recycle any of this food. A few minutes later I look up from my plate, glancing around the room. I spot Ja'Meer over at the salad bar. He catches my eye, giving me a head nod. It doesn't take him long to make his way over to the table, carrying a tray with two pieces of chicken on it.

"Wassup, Green Eyes? I know you not gonna throw that chicken out. Let me get it, man."

I smile, sliding him my tray. He scoops off the chicken, placing the plate back on my tray. "Man, this here is good eating. You really don't know what you're missing."

I sit back in my seat, and watch him as he shovels food in his mouth, wondering if he grew up not having food in his house.

"So you up for a game of chess? Oh, wait. You're still on that loss of rec shit, right?"

I nod.

He laughs, shaking his head. "That's the dumbest shit. You get in trouble for that bum-ass nigga getting up in your face. Makes no damn sense. But, I guess it's good for you 'cause now you don't have to worry about the butt-whoopin' I was gonna put on you tonight."

I smirk at him. *He'll never learn.*

I get up to leave. "Let me guess. You're going to the room to study."

I nod.

"Man, your brain's gonna explode from all that learning. You need to kick back and do nothing sometime."

Yeah, okay. Doing nothing isn't what's going to get me into Yale or Harvard. I walk off carrying my tray over to the trash. I spend the rest of the night studying and doing Calculus homework, then reading *Monster*. It's a story about a sixteen-year-old kid who is accused of being a lookout for a four-person drugstore robbery where the owner is shot and killed. Even though he wasn't even in the store when the owner was killed, he sits in jail during the trial while the prosecutor paints him out to be a monster. So far it's a really good book. Well, I'm only on page fifteen, but I like it so far. I like when he says in the beginning, "The best time to cry is at night, when the lights are out and someone is being beaten up and screaming for help. That way, even if you sniffle a little, they won't hear you." That right there is what hooked me to read more. I can relate to him in some ways; especially when he talks about looking in the mirror and seeing a face looking back at him that doesn't look like him, wondering if he will ever look like himself again.

Wow.

I read another thirty pages of the book, then close it.

That's what he was, a monster! I don't know if I'll ever forgive him for that.

For some reason I get up and search through the jeans I had on the night Kyle and Grandma Ellen came to visit me with him. I dig into the back pocket until I retrieve what I am looking for. I almost forgot I had it. The letter from Tabitha. I open it and catch a faint whiff of perfume lingering on the pages. I put it up to my nose and inhale, then open up the one page letter.

Hi, Big Head—

When are you going to get out of that place? Everyone at school misses you. Even me, Yuck! But it's true. You know, if you stay gone too long, I'm going to end up having the highest GPA in our freshman class; technically, I already do since you're not here. Ha! Told you I'd jump ahead of you. So what if it's only by default. Anyway, what is it like in there? Are they treating you nice? Are there a bunch of violent kids there with you? Are you scared? I don't know, like I have these crazy dreams that you're in there fighting for your life. But I know you can handle yourself with all that kung fu you do. Hahaha!

Kyle told me you like me. Is that true, K'wan? Do you like me? You probably wanna kiss me, too, right? Well, if you wanna be my boyfriend, you better write me back, or else it's your loss. Hahaha! lbvs!

Okay, gotta go. I have to get ready for dance rehearsal. TTYL! You better write me back, Big Head. With your ugly self. Hahaha! Sike!

Tabitha

I fold the letter back, put it to my nose again, then go to place it back into its envelope. A small picture falls out. It is a picture of her in her tights standing in some kinda ballet pose. She looks really pretty. I stare at the picture, smiling. *She wants to know if I like her.*

⊕

"So do you like her, man?" Ja'Meer asks as he hands me back the letter. I don't know why I showed him, but I did. No. I know why I did it. Because I have no one else here to share it with besides him, and I trust him.

I shrug.

He gives me an incredulous look. "Man, you better hop on shorty 'fore someone else does." I show him the picture. "Oh, shiiiiiit, hell yeah, you better snatch her fine-ass up. Man, you crazy. You better stop the dumb shit and start talkin', yo. She's lookin' all kinda sexy in them tights, man."

I smile, snatching the picture outta his hand when he tries to stick it into his front pocket. He bursts out laughing. And for the first time, I am laughing, too. Then he gets serious. "Yo, keep it a hunnid, you ever smash?"

I frown, giving him a confused look.

"You know, rock them sheets with a chick; have sex?"

I blink back my embarrassment.

"Oh, damn. You still a virgin, huh?"

I shift my eyes.

"Yo, it's all good. Don't rush that shit, ya heard? Sex is over-rated anyway. Chicks start buggin' once you hit 'em real good with the sausage. So you better off not goin' there. Trust me."

Sausage?

I blink.

I never really thought about sex. I mean, I have. But not like about having it, not right now. And I don't think I'd wanna be with a girl who was fast, either. I don't wanna rush into anything and get a disease or have kids. I'm still a kid. I don't think Tabitha's like that, all fast and nasty and whatnot. At least, I hope she's not. I don't know if I even like her like that—like a girlfriend. But if I did, I wouldn't want her to be like that.

Anyway, I can't even think about stuff like that right now. I'm not even allowed to date for two more years, so what's the point?

Besides, hearing all those stories in group with how their girls turn all crazy, and now hearing Ja'Meer say it, makes me wanna never have sex.

"I'm telling you, man," he continues, flopping back onto his bed, "stick to masturbation for as long as you can. Whack that shit off, bust off and keep it movin'. It'll cut down on the stress in your life."

I frown. *This guy is kinda nasty.*

"Yo, let me see that honey's pic, again," he says, sitting up. "I'ma need to handle some thangs in the bathroom later."

I blink, regretting I ever showed him her picture.

He cracks up. "Yo, Green Eyes, I'm fuckin' with you, man. I wouldn't do you like that. You my peeps. But anyone else, I'd be schemin' on tryna get in them drawers."

"Do you like me?"

Not if you're having sex, I think, quickly tucking her letter under my mattress while Ja'Meer's not looking. I don't want him touching his sausage or anything else, reading her letter or looking at her picture. The thought makes me wanna throw up. Nasty!

I grab *Monster* and go back to reading about the life of Steve Harmon. Even if it's only for a brief moment, I don't have to worry about my own for a while.

Thirty-Six

I am walking the hall, listening to my sneakers squeak and squeal against the white, waxed floor as I make my way to Mrs. Morgan's office. Today is my IPC. And as much as I find her interesting to look at, I don't feel like listening to her; not today. I want to turn around and go back to bed. I am exhausted. I tossed and turned all night. My mom was dead, again. But this time she was dressed in all white. And she had a black eye. Her lip was busted. Her arms were open. She wanted to hug me, and I tried to run away from her, but she grabbed me and held me close to her, telling me over and over and over, "Your father killed me."

She was crying and apologizing over and over for letting him take her from us—my brothers and me. She told me he had beaten her to death. And I believed her. Believed it. The dream, no, the nightmare; it was real. All I could do was cry. He had finally done what he said he would. Kill her. My brothers were missing. I remember running through these woods looking for them, calling out their names. It was dark and raining. And I was screaming at the top of my lungs for God to help me. He didn't.

When I opened my eyes, Ja'Meer was standing over me, shaking me. I feel really bad for waking him. He said I was groaning. Said I was yelling, then mumbling. I am always afraid to know what it is I am saying or doing before he wakes me. Last night, all I could do was jump up out of bed and run into the bathroom, lock myself in and cry until I couldn't cry anymore. When I came out he was sitting up waiting for me, wanting to talk. So I listened to him.

"Yo, for real, man, you gotta talk that shit out. I mean, like damn. Something's really eating you up. And it's not good." He shook his head, staring at me. I shifted my swollen eyes. "Damn, man. You can trust me, yo. All you gotta do is talk, man. I promise you, it'll make you feel better. Maybe it won't change shit, but at least you don't have to walk around carryin' all that shit by ya'self; feel me?"

I nodded.

He continued, "I really feel bad for you, Green Eyes. I wish there was something I could do, but this is something you gotta work through on your own, man. Just talk to me, yo. I promise, man, whatever it is botherin' you, I ain't gonna put ya business out there like that. You already know I don't fuck wit' nobody in here like that, anyway. But, for real, K-man, you need to talk to your counselor, today, aiight?"

I nodded, then waited for him to go into the bathroom to take his shower and crawled back into bed, burying myself underneath the sheets.

Then while everyone was having breakfast, I went to the payphones and called home. I had to hear her voice. Had to know she was okay. Even if I'm not speaking to her, I still worry about her. I'm still scared for her. But no one answered. So now, I am frightened even more. What if something's happened to my brothers, too? What if he killed them, too?

I take a deep breath and try to think positive thoughts. That she is okay. That he hasn't done anything to hurt her. That my brothers are okay; that they are unharmed. But it doesn't take much for my thoughts to take a turn for the worse. What if running out of visits pissed him off? What if he blames her for me not talking to him and takes it out on them? What if he shoots her in front of my brothers, like this kid Aaron's father did his mom? Shot her in the face with a shotgun in front of his two sisters and brother, then he turned the gun on himself. But what if he turns it on my brothers first, then himself. I keep having dreams that I will be all alone. I couldn't live with that. It would all be my fault; something else to add to my list of blames.

Before I know it, I am standing in the doorway of Mrs. Morgan's office. My mouth drops open.

"Come in," she says, waving me in. She offers a smile. But my feet are stuck beneath me. My mom is here. And I am surprised. And mad that Mrs. Morgan didn't tell me—warn me—at least, that she'd be here today. *Did someone call her? Is she here because of what I did at visits?*

My mom smiles at me, getting up from her seat. I am happy to see her. Happy to know that she is safe. I steady myself, then walk through the door. And without any thought, I rush into her arms and hug her tightly. She holds me like she used to when I would wake up from a really bad dream. Something inside of me relaxes, then breaks open. And I am crying. I know boys aren't supposed to cry. Tears are for punks and sissies; that's what these kids here say. That's what *he* used to say, that's what Mom used to say—not that I was a sissy or punk, but that big boys don't cry. But I do not care. I do not feel any less than I already am. I am not a punk or a sissy; I am alone and sad.

"Oh, sweetheart," Mom says, rubbing my back. "It's okay, baby. Mommy's here." My shoulders shake. I am overcome with emotion. It is the first time I have cried like this—since that night—the night I stabbed *him*. The night I thought my mom was dead.

She holds me and rubs my back and lets me cry until I get it all out. She hums and, for a minute, I forget that someone else is in the room. It is just my mom and me. Mrs. Morgan doesn't say anything. She lets her comfort me. And I breathe in her scent, peaches and vanilla, and realize how much I miss her. How much I miss home. And, right here, for the briefest moment, I feel human again—alive.

When I have stopped crying, Mom steps back, holding my face in her warm hands. "K'wan, baby. I am so sorry, sweetheart. You are loved very, very much. Don't you ever forget that, okay, baby. Promise me."

I nod.

Mrs. Morgan pushes a box of tissue over to us. "Thank you," Mom says, pulling out sheets of tissue and handing them to me. I wipe my face and blow my nose, reaching for more. Mrs. Morgan waits for me to get myself together, then asks me to have a seat. I do. Mom reaches over and grabs my hand.

"K'wan, I called your mother and asked her to come to your session today because I think it's time. I have discussed it with the treatment team, and they also believe it's time to begin your family sessions. I also spoke to Dr. Curtis and he shared with me your breakthrough in session with him. So we feel that is time for you to confront your fears. I would have liked to have told you, first, about today's session. But after seeing you last session, I had decided against it." I frown. "I knew you wouldn't come if I had told you." She smiles at me. "Now would you?"

I lower my head, then push out, "No."

My mom's hand flies up to her mouth in shock. "Ohmygod, K'wan, sweetheart, you're talking. Oh, this is so great, honey. When?" She looks over at Mrs. Morgan.

She simply says, "When he was ready."

"Yes," she says, nodding and smiling. "When he was ready. I knew you'd eventually come around. All we had to do is keep praying and waiting. Stay patient. God heard me. He answered my prayers."

Mrs. Morgan glances over at me. Today she isn't wearing loud colors or wearing a buncha heavy bright makeup. She looks like a professional. She looks really nice. She smiles at me and I smile back. "Are you ready to talk to your mom, K'wan?"

I nod. I feel my throat and chest tightening. I am afraid no words will come out.

Mom squeezes my hand. "It's alright, sweetheart. I have so much to tell you. So much I've wanted to say to you."

My heartbeat speeds up. A part of me is scared of what I might hear. I'm afraid of hearing that she's dropped the restraining order, again. That she wants him to move back home again. That I can't ever come home because she's chosen him over me, the way some of these kids say their mothers have done with them. Chosen their men over their kids.

"Mrs. Taylor, let's start with you looking at your son and telling him everything you feel. K'wan, I want you to look at your mother and give her your undivided attention. Can you do that for me?"

I nod.

She smiles. "Mrs. Taylor, what would you like to say to K'wan?"

"First, I want to tell him how sorry I am for everything's that happened. Then I want him to know how much he is loved and missed."

"Then tell him."

My mom reaches for my hand. She shifts her body and chair so that she is facing me. She repeats it to me, getting emotional. She dabs at her eyes. "K'wan, sweetheart, from the moment the doctor laid you in my arms, I always knew there was something remarkably special about you. You were my beautiful baby boy, who I knew would one day grow into a handsome young man. And I have prayed and prayed that my choices, staying with your father and taking him back..."

I hold my breath, waiting for the worst. I shift my eyes.

"K'wan," Mrs. Morgan says. "I want you to try to keep your eyes on your mother, okay?"

I look back at her.

"None of this is your fault, sweetheart. None of it. Not a day goes by that I am not missing you. This is killing me. I feel so very sad that you are here, instead of home with your family. I am so sorry for putting you through all of this, for putting your brothers and myself through all of this. None of you deserved this. I am working on forgiving me for my choices, and I am working on forgiving your father for his. Not because I am letting him off the hook for what he has done to his family, or for all I have allowed him to do to me, but because I am letting go of him. Forgiving your father and forgiving myself allows me to move forward in my own healing. I only hope you can find forgiveness in your heart for your father and me. And forgiveness for yourself."

I blink, then swallow. I do not know if I can forgive. Do not know if it is in me. But I don't like seeing my mom like this.

"I know you blame yourself, sweetheart." She pauses, attempts to contain her tears. But they fall, slowly at first. But then they erupt into a heavy sob. I have never seen my mom cry like this. "None of this...is...your...fault...Oh, God...I am so...sorry, K'wan...I know you're angry with me. I'm angry with me..."

Her crying tugs at my heart, and I find myself trying to hold back my own tears. But they fall as well. I am not sure if my tears are for her, for me, or for the both of us. I just know that she is hurting. And I am hurting, too. I reach over and hug her. And, for the rest of the session, we sit hugging each other, crying. She hugs me tightly to her chest, rocking me in her arms. "I love you so much, sweetheart."

Finally, I look up at her, seeing my reflection in her wet eyes. And for the first time, I am not seeing a potential abuser. I am seeing her son. I am not seeing black eyes or bruises around her neck. I am seeing my mom. I am seeing everything good about her, and about me. I am seeing her love. I hug her tightly and whisper, "I love you, too, Mom."

Thirty-Seven

After seeing my mom with Mrs. Morgan the other day and crying with her, I feel…drained. That word *cathartic* comes to mind. But it was overwhelming for me. It still is. I am trying hard to take everything without being angry or blaming. It's hard. I have another session with her today, and then my first session with *him* tomorrow. So I am having sessions back to back this week. And honestly, this is the first time that I wish that I was going to be in group instead. I'd rather be sitting in a circle with a buncha guys I don't feel any connection to than to have to face *him*.

I walk into the bathroom, brush my teeth and wash my face, then finish getting dressed. Today I wish I could wear one of my favorite fitted caps. But hats aren't allowed to be worn here. Still, a hat would be nice. I need a haircut. I avoid looking in the mirror any longer than I have to. I quickly make my bed, then head out the door.

Mom is already sitting in Mrs. Morgan's office. She stands up and gives me a big hug when I walk in. I hug her back. "Hi, baby."

"Hi," I say back in almost a whisper.

"Hello, K'wan," Mrs. Morgan says, smiling. I say hello back. Again, she isn't dressed in anything loud or crazy. I wonder if she only dresses like that when she isn't seeing parents. I toss the idea. She doesn't seem like someone who'd care either way.

I am surprised when she gets up from her desk and wants to

make a little circle—well, it's more like a triangle, with the three of us.

I am still not sure what to expect, but I am happy to see my mom. "K'wan, is there something you'd like to say to your mother?"

I shake my head. "No." Mom reaches for my hand and, for some reason, my heart skips three beats.

Mrs. Morgan nods. "Let's talk about that night."

I feel the blood rush from my head.

"Are you comfortable with talking about the night this all happened?" Mrs. Morgan wants to know.

I shake my head, holding my breath.

Mom says, "K'wan, we have to talk about what happened. Too much time has gone by. We can't let any more go by without talking about it."

I feel lightheaded.

"I don't want to."

"Then let me talk about it, okay?"

I swallow, then slowly nod my head.

"That night," she starts, then pauses, closing her eyes. She takes a deep breath. "Your father had come home from work late. I had been waiting all day on pins and needles. He knew I wanted to talk to him, but that night he deliberately got home after ten, thinking I would already be in bed. But I wasn't. I was downstairs waiting for him. I had checked in on you and your brothers and you all were sleep. At least I thought, hoped, you all were."

I shift in my seat.

"I heard your father go into the kitchen and I came up from the family room. I told him I wanted a divorce."

I blink, shocked to hear this.

"I had let your father back home, but started noticing things that didn't feel right to me. He hadn't changed. He had stopped his abusive behaviors just long enough to get back in the home. I was still going to see Dr. Curtis every week, working on a safety plan. I had already contacted a divorce attorney and had the papers in hand when I confronted him. He threw the papers in my face and said he wasn't going to sign them.

"I told him that I was still divorcing him whether he signed them or not. That I wanted out of our marriage and wanted him to move out. That's when he slapped me..." Her voice trails off. "I loved your father, but not in the way I needed to stay married to him. I was different. He was not. There were plenty of nights that I didn't sleep in the same bed with him. I wanted out, and I wanted him out."

Her eyes are filled with tears.

"Why'd you take him back?" I ask, holding back my own tears.

"Because I wanted to believe he had changed. I wanted to believe our marriage still had a chance. And that we could still be this happy family. I wasn't ready to give up on my marriage, or him. But it was all a lie, my lie. And his. And for almost two years I tried to live in it, pretending that everything would fall into place. But it didn't. And I got tired of pretending; pretending for him, pretending for me, pretending for your grandma Liz. It was draining. After a year into him moving back home, I realized I wasn't happy. That that wasn't what I wanted, but I allowed him to convince me to keep giving it a chance.

"We went to a few sessions of marital counseling. But it was too late for that. I was done. So earlier that day, I picked up my divorce papers, then gave them to him when he got home. I didn't expect him to hit me. Didn't expect him to choke me and try to strangle me. If I would have thought that, I would have called the police and had him removed. Everything that night happened so fast."

She bursts in tears. "I-I...remember thinking, *Oh, God, my sons are going to find me dead in the morning.* I tried to fight him off of me, but he was too strong for me. I remember seeing it in his eyes...he was really going to kill me and there was nothing I could do.

"I-I-I couldn't scream. All I heard was him saying over and over how he would never let me leave him. I had never seen your father like that, like he was possessed or something."

I take a deep breath, wiping my own tears. "I knew," I say, getting choked up. "I knew something wasn't right. I always knew when something wasn't right. That night I had a bad dream and woke up. I knew...I saw him over you, shaking you, his hands around your neck...and I-I-I..." I break down. I have not once cried about stabbing him, only about him trying to kill my mom. Talking it out in my head, repeating to myself is one thing. But to actually say it, to actually replay that night word by word, moment by moment, is a different story. "I kept stabbing and stabbing and stabbing him until he let you go, but I couldn't stop. I didn't wanna stop. I. Wanted. Him...dead for hurting you."

"I'm so sorry," she sobs, reaching for me. She pulls me into her. "Not a day goes by that I am not regretting taking him back. I have beaten myself up over and over again, thinking that maybe if I would have done things differently that maybe things would have turned out different, but in my heart, I know it would have probably been the same outcome, only worse. He would have killed me."

"I know." I sob onto her shoulder. "I'm not sorry for stabbing him. I'm not sorry for wanting him dead."

My mom's sobs turn into wails. And my heart aches. "You have to try to forgive him, sweetheart. Please. You have to try to let it go, your hatred, your anger. Please, sweetheart. Can you try to do that for me?"

I am exhausted. I am drained. But there's a part of me that feels relieved. I look my mom in her eyes and say, "I don't know if I can."

🌐

"Okay, K'wan," Dr. Curtis says the following morning. "Are you ready to get started?"

I shrug, cutting my eye over at *him*. He is sitting in a chair across from me, a foot or so away from Dr. Curtis. They are the base, and I am the point in our triangle. I am the focal point. I feel like I am sitting under a thousand spotlights.

He speaks. "Hey, son."

I swallow. Do not acknowledge him, shifting my stare from his.

"I know you're upset with me..."

I shoot him a nasty look.

"Angry at me. I get it. I deserve it. But I am still your father. You are still my son. And I love you. And I am willing to do whatever I have to do to fix what I have damaged. It's not going to happen overnight, but I'm hoping you're willing to let me in. I hurt you, son. And there's nothing I can do to take back what I've already done. I'm hurting, too. I caused this—your pain, your mother's pain; my own pain. I have no one else to blame but myself."

I don't look at him. I am exhausted. I did not sleep much last night. Not because I was having bad dreams, again, but because my mind was racing, replaying everything in my head. I sat up all night and, for the first time, I was the one doing all of the talking. Ja'Meer was surprised and glad that I spoke.

"Oh, shit!" He jumped up, doing a two-step kinda move. "Look at you tryna get a deep voice. Aaah, shit. That's what it is." He gave me a pound, then a big hug. "It's about time you got ya mind right, muhfucka."

I cringed, not used to that kinda talk. But he laughed it off.

"Yo, you too damn preppy, Green Eyes. But, it's all good. I'ma school you as soon as we get outta here; real shit. We gonna hang, son. I know some bad bitches who I already know gonna wanna give you some hood pussy."

I blinked. And he started laughing again. "I'm only fuckin' with you, yo. But man, this is great. I knew ya lil ass would finally come around. I told my counselor you would start talkin. She knew it, too. Speakin' of which…"

I stopped him before he could say anything more. There was no need for him to apologize for saying anything to his counselor about my nightmares. Well, at least that's what I think he was going to tell me. That he was sorry for telling her. If he wasn't, he didn't say anything otherwise.

"Yo, real shit, Green Eyes. You had a muhfucka mad stressed about you. I kept beatin' my counselor in her head about you. Shit, I might wanna get me some degrees and be a counselor, too. I already told her I'm goin' back to school when I get outta here. I owe that shit to you, yo. Shit, I ain't no dumb-ass nigga, either, yo. I just don't let muhfuckas know what it really is wit' me. That shit ain't cool in the hood, yo."

I stared at Ja'Meer while he went on and on until he finally shut up and let me tell him about my session with my mom. And about the one I would be having today.

"Yo, for real. You feelin' some kinda way at your pops, but, he's still ya pops, no matter how you look at it. You should try to hear him out. Before you go cuttin' muhfuckas off, listen to what he has to say, first. Then decide. Fuck, we all make mistakes. No one's perfect. Your pops fucked up; tell him how you feel, then peace that shit up, yo. Ya moms is done with him, right?

"Yeah, cool. If he wanted to get at her, he woulda by now. Isn't he on probation?" I told him that he was on probation for five years. "Oh, shit…you good, then. Dude ain't tryna sit in prison. But he's a damn fool, if he is. Fuck, I'm stressin' just bein' up in this dip all this time. Yeah, you definitely need to work that shit out."

I tried picturing him as a counselor, with every other word a curse word, then shook the idea from my head. Then again, anything's possible.

"All I'm asking for is a chance, son," I hear him say, bringing me back to the session. I blink. Dr. Curtis is watching me as he keeps talking. "I'm so sorry for everything I put you and your brothers through. I am so sorry for everything I ever did or said to your mother. All the times I apologized to her in the past didn't mean anything because they weren't real. They were for that moment, but I still found ways to blame everyone else for everything I did.

"I swore to myself that I would never ever raise my hand to a woman, or ever put my kids through what I went through."

My eyes widen. *Is he saying what I think he is? Ohgod, please don't tell me…*

"My dad used to yell and scream and curse at your grandmother. He would make her cry, and I hated him for it. I'm so sick for being no different than him."

I feel lightheaded.

Abuse is generational. Abuse is learned behavior…

"Boys who witness domestic violence are twice as likely to abuse their own partners and children when they become adults."

I think I am going to be sick!

How could he do this?!

"I heard your grandmother beg and plead and scream for help. I saw her bruises." He lowers his head, and I think he is fighting back tears; maybe guilt, maybe both. "I swore I would never be him, and I turned out to be worse than he ever was." He tells me my grandma Ellen left my granddad three times and kept going back. That the last time she had left him, they stayed gone for almost a year before moving back home with him.

I blink. This is all too much for me to handle.

"The last time your grandmother went back, your grandfather swore he'd never put his hands on her again, and he didn't. He changed. I was thirteen when he stopped being abusive. But before that, I lived through twelve years of hell."

And you put me through almost twelve years of hell, too!

"The only thing I tried not to do that he did was hit your mother in front of you. Your grandfather would make me watch as he yelled and screamed at your grandmother. A few times he punched her in front of me, practically knocking her out. I hated him. The same way you hate me. And now I hate myself even more."

And you should! I cannot believe I am hearing all of this.

"I kept all of this a secret. I went through the rest of my teen years, pretending I had this perfect family. Then I went off to college and pretended I came from this wonderful life. And, I married your mother and pretended to be everything I was not. I had everyone fooled, including your grandma Liz. I charmed everyone in your mother's family. They all loved me and thought I was a loving husband and father. No one knew what I was like behind closed doors. And your mother pretended right along with me. It was our own little perfect world. But the only thing that was perfect in it was the lies, the ones I concocted and the ones your mother wanted to believe.

"You are nothing like me, K'wan. Nothing, do you hear me? You're better than me. You don't ever have to become me or your grandfather unless *you* choose to be. I abused your..."

I get up.

"...mother because..." I've heard enough. I open the door and walk out, leaving behind a trail of anger.

Thirty-Eight

am afraid of closing my eyes. If I close them, I am certain the
nightmares will find their way to me. I do not want to toss
and turn. Or thrash about in the middle of the night. So I
will wrestle with sleep for as long as I can. I will stay awake. And
I will try not to think. But what else can I do when all I have are
my thoughts?

My session with Dr. Curtis and him plays in my head. I don't
know why seeing him cry bothered me. But it did. I am more
confused now than I was before going into the session. At least
before I knew what I felt for him. Hate. There was no question,
no room for mistakes. But now...now I am not certain what I feel.

When I look into Mom's eyes, I see me. When I look into his
eyes, I see me. I am a culmination of the two. Wounded and lost.

I can't get over knowing Grandma Ellen was abused, too. And
that *he* witnessed it. I can't believe he kept it a secret.

"Silence is a batterer's best friend."

I am afraid that I will not find a balance. I am afraid that I may
end up worse than he was, the way he ended up worse than his
own father was.

"Abuse is a cycle."

I can't get the image of him crying out of my head. He seemed
pained and hurt and ashamed. He seemed remorseful. At least
that is what I hope. But why should I care?

I hold my head in my hands, running my hands back and forth over my head, trying to massage out the beginnings of a headache. *"Forgiveness isn't about him. It's about you. Forgiveness allows you the freedom and permission to heal and let go."*

"K'wan, how is staying angry at your father useful to you now?"
Shut up! Get out of my head!
Then answer the question!
Alright already! It's not! Staying angry with him is not useful to me.

"What are you going to do, be condemned to hate your father for the rest of your life? Who are you really punishing, him or you?"

I do not know what I am going to do. Ambivalence. That's one of those words Mrs. Morgan used in one of my sessions when I first came to Healing Souls. She said I was ambivalent. I remember looking the word up, even though she had explained to me what it meant. Still I needed to see it for myself. "A state of having both positive and negative emotions, or having thoughts and actions in contradiction with each other." Like my feelings toward *him*. Mrs. Morgan said then she believed that deep down I still loved my father, but was so deeply hurt by the things that he had done that I had learned to hate him. That hating him would be easier than loving him because I wouldn't have to feel any guilt for feeling how I felt about him when he was hurting my mom.

I don't know what I feel anymore.
I don't know what I'm supposed to feel.
I don't wanna fall asleep, though. Dr. Curtis has been tryna help me rewrite, or *rescript* the endings to my nightmares. He says it's some kinda cognitive behavioral technique. He says it can help reduce the frequency of nightmares I have. I wanted to tell him that talking has already helped some. I'm still having them, and I can almost tell when they will come, when I spend too much time thinking or worrying about the past or about the future. I

am starting to believe Mrs. Morgan when she says guilt and worry are useless emotions. That they keep a person stuck. Because that is exactly how I feel—stuck.

Tonight if I were gonna go to sleep, I would change the ending of the nightmare with my mom dying. I wouldn't be standing at a tombstone with her name on it. There'd be no open ground. There'd be no casket. I wouldn't hear him saying he would kill her over and over and over in my head. Instead, he would be telling her how much he loves her. How much he loves us. My mom would be smiling and laughing and happy. I wouldn't be crying. Kyle wouldn't be crying. We'd be hugging Mom, not because she was being hurt or because we were afraid that she was dying, but simply because we were her children and she loved us. We would all feel safe, and be safe.

I get outta bed and sit at my desk, turning the desk lamp on. Ja'Meer is snoring, like he's wrestling wild boar. Lucky for me since I don't wanna fall asleep. I open the composition book and read the Ralph Emerson quote at the bottom of the page, again: "BE NOT THE SLAVE OF YOUR OWN PAST..."

Do you like me?

I tear out a sheet of paper, then pull out a pen and start writing:

Dear Tabitha,

Thanks for writing me. I'm okay, I guess. Things would be better if I were home. Sorry it took me so long to write back. No, I am not getting into a lot of fights here. I had one fight since I've been here. The kid was a real bully. And yes, I punched him out.

This place isn't that bad. At first I didn't wanna be here. But now I think I need to be here, at least for a while longer. So you can hold onto the number one freshman GPA spot for now, but don't get too comfortable because I am coming back to take it back. Hahaha!

Do I like you? Maybe, maybe not? Depends on some things. But I don't

wanna say in a letter. And no, has nothing to do with me kissing you.
Do you want me to kiss you? Anyway, ask me the question, again, when
I come home, okay?

Write back!

K'wan

I neatly fold it in two, place it inside of an envelope, then address
it. I'm not sure if I will actually mail it off, but it felt really nice
writing it. I stick it inside my composition book, closing it, then
shutting off the light. I've decided to go to sleep with positive
thoughts on my mind.

Thirty-Nine

"I hate you!"

At first I am not certain it is my voice that I hear. But when more words push out, this time with force and purpose, I know for sure. It is me. I am speaking. This is my third session with him. And it's the first time I am talking. I can tell that I have shocked him and Dr. Curtis.

"Why did you hit her? Why did you try to kill her?"

"I don't blame you for hating me," he says, painfully. "Every day that you're here, I hate me. I caused this. And if there was something, anything, I could do to take back all the hurt and pain that I caused you, your mom, and your brothers, I would. Not once, did I ever think about you or your brothers and how what I was doing to your mother was affecting you. I fucked up, K'wan. I really did, son. Sitting here, seeing how much hate you have toward me, it kills me."

"You haven't answered my question. Why. Did. You. Try to kill her?"

He holds his head in his hands. "That night your mother told me she wanted a divorce. And it took me by surprise. And I didn't want to let her go. I didn't want her to give up on us. I loved your mother. I still do."

"So you tried to kill her?! You tried to strangle her to death instead! How's that love?"

He gives me a pained look, then lowers his eyes. "It's not."

"Then how can you sit here and say you love her? I don't wanna be disrespectful to you, but I am angry at you. You make me sick. And I hate everything you stand for. Why couldn't you just let her go? Why did you have to destroy our family like that? Do you have any idea what you did to me? To us?"

He looks at me as if it he is seeing me for the first time. And in some ways he is. I'm not a little boy anymore. And I am not a man, yet. I am somewhere in the middle. And I am trying to learn how to balance the two worlds while trying to become my own person, one who is not angry and hurt and filled with hate toward him. But I do not know how. I do not know how to be his son and still be angry with him. I don't know how to let him be my father and still hate him. I don't know how to let go. And yet, I think that is what he sees. Me trying to find my way.

My chest heaves in and out.

"Truthfully, because I could and I thought I could get away with it. And for a long time, I did. I felt invincible. But, then your mother started changing. She started speaking up for herself and I started feeling like I was losing control over her." He looks over at Dr. Curtis. "I hated you. And I resented the fact that she was going to see you. You were giving her the freedom to think for herself. You were empowering her. Teaching her ways to be her own woman. And I saw her slipping through my fingers. I saw myself losing control over her. It was always about control. I had to keep her in line. That's what I thought." He looks back over to me. "Even when I realized that I was wrong, I always found a way to convince myself that I was right. That she was the problem. Your mother was never the problem. I was."

I blink.

"You were fucking selfish!" I scream at him, surprised that I have cursed at him. But I am angry. And I do not care. I want him to know what he did to me. I want him to feel what I've felt all these years. I want him to know what my anger is like. "I hate you because I was scared of you. I was scared of what you would do to Mom. You shut us out; didn't talk to us! When you ignored Mom, you ignored us, too. And I hate you for that!"

"I'm so sorry, son. I stayed in my own feelings. Shutting your mom out was another way I tried to control her. I knew the silence, making her invisible, hurt her more than anything else. But I felt that was better than putting my hands on her. I know it wasn't. Still, I did it, deliberately."

"Well, you're right. It wasn't. It was worse than you hitting her. I don't know how it made her feel. But it made me feel unimportant to you. It made me feel invisible to you, too. It made me sit up at night, waiting and wondering when you were going to explode. When you were going to beat up on her. You threatened to kill her. I heard you! That scared me! I heard you tell her that more than once. And I believed you would do it. Even when she tried to tell me you really didn't mean it. I knew you did. I felt it. And no matter how many times Mom tried to make me think otherwise, I know she felt it too. Fear. Why would you do that?"

He lowers his head and holds his face in his hands. His shoulders shake. He's crying. I stare, surprised by this. Dr. Curtis and I wait. A few seconds, maybe minutes, go by, then he finally lifts his head and wipes his face with the back of his sleeve.

"I can't stand what I did to your mom. I would have killed her. In that moment, in all of my rage, I wanted her dead. And I would have taken her life without a thought. Then who knows… maybe my own. You saved your mother, K'wan. And you saved me from making the biggest mistake in my life…." he pauses, choking back what look like more tears. "I fucked up, son. I can't ever repair the damage already done. I've already hurt you and your brothers enough. And I've put your mother through hell. I loved your mother, I still do. I just loved her the wrong way. She's all I obsessed about. The idea of her leaving me, or another man coming into her life and taking her and my family away drove me crazy."

He looks over at Dr. Curtis. "I was afraid of losing my wife and family, but I didn't know how to say that without sounding weak. I have to live with what I've done for the rest of my life."

Dr. Curtis nods.

He looks at me. And I stare back. There's a slow-burning fire that singes the back of my throat. I try to swallow it back, but it erupts and everything I've felt spews out of my mouth, like hot, angry flames.

"I fucking hate you! You were supposed to be my dad, someone I could go to and feel safe around. Not some fucking monster. Not some man I was afraid of. Every time you beat up on Mom, you were beating on me, too. No, not physically, but mentally and emotionally."

He keeps apologizing over and over and over. And the more he apologizes, the angrier I am getting. I don't want apologies; I want answers.

"I don't want your fucking apology! I want to know why. Why did you fucking put us through that?! You have no idea what kinda hell you put me through. You have no idea how many nights I stayed on edge. How many times I stood at your bedroom door with my ear pressed up against the door, trying to hear if Mom was okay. You have no idea how many times I promised to keep her safe from you. How many times I was afraid to go to school. I played sick to stay home! Did you know that? No, of course you didn't. You didn't give a damn about anyone except yourself. You didn't give two shits about how your behavior hurt Mom and was hurting Kyle and me. I was so scared and so stressed out that I would get sick because of *you!*"

He and Dr. Curtis let me get it all out. It hurts. It burns. But I push past the pain and purge. Rage sweeps through me and I feel like fighting him. I want to punch, and kick, and slap him the way he had done my mom. I tell him this. Tell him how I had rehearsed in my head killing him. How he had turned me against him. Turned my love for him into hate. I tell him this and more. I yell and scream at him until I am exhausted and in tears.

"If I didn't know then, I know now how badly I hurt you, son. And I will do whatever I have to do to make it up to you, or at least die trying. Accepting and owning up to what I've done has been the most painful thing I've ever had to do. I am hurting that I hurt you, your mom, and your brothers. Because of me, I've lost everything. My wife and family, my dignity, my self-respect, and you. I have no one else but myself to blame.

"The first time I hit your mother, she threatened to leave me and I begged her to stay. We had only been married for six months. I promised her that I'd never do it again. And I didn't for almost two years, then something happened and I snapped."

"Nothing just happened," I shoot at him, repeating what I learned in group. "You didn't snap. You knew what you were doing. So don't lie and don't use that crap as an excuse."

Dr. Curtis eyes me.

"You're right. I did know. But I didn't care. I hit her anyway. And when she didn't leave me like she said she would, I knew there wouldn't be any consequences. I knew that I had her. And each time I hit her, I promised her a hundred times over that I'd never put my hands on her again. And I did, again and again and again. When she finally called the police on me and had me arrested,

I swore I'd learned my lesson. And I agreed to go to that six-month domestic violence group, not so that I could learn anything about domestic violence or how not to be violent, but to get my family back. I did and said whatever I needed to. I was desperate and willing to do whatever it took to win your mother back. But, I still had no intentions of changing. I didn't think I needed to change.

"She needed to change. She needed to do what I expected and not have any opinion other than the ones I allowed her to have. She didn't need outside influences trying to get in her head to see things differently. All she needed was what I constructed for her. All she needed to do was believe in my lies, in my realities, in my twisted way of thinking and everything would be fine. I smothered your mother. I kept her trapped. Didn't allow her to have a life of her own outside of mine. I knew keeping her pregnant would keep her with me. Not because that's where she wanted to be, but because it's where she needed to be."

He hangs his head, pausing, then starts bawling. I blink back my shock. This is not the man I remember. I have never seen him like this...broken.

Dr. Curtis lets him have his moment. He eyes me. I'm sure to see what my reaction is to everything that is happening in here. Truth is, I don't know what I am feeling. I don't even know if I should be feeling anything at all. But I do not give him his moment. I start screaming at him all over again. I start punching my fist into my hand. "I don't wanna ever fucking be like you, but I'm scared that I am already you! And I hate you for it! You did this to me! You made me hate you! Hate me! You fucked my life up! This tore our family apart. Why couldn't you love us? Why couldn't you love mom?"

"I do love you and your brothers. And I've always loved your mother. She's the only woman I have ever loved."

"Not enough to keep your hands off of her. Not enough to care about how Kyle and I would feel seeing her face beaten or her body bruised; how that would affect us. Why couldn't you just let her be a wife and mother, or whatever else she wanted to be, without making her your punching bag, too?" I do not realize I am crying until I feel tears hitting my forearm. They feel hot and heavy with each drop. And for the first time, I feel like a ton of weight is being lifted up from my chest.

We are both crying, sitting across from the other in our own space. He keeps his eyes on mine. "I know apologizing will never take away the hurt I've already caused you, but somehow, someway, K'wan, I will make it up to you, if you let me." I don't look at him.

"Mr. Taylor," Dr. Curtis says, getting up and handing us both a box of tissues. "Why don't you tell K'wan about your own childhood."

He nods, wiping his face, then blowing his nose. "I-I was..."

I stand up and walk out before he can get the rest of his words out, fighting back the rest of my tears with every step.

I hear Mrs. Morgan's voice in my head, "Forgiveness isn't about anyone else but you...you don't have to be consumed by your anger toward him. All you have to do is release it."

I stop in my tracks, turning back around. I walk back into Dr. Curtis's office. They are talking. They both look at me. Dr. Curtis with approval in his eyes. Him with tears still in his.

I sit back down. I am not gonna run. I hear Dr. Curtis telling me it's time to confront my fears. He is who I have feared. So this is where I have to start.

Dr. Curtis sits back in his seat. "I'm glad you came back. What does this mean?"

I take a deep breath. I stare my fear in the eyes and say, "I don't wanna ever be like him."

Dr. Curtis nods. "Then you don't ever have to be."

He gets ready to say something, but I stop him. "I don't know if I can forgive you. I don't even know if I want to. And I don't know if I will ever like you. But I don't wanna ever be afraid of you or of what you might do to my mom." I can feel my emotions getting the best of me. I don't wanna cry. But he has hurt me. "I used to love you," I tell him, letting my tears fall uncheck. "I looked up to you, Dad. And you hurt me."

"I'm so sorry, son. I never wanted to hurt you, or your mother."

"But you had to. You knew what you were doing. You could have stopped it at any time, but you didn't. That's what I am learning here. That we all have choices, even if we don't like them. I wanted to kill you. I felt like I had to kill you to stop you from hurting Mom. I wished you were dead. That's how much I hated you." I lower my head. And before I know it, I am sobbing.

I hear Dr. Curtis say, "Go to your son."

And he does, and I do not stop him. He kneels down in front of me and pulls me into him. And I let him. The room fills with my sobs and his. I cry and I cry and I cry.

I curse him and scream at him and he lets me get it all out. He lets me cling onto him, like I have never before. And, for the first time, crying doesn't feel like it's only for sissies or babies. This time he makes it feel right. That it is okay to show emotions. That it is okay to cry. Maybe this time it is okay because he knows I am hurting. That I am angry. That he has hurt me. Maybe this time it's okay simply because I am his son.

Epilogue

Two months have passed and I am still here at Healing Souls, working on me. I still have two family sessions a week, one with my mom, the other with my dad. My mom is gonna drop the restraining order because she wants the three of us to have a session together. She says she will always love him, but she assures me that her love for him isn't greater than the love she has for herself or for my brothers and me.

And this time I really believe her.

I open the composition book that Mrs. Morgan had given me, and open to the first page. My eyes shoot down to the end of the page. I read the quote by Ralph Emerson: "Be not the slave of your own past. Plunge into the sublime seas, dive deep and swim far, so you shall come back with self-respect, with new power, with an advanced experience that shall explain and overlook the old," then shut the book, smiling.

When I read it now, I can grasp what it means for me, what it says to me. That no matter what, I have to push forward, fight my fears, and embrace whatever life might have in store for me. I'm only fourteen, so I have my whole life to figure that part out. But, at least I understand. At least I know I don't have to stay stuck in my fears. I don't have to be afraid of what's ahead. I can acknowledge what I am afraid of and not be consumed with it.

I still wanna go home, but not as bad. I am in good hands here.

I really do believe it. I trust Dr. Curtis and Mrs. Morgan and Miss Daisy. They really do care about me here. It still saddens me every time my mom and brothers leave after visits, but I know that this stay—although it's where I am supposed to be, where I have to be, right now—it isn't gonna be forever. I am going home, one day soon. But for now, this is where I will continue to work on me.

I never thought I'd say this. But being here has really helped me. It has helped me learn a lot about domestic violence and why people do it. I still don't agree with it, but at least I have a better understanding of it.

I still have a lot of anger inside of me toward my dad. But I am working on letting go of it. Not for him, but for me. I am trying not to hate him. And I still don't like him. But I realize that he is still my dad. And, no matter what, I should be respectful. In spite of everything, I know that he loves me. Maybe one day, I can love him back. Right now, I'm not there yet. But at least I am talking to him. I am listening to him and he is listening to me. At least I am not refusing his visits or walking out on him in sessions. Still, I know I have a long way to go, but I'm getting there. And he wants to get there with me. And deep down inside, that's what I want, too. I'm just not willing to admit it to him, not yet. I still don't trust him. And I am not sure if I ever will. But if nothing else, I will forgive him.

I owe so much to Mrs. Morgan, Miss Daisy, and Dr. Curtis… oh, and Ja'Meer. The four of them have really helped me see that the best thing I can do is let go of the past. And the best thing I can ever do for me is to let go of my hatred so that I can get on with my life. Ja'Meer got released last month, and it's not the same. He really looked out for me here. And I miss him. But, it's okay because I have this new kid in my room. He's fourteen like me, and he seems frightened about being here like I was when I first got here. But I am going to help him like Ja'Meer helped me. I only hope I can be half the roommate that he was to me.

I really wanna go home. But I know everything happens when it's supposed to. So I am being patient. But I'll be fifteen in three more months and the last thing I wanna do is spend my birthday here. But I can't worry about that. I am learning a lot about guilt and worry, and learning to not let either control me. It's not easy, though. Like Mrs. Morgan said, "They are useless emotions" to me. So I have to live in the present. Something I am still working on. Dr. Curtis and Mrs. Morgan are helping me with that.

I feel like I have changed so much over the last year. Shucks, so much in the last three months. And I am still changing. And, hopefully, one day, I will become the kinda man that treats his family with respect. Hopefully, I will become the kinda man who won't let his pride or ego or insecurities control him. I don't know how I will get there. But somehow that's the kind of man I will need to be.

But right now, I'm still a kid. I'm fourteen, a freshman. And that's really all I wanna be. I don't wanna worry about what kinda man I might become. I only wanna focus on the kinda kid I am today. And hopefully that will help me make the right choices so that I can grow into the man I hope to be; if that makes any sense.

I don't wanna be stuck obsessing about the future, worrying about something I can't control or predict. I really just wanna be in the moment. Speaking of the moment, Tabitha wrote me again. Well, she's written me like six times. And I have written her back. I decided to mail off that letter to her after all. And I am glad I did. I really do like her, but I still won't tell her until we have "the talk." I don't wanna be like Jackson and Westley and Corey and the rest of them who have all those grownup issues with their girlfriends. I am too young for that kinda stress.

I asked my mom if I could date when I turned fifteen instead of sixteen, and she told me to ask my father. I did, and he said I can. So, that's why I really wanna get home. I mean, I miss my family, but I wanna spend time with Tabitha, too. And I wanna kisss her. But that's it.

"Yo, Green Eyes," Nelson calls out. "You have a visit."

"Okay, thanks," I tell him, slipping on my Jordans. I walk out the door and head down the hall toward the visiting room. I walk in, and see my brothers first. Kyle waves as the triplets run over to me. "K'waaaaaaaaaaaaaan, are you gonna come home soon?" Kavon wants to know.

"Mommy said you can come home 'cause you talking now," Karon says this.

"Are you gonna stop talking again?" Kason asks.

"No, I'm not ever gonna stop talking again," I tell them as I bend over and wrap my arms around the three of them.

"Kyle says you have a girlfriend," Karon teases. "And her name issssssss Tabitha."

"I do not." I laugh as Kyle walks over to me. We hug. "Hey, man," I say, giving him a pound.

"Man, you need to hurry up home. Tabitha is stressing me out." He shakes his head. "That girl is nuts about you. All she wants to do is talk about you. It's sickening, man. But guess what? Her cousin likes me. And she's older than me!"

"How old?"

"She's in the eighth grade." I smile. "Do you think Mom will change her mind and let me date at thirteen?"

I laugh. "Nope."

He shrugs. "Dad might."

"Did you ask him?"

"Yeah. But he said it's up to Mom. But if I keep bugging him, he might change his mind."

I see Ja'Meer in my mind, shaking his head. I smile, draping an arm over his shoulder. "Man, don't rush. Dating isn't all what it's cracked up to me. Trust me, I know."

"Hey son," Dad says, getting up from his seat. This is his week to have my brothers. Mom lets him have them every other weekend now instead of one weekend a month.

"Hi," I say back. We hug. And it's not one of those awkward hugs. It's the kinda hug that lets you know that you are cared about. Still, I'm not sure if I will want to spend the weekends with him when I get home. We'll see.

Grandma Ellen stands up, and hugs me next. "How's my handsome grandbaby doing?"

"I'm good, Grandma." I kiss her on the cheek. And the truth is, I really am. I'm not having the nightmares as much. And when I do, they aren't as frightening. The more I talk in counseling, and in group, the less frequent they are. I can't wait for the day when I am no longer having them. The triplets jump up on me, and I tickle them. It's really good to be surrounded by my family. Tomorrow, my mom and Aunt Janie will visit me. I look up from playing with the triplets. And Grandma Ellen is crying. Dad wraps an arm around her. Asks her what's wrong.

"I'm so happy to see my boys all together. I don't want anything to ever tear y'all apart again. Do you hear me? Nothing."

"It's not going to happen," Dad assures her, kissing her on the side of her head.

"Family is all we have," she says, eyeing us. "And there is nothing like the power of love."

"Or the power of forgiveness," I imagine Mrs. Morgan saying. I smile, looking over at my dad. Forgiveness may not come easy, if at all, but we might be on our way. But for now I take a deep breath. I am going to stay in the moment. I am not gonna lose my voice again, or be silent. I will not suffer in silence. I will continue to face my fears. I am gonna keep purging and keep working on me. Yup, until I can get it right. Until I can look in the mirror and only see the reflection of myself staring back at me...K'wan Elliot Taylor. Not my father, not my mother, but me.

About the Author

Dywane D. Birch, a graduate of Norfolk State University and Hunter College, is the author of *From My Soul to Yours*, *When Loving You is Wrong*, *Shattered Souls* and *Beneath the Bruises*. He is also a contributing author to the compelling compilation, *Breaking The Cycle* (2005), edited by Zane—a collection of short stories on domestic violence, which won the 2006 NAACP Image Award for outstanding literary fiction; and a contributing author to the anthology *Fantasy* (2007), a collection of erotica short stories. He is the author of the novella *The Goddess of Desire* in Zane's erotica anthology *Another Time, Another Place*.

He has a master's degree in psychology, and is a clinically certified forensic counselor. A former director of an adolescent crisis shelter, he continues to work with adolescents and adult offenders. He currently speaks at local colleges on the issue of domestic violence while working on his next novel and a collection of poetry. He divides his free time between New Jersey and Maryland.

You may email the author at bshatteredsouls@cs.com